ALL OUR MISSING PIECES

SOPHIE RANALD

Storm

This is a work of fiction. Names, characters, businesses, places, events and incidents are either the products of the author's imagination or used in a fictitious manner. Any resemblance to actual persons, living or dead, or actual events is purely coincidental.

Copyright © Sophie Ranald, 2025

The moral right of the author has been asserted.

All rights reserved. No part of this book may be reproduced or used in any manner without the prior written permission of the copyright owner. This prohibition includes, but is not limited to, any reproduction or use for the purpose of training artificial intelligence technologies or systems.

To request permissions, contact the publisher at rights@stormpublishing.co

Ebook ISBN: 978-1-80508-976-6
Paperback ISBN: 978-1-80508-977-3

Cover design: Rose Cooper
Cover images: Shutterstock

Published by Storm Publishing.
For further information, visit:
www.stormpublishing.co

ALSO BY SOPHIE RANALD

The Love Hack

The Fall-Out

The Girlfriends' Club series

P.S. I Hate You

Santa, Please Bring Me a Boyfriend

Not in a Million Years

The Ginger Cat series

Just Saying

Thank You, Next

He's Cancelled

The Daily Grind series

Out With the Ex, In With the New

Sorry Not Sorry

It's Not You, It's Him

No, We Can't Be Friends

Standalone romcoms

It Would be Wrong to Steal My Sister's Boyfriend (Wouldn't It?)

A Groom With a View

Who Wants to Marry a Millionaire?

You Can't Fall in Love With Your Ex (Can You?)

ONE

Beatrice looked down at the notebook on the open seat-back table. She had always loved stationery; as a little girl, she'd had a huge collection of sparkly notebooks, sheets of stickers and erasers in every shape, colour and scent. Every birthday had brought a new pencil case, set of luminous markers or notecards with matching envelopes. Later, she'd begun to accumulate a collection of sketchpads, sticks of charcoal and enticing, plump tubes of oil paints.

Her current notebook was bound in scarlet leather with her name embossed on the front in silver foil, a present from her mother for her twenty-first birthday, and she had hoarded its pages so that now, over a year later, it was still only half full. On the open page in front of her was just one word, which she had noted down in the teal-coloured ink she currently favoured in her Montblanc fountain pen before leaving home.

Clonmara.

She craned her neck to look past the woman on her right, who was engrossed in a book and apparently indifferent to the excitement of flying. Her flight from Philadelphia to Dublin had been a night-time one, and Beatrice had hoped that now, on the journey from Dublin to London, she would be able to see the world from above, stretched beneath her like one of her mother's handmade patchwork quilts. She'd imagined drawing it – the blocks of fields, arcs of rivers and sprawls of cities – even if all she had to hand was her fountain pen and notebook.

But through the window she could see only grey cloud.

She turned back to the page. *Clonmara*. That was all she'd had to go on. Over the years, the word had acquired a kind of mystique – she'd pored over it in atlases, tracing the route from Dublin out into the surrounding countryside, looked it up on Wikipedia, even attempted an unsatisfactory watercolour landscape based on a photograph she'd found on Flickr. It had all felt impossibly distant, the words she'd read describing a small village surrounded by farmland, forty miles outside Dublin and twenty from an industrial area that apparently specialised in the manufacture of wool and linen cloth, seeming to have little connection to reality.

Now she had seen it for herself, and come away disappointed.

But Beatrice wasn't one to give up. She had persuaded her parents to pay for her flight from Philadelphia to Dublin without disclosing the true reason for her trip – although they must surely have guessed. Eventually, their objections overcome, they'd agreed, encouraging her to see the city where she'd been born and explore Trinity College, where her dad had worked all those years ago.

She hadn't mentioned Clonmara to them.

The first time she'd said the name out loud had been to the receptionist in her Dublin hotel, the morning after her arrival.

'Sure, you'll need to get the bus there,' he told her, noting down where it would depart from and what time it left, then smiling the way men always smiled at Beatrice before adding, 'Mind you don't miss it. There's not another until tomorrow.'

'Thank you. I'll leave in fifteen minutes, then.'

She took a seat in a brocade armchair and flipped through the glossy tourist brochures on the varnished table next to it, glancing around at the other occupants of the lobby with idle curiosity.

At a table by the window, sipping a cup of tea, Beatrice noticed a woman on her own. She was middle-aged, dressed in navy trousers, a cream polyester blouse and black shoes with a low heel. She looked uncomfortable in this upscale hotel lobby – like she had never been in a place like this before, except perhaps to work as a waitress or housekeeper. When her teaspoon clinked against her saucer she looked around anxiously, as if she'd committed some faux pas.

Then the woman's eyes lit on the door, her face suddenly alight with hope.

Beatrice watched as a couple walked into the lobby from the street: a bearded man in chinos and a jumper, a think manila folder tucked under his arm, and a slim young woman in jeans and a trench coat. She was unmistakably related to the older woman – they had the same slight figure, the same curly almost-black hair, the same brilliant blue eyes.

Her daughter? Perhaps the young man was her fiancé, meeting his mother-in-law-to-be for the first time? But fiancés didn't carry folders bulging with documents to meet prospective mothers-in-law.

As Beatrice watched, the older woman stood, almost knocking over an occasional table in her eagerness. She turned towards the door and took a step forward, her arms outstretched, then let them fall awkwardly by her side. The younger woman had no such hesitation. She hurried over, reaching out, smiling radiantly, and took her mother's hands – of course she was her mother, who else could she be? – in hers.

'Well, I don't need to introduce you two,' the man said, smiling. 'But that's my job. Mary, Bronagh.'

Introduce? Beatrice's curiosity shifted from idle to intense.

She stood up and walked casually to the door, pausing with her back to the group and pretending to admire a flower arrangement as she listened.

'We'd never have recognised each other otherwise,' the younger woman – Bronagh – laughed. 'Would we, Ma-Mary?'

'Sure it's like looking at myself in the mirror,' Mary marvelled. 'Or like myself twenty years ago. I knew you'd be beautiful, but not...'

Mary's voice trailed off, and Beatrice glanced over her shoulder to see her fishing a tissue out of her sleeve at the exact moment Bronagh fished one out of hers.

'I'll leave this with you, ladies' – the man handed over the folder to Bronagh; Mary was vigorously blowing her nose – 'and let you get acquainted. Please feel free to get in touch with me or any of my colleagues if there's anything at all we can do.'

The two women thanked him – their voices identical – and he walked past Beatrice with a satisfied smile, raising his hand in a wave then pushing out through the door.

'Would you—' Bronagh began, then started again. 'I mean, would you like another tea here, or shall we go somewhere else?'

Beatrice strained to hear Mary's voice, lowered to a whisper. 'I'd just as soon go somewhere else. This place is... it's...'

'I know what you mean,' Bronagh agreed, adding decisively, 'We'll be off to Bewley's then.'

'Bewley's.' Mary blew her nose again, then laughed. 'Haven't I waited twenty years to buy my daughter tea and scones at Bewley's?'

'Then you shouldn't have to wait a minute longer.'

Laughing, their faces wreathed in carbon-copy smiles, the two women left the hotel, walking past Beatrice and shoulder to shoulder out into the rain.

Beatrice stood where she was, frozen, the flowers blurring into a kaleidoscope of colour in front of her eyes.

What did I just see?

But she knew: there was no doubt what had happened, no other possible explanation.

Hoisting the strap of her purse more securely over her shoulder, she left the hotel and hurried down the rainy street, heading towards the destination she hoped would hold the key to her own past.

But the door remained firmly closed.

Impatiently, she sat back and took another sip of her British Airways coffee, weak and bitter. At least in London there'd be Starbucks. Starbucks and Big Ben and Madame Tussauds and red buses and Arctic Monkeys gigs.

Her time in Dublin and expedition to Clonmara had, on the surface at least, been a failure. Her own replaying of the moment she'd witnessed in the hotel lobby hadn't happened – was no closer to happening than it had been when she had left Philadelphia. The scant information she'd left home with – the name of the village, the mention of a big house where a family lived, made rich by the textile industry that had flourished there – had barely been augmented at all by the information she had gleaned from a few old men she'd talked to in a Clonmara pub.

Instead, she had a whole load of new questions.

Her hands twisting in her lap with impatience, she glanced towards the window again, but she could still see only grey nothingness.

Along with all the other things waiting for her on the far side of the Irish Sea, she reminded herself, was the need to work, to support herself while she tried to uncover the truth about her past. It wouldn't be all fun and games – she'd have responsibilities, too. She thought about the letter, printed off from her email, her mother copied in, folded carefully in her hand luggage along with her passport and boarding card. She had a job to go to – although not a place to live.

That was for her to arrange.

Beatrice felt herself smiling as she remembered the conversation with her mother a few days before.

'They're a lovely family,' her mom had said, and Beatrice could picture the smile of approval, even though thousands of miles separated them. 'Two children, four and two, a girl and a boy. Father's in finance and she works in fashion. And you'll be able to live in.'

Beatrice's heart had sunk. This wasn't quite the freedom and independence she'd imagined. Being a nanny was one thing – being nannied by her employer was something else entirely.

'But I—' she began.

'Now, sweetheart.' Again, Beatrice could picture her mom's face, the serious expression that preceded a mild scolding. 'You've not lived away from home before and—'

'I lived away for four years at college,' Beatrice pointed out. 'No one died.'

'That was different. You were only in Boston and you were living with other girls.'

'Exactly! Other girls, as opposed to a strange man. Anything could happen. I've been on the nannying forums online, Mom. I've read the stories.'

'Beatrice!' Now there was a hint of alarm in her mother's voice, and Beatrice wondered if she'd played her trump card too soon. 'Perhaps it won't be suitable after all. Maybe you should—'

'Calm down, Mom. It'll be fine. I just feel like it might be better if I don't actually live with the family. I could find a room somewhere nearby – in a youth hostel or something. A YWCA.'

Her mother sighed. 'Perhaps you're right. You know your dad and I—'

'Worry about me. Of course you do,' Beatrice soothed, sensing victory. 'But I'm an adult. I can look after myself. You don't need to worry.'

Her mother laughed. 'Worrying about you is my job. One day you'll understand.'

But right now, Beatrice couldn't imagine ever worrying about anything. What lay ahead of her was an adventure – a literal journey of discovery. The next time she saw her parents, she'd be a completely different person.

Or the same person, but with a completely different identity.

She turned the page of her notebook. Unlike the previous page, which held only one word, this held four. She ran her fingers over them but the ink had long dried and her pen had left no impression on the paper.

Big house in Spittlefields.

Since writing the words, Beatrice had looked online and discovered her misspelling; now, she used her fountain pen to strike through the word and write it carefully again.

Spitalfields.

The wing of the plane dipped and Beatrice's stomach lurched with fresh excitement. Through the window, she saw a glimpse of bleached blue sky and then, suddenly, the earth below – a margin of sea then stretches of green interspersed with the grey patches of buildings.

It all stretched out like her future – like a promise.

TWO
5 MARCH 2005

My first thought when I woke up this morning was, What have I done?

My second was, I need to write my Morning Pages. So here I am, marking this new start with a fresh page – though not a new notebook. If I'd started one with every new beginning over the past ten years, I'd have left hundreds of pages empty, and that would have been a shameful waste of the planet's scarce resources.

As it is, I've filled almost fifty of them – a pleasing array they'd make, all more or less the same size but with different colours and bindings. They're stashed away in a tea chest somewhere in the cellar, in this house where I am waking for the first time and filling my pages as I do every morning. Three pages of longhand writing, no more and no less, every single day.

I thought, after all the excitement – to put it kindly – of yesterday, I'd sleep like a baby. Not that babies sleep, according to those who know more about them than I do. Like a log, then. But I didn't. The unfamiliar sounds of this house – the scrape of a tree branch on a windowpane, the shouts of a group of young people making their way back from the pub late last night, the intermittent drip, drip, drip of rain coming through the roof on to the floor of the attic above me – all kept me awake last night for hours and punctuated my dreams.

Not to mention the whistling of wind coming from across the room: I thought I'd closed the window tightly last night, but it appears I didn't – or that the wooden frame is rotten, letting draughts through around the edges of the glass. Rotten, like so much in this house, from the ceiling joists to the floorboards and just about everything in between.

What have I done?

But what choice did I have? It has been bequeathed to me, as much a duty as a gift, and I already feel as if I have a responsibility to it – to nurture it, restore it, make it whole again. Because none of this – not the leaks or the rotting window frame or the disgusting bathroom – is the house's fault. It's no more to blame than a stray cat would be for wandering the streets scrawny and threadbare, its ears torn from fighting and its eyes rheumy. The house has been neglected too, unloved and uncared for, fifty years of tenants leaving clutter and botched renovations but no memories that I can discern.

Only the cellar is sound, if damp, so that is where I have stored the possessions I have accumulated over the years, as well as those Mr Murphy had shipped over to save on storage costs.

Already, for all its faults, it feels like home. It feels as if it has been waiting for me – which, of course, as a matter of actual fact, it has. More than that though – it feels as if I have been waiting for it. As if all those moves, from country to country, hemisphere to hemisphere, pillar to post, were all leading me back here.

I couldn't just walk in, however. I had to wait for events to unfold, for the formalities to be completed, for Mr Murphy to track me down and tell me that it was mine. And so here I am, lying on a stained old mattress in the most habitable room of a house that would probably fall down if I let it. I'm not going to let it. I feel fiercely protective of it – almost maternal, which is an absurd way to feel about five storeys of bricks and mortar.

An absurd way for me to feel about anything.

And, of course, I have no more of an idea how to care for it than I would if it were a baby. Instead of feeding and nappy changing and winding and settling down for naps, it'll need plastering and rewiring and rodent extermination and no doubt repointing and other things I can't begin to understand. But first it'll need a damn good clean, and I've filled three pages now so that is what I'm going to give it.

I will love this house. I swear I will – if only it will allow me to.

THREE

It would never have occurred to me that I'd live somewhere beautiful. I'd never put the thought into words – not, *Beautiful places aren't for the likes of you, Livvie*, or anything like that – but it had still become somehow internalised. Besides, I already had somewhere to live – that is, until I came to the realisation that I'd rather live anywhere at all than there. Well, almost anywhere.

I'd been renting the top right-hand bedroom in a house just off Mile End Road for three months by then. In the room opposite mine, on the other side of the landing, was Samantha and often Samantha's boyfriend, Gary. Half a flight of stairs down was the back bedroom that was Amanda's.

Even though we didn't know one another, it should have worked. We should have become mates, borrowing each other's hair straighteners and comparing hangovers while we cooked fry-ups on Saturday mornings. Or even if that didn't happen, we could have rubbed along, barring the occasional row about who'd left hair in the plughole and who was late with their share of the rent.

But we didn't. Not from the beginning.

It started a week or so after I moved in and never really stopped; something had made Samantha decide that Amanda was her friend and I wasn't. When I arrived home from work, I'd find Samantha in the kitchen, either with Gary or Amanda or both of them. And always, when I walked in, they'd stop talking about whatever they'd been talking about, look at me for a second, then laugh.

I didn't know what I'd done wrong, but clearly it was something. I did my best to ride it out, to rise above it, and so it took until March before things went from tense to explosive.

One morning, when I managed to catch Amanda alone, I tried asking her about it. It was a Saturday; I'd slept in – or not slept so much as lain in bed, listening carefully to the sounds of the house, trying to judge when it was safe to emerge from the refuge of my room, use the bathroom and go downstairs.

When I eventually did, I found Amanda there, eating toast and peanut butter at the kitchen table, apparently engrossed in *Heat* magazine.

'Morning.' I smiled. 'Tea?'

She shook her head. 'I'm all right.'

I flicked the kettle on, glancing at the open magazine next to her plate.

'Oh my God, Jordan and Peter Andre,' I exclaimed, although I couldn't have cared less about either of them. 'Do you think they'll get married?'

'Hope not,' Amanda said. 'She's a slag and he's too good for her.'

'Maybe he's what she needs,' I suggested, pouring water on to a teabag. 'Maybe he'd settle her down, and be a good dad for...'

My knowledge of the celebrity couple had run out.

'Harvey,' Amanda said.

'Harvey,' I echoed, taking a seat opposite her. 'You up to anything fun today?'

A shadow of something flickered over Amanda's face, and it was only when she spoke that I realised it was guilt.

'Sam's party tonight, innit,' she said. 'She and Gaz have gone out to buy booze.'

'Oh.' My voice came out sounding not like me. 'I didn't know... is it her birthday or something?'

Amanda shook her head. 'Just having some mates round. It's no big deal.'

Except it was a big deal – I hadn't been told about it and I literally lived in the same house as her.

'Is there...' I began. 'I mean, have I done something to annoy Samantha? She seems... I don't know. Off with me.'

Amanda actually blushed, before muttering, 'I dunno, Livvie.'

'There must be something, though.'

'I guess she thinks...' Amanda looked cornered, and I had a flash of understanding of how she must feel. Samantha was the one with the power – the power to shut her out like she'd shut me out, to cut off her friendship as she had done with me.

'Thinks what?'

'Thinks you're after Gary.'

'I what?' I burst out laughing. Gary, with his receding chin and his habit of standing over you with his crotch at your eye level, thumbs hooked into the belt loops of his jeans? Gary, whose snoring sometimes kept me awake at night? Gary, who was – even if none of the other things had been the case – my flatmate's boyfriend?

'Apparently he said something to her about you.' Now Amanda had started, it seemed she thought she might as well carry on. 'That he totally would, and maybe if someone gave you one you'd be a bit less standoffish.'

I suppressed a shudder of revulsion at the idea of being given one by Gary.

'Look, Amanda,' I said, 'I couldn't be less interested in him. Really. I just want us all to get along. Thanks for telling me, though. I won't be here tonight – I'll go out. I'll try to talk to Sam in the morning. And have a great night, okay?'

I did as I'd promised. I texted my friend Emily and arranged to meet up with her that evening for a pizza and a movie, and only returned home just before midnight. A wall of noise greeted me – music, laughter, raised voices and the crash of a breaking bottle. Praying that no one had heard me come in, I made my way upstairs.

But I only made it as far as the landing. As I was passing, the bathroom door opened and Gary lurched out, a can of Carlsberg in his hand.

'Evening,' I muttered.

'Where've you been?' he demanded. 'Wasn't our house party good enough for you?'

'I was out with a friend.'

'Boyfriend? You look hot.'

I was wearing jeans, a jumper and Converse, and I certainly didn't. I just said, 'Thanks.'

'Very hot.' He took a step towards me and I stepped back, but the wall was in the way.

'Thanks,' I said again. 'Anyway, have a good rest of the—'

But before I could finish, he'd leaned in and kissed me.

It was horrible. I'd had my share of unwelcome snogs, of course, but this was up there with the worst of them. Gary smelled of stale Lynx, beer and fags. His stubble scraped my skin. The hand that wasn't holding the beer can was pressed against the wall next to my head, trapping my hair.

I fought to escape and, after a few horrible seconds, I managed it. But I wasn't quick enough.

As I snaked away from him, I heard Samantha's voice calling from the stairs, 'Gaz, where the hell are— What the fuck?'

Desperately, I ran the rest of the way to my room and ducked inside, locking the door behind me.

FOUR

17 MARCH 2005

St Patrick's Day. Well, I shan't be carousing in the street with pints of Guinness and a sexy leprechaun outfit this year – or any year, come to that. But I find myself, as I huddle under the duvet – which at least, now, covers a new mattress and a proper bed – considering breathing a prayer to him, the patron saint of engineers.

Yesterday a surveyor visited and the news he left was not good. The house, it seems, is practically falling down. There's dry rot in the floors and rising damp in the walls, as well as evidence of woodworm and rodent infestations, not to mention the fact that the entire roof needs replacing before the top floor gets even more sodden than it already is and the ceiling above me collapses.

Then something else happened – something better. Maybe St Jude, patron saint of lost causes, has been looking out for me after all? It was when I visited the newsagent, not just because I'd run out of bread and milk but because Imran, the shopkeeper, was likely to be the only friendly face I'd see all day.

For the first time, I stopped outside Imran's shop and took a proper look at the cards stuck in the window. Many of them were faded, curled at the corners and dusty – it's a quaintly old-fashioned way to advertise one's services, whether as a painter or a prostitute, now that everything happens on the internet. But one looked relatively new and freshly lettered, carefully handwritten with what looked like a permanent marker. I can't remember now exactly what it said, but two things jumped out at me: Handyman Services and a mobile number.

I hadn't been praying but it was like an answer to prayer.

I dialled the number. A young man's voice answered and I gabbled out the fact that I was in desperate need of his services. Then he dashed my hopes: his circumstances had changed, he said, his accommodation in London had fallen through and so he was going to return to his family in Leicester.

Some kind of desperation possessed me. In that moment, it seemed like this boy – Luke, he'd said his name was when he answered the phone – was my only hope.

Don't do that! I begged. You can come and stay in my house for free if you'll do some of the work that's needed.

He must have thought I was mad. I think I am mad!

But he must also be just as desperate as I am, because he agreed to come and meet me and see the house. I will have to pay him, I'm sure, in addition to putting him up in one of the rooms here – the one across the landing is probably the most habitable. There is far too much work here for one man to tackle, however desperate he is for a roof over his head, and I know absolutely nothing about this Luke – he could be a fraudster or even an axe murderer. But even if he is, I have nothing to be defrauded of and his axe-wielding skills might come in handy getting rid of some of the crumbling dry-walling left over from when this place was a warren of cheaply rented offices.

What's more, he mentioned that his ultimate goal is to become an artist – almost as if he knew that would instantly make me look kindly on him, given my own mothballed ambitions.

Best of all, my conversation with him has given me an idea. I may have almost no money, but I have all the space I could want. Eventually, I may be able to find other people who are desperate enough to want to live here – people who will pay me actual money. I can cook and clean for them, like a proper old-fashioned landlady. The prospect makes me feel almost hopeful. Perhaps we have a future together, this house and me. I will put a card of my own in the newsagent's window and see what happens.

FIVE

I stayed in bed as long as I could the next day. I felt like a child who was about to be called into the head teacher's office for a misdemeanour she hadn't committed – I knew I'd done nothing wrong. But, with equal certainty, I knew that Samantha wasn't going to see it that way. Still, the only alternative I had to getting up and facing whatever there was to face was staying locked in my room for the rest of my life – a prospect that wasn't without appeal.

It was the sound of Gary snoring that finally propelled me out of bed. Even through my closed door and Samantha's across the landing, I could hear it as clearly as if he was in my bed, not hers. A grinding inhale, a pause, a snorting exhale. Over and over.

Abruptly, I sat up. It was pathetic to hide away in here like I was some kind of criminal. Besides, I needed to wee and clean my teeth. I opened my bedroom door tentatively, peering out on to the landing then scuttling furtively to the bathroom.

Fifteen minutes later, showered and dressed, I made my way downstairs. My trepidation had eased now, and I was feeling resolute if not exactly confident. I'd take myself out, buy a copy of *Loot* and read the accommodation section.

I'd make a plan.

It came almost as a shock to see Samantha when I got downstairs. She was sitting on the sofa in her pyjamas, last night's make-up still smudged under her eyes, her hair hanging lankly over her shoulders, eating tuna mayonnaise out of a cereal bowl with a spoon.

'Good morning,' I said, as calmly as I could.

She didn't respond to my greeting. She looked straight through me, as if I wasn't there. I saw right then what lay ahead – weeks and weeks of being shunned and ignored, treated as if I was invisible, until eventually I gave up and moved out.

'You don't have to bother sulking,' I said. 'I'm going to find a new place to live. And you might want to find a new boyfriend.'

Then I put on my coat and headed out into the cold, bright morning.

Anger and adrenaline carried me to the end of the road, past the corner shop with its stacks of newspapers outside, past the greasy spoon where solitary old men and groups of students were piling into bacon and eggs washed down with cups of tea, through the park where daffodils turned hopeful faces up to the thin sun, and across the bridge over the canal, wanting to put as much distance between me and Samantha and Gary as I could. I walked on and on, not really noticing where I was going. Red buses roared past me, women in black abayas stood chatting in doorways, a group of men in Lycra whizzed by on racing bikes, but I barely saw any of them.

I must have walked for almost an hour before hunger made me slow down, pausing to take stock of where I was. I'd passed through the run-down bustle of Whitechapel and almost reached the City. Over the hum of traffic, I could hear market traders' shouts, and a small stream of people seemed to be making their way down a side street to my left. I followed them, deciding to find a shop where I could buy a paper and then get some food.

It didn't take long for me to find what I was looking for. On opposite street corners were two shops. One was an off-licence, a dishevelled old man emerging from it clutching a can of extra-strength lager and rolling a cigarette. The other was smaller, a traditional newsagent with metal racks outside holding Sunday papers from all over the world and shelves laden with magazines inside. As I approached the doorway, the comforting smell of paper and ink drifted out, mingling with incense.

But I didn't go inside. The window, I noticed, was full of cards that had been stuck to it from the back. They were all colours: mostly white but also pink, pale blue, light green and yellow. Some were handwritten and others printed. I couldn't get close enough to read any of them because a woman was standing by the window, hands on hips, gazing at the cards.

She wasn't tall, but the way she held herself and her wedge-heeled boots made her look that way. Her hair was cut short, in a spiky pixie crop, deep brown threaded with grey. She was wearing a long tweed coat, the cuffs of her wide-legged trousers just visible below it. Above the collar of her coat, the line of her jaw was sharp and clean and her full lips were bright red.

My first thought was, *She looks like a film star.* But she couldn't be, of course – not here, in the melting pot of East London on a Sunday in March. She was just some random lady out for a walk, curiosity leading her to stop and browse in a window not for clothes she might buy but for the details of people's lives she might glean from reading the display of cards.

But she wasn't browsing, I realised. She was gazing intently at one of the cards, right in the centre of the window, the Blu-Tack that held it there still fresh. As I watched, she nodded as if in satisfaction, then abruptly turned on her heels and strode away.

At least, she would have stridden if I hadn't been there,

loitering right by her shoulder, trying to see what was written on the card she'd been studying so closely. Instead, she cannoned into me and almost sent me flying.

'Oh my God,' she gasped, torn between shock and embarrassment. 'I'm so very sorry. I just didn't see you there.'

'It's my fault. I was standing too close, practically breathing down your neck trying to read those.'

'Are you all right?' Her voice was breathy, with the hint of an accent I couldn't place. 'I didn't hurt you?'

'Really, I'm fine,' I said. Up close, I caught the vanilla scent of her perfume and could see the colour of her eyes – a hazel so bright they were almost golden. 'I was just waiting for you to…'

I gestured towards the window.

The woman smiled. 'I just put a card in there. Or rather, Imran did on my behalf. Probably nothing will come of it, but I had a stroke of luck with one the other day and I thought I'd try the same thing myself. Serendipity, you know. Or more likely superstition.'

I took a step closer so I could read the card she'd been staring at.

Rooms for rent in house on Damask Square. Reasonable rates. Call Orla. And a phone number.

Serendipity, I thought.

I said, 'Orla – is that you? My name's Livvie.'

SIX

Beatrice stepped into the elevator, which had been opened by a uniformed doorman using a code. Because it only led to the penthouse level, it was small and had no buttons to press.

But it did have a mirror. As the doors glided shut in front of her, she turned and scrutinised her reflection: her make-up was carefully toned down, her blonde hair in a ponytail. She knew her tailored wool pants were carefully pressed and she could see that her primrose-coloured cashmere sweater was clean. She reckoned she'd nailed the nanny aesthetic: smart but homely, conservative yet relaxed.

The elevator was warm. Beatrice could feel the fibres of her sweater prickling her armpits under her charcoal wool coat, and realised she was sweating. She had no reason to be nervous, and yet she was. These people, who she'd only met over Skype, would be not only her employers but as good as her family. She'd be expected to change the smaller one's diapers, kiss them both goodnight, cook their meals and dry their tears.

Hopefully they wouldn't cry too much. Hopefully they wouldn't shit too much either. But there wasn't much chance of that.

The elevator came to a stop with a barely perceptible jolt and the doors silently parted. Beatrice stepped out on to an expanse of polished parquet, a white-walled hallway stretching ahead of her. She could smell something cooking – a casserole, maybe. She wondered if they'd ask her to stay for dinner; part of her dreaded that prospect, but she was also hungry.

'Beatrice!' A woman hurried into view, her high heels clicking on the hardwood floor. Her face was familiar from the Skype calls – a sharp dark bob, heavy brows, pale lipstick – but Beatrice hadn't seen the rest of her before, and she was reluctantly impressed by the tight black leather pants, cream silk blouse and catwalk slimness. 'I'm Frances.'

Frances leaned in to embrace her, and Beatrice cautiously returned the hug. She didn't like touching people much, especially not strangers.

'Great to meet you,' she managed.

'May I take your things?' Frances helped Beatrice off with her coat. 'Did you find the place okay?'

'Not really,' Beatrice admitted. 'It's kind of confusing out... down there.'

'Tell me about it!' Frances laughed. 'When we first moved here from New York, I used to lose the building every single time. But you'll get used to it. Let me show you round and then we'll have a chat.'

Frances slid open a concealed door and hung Beatrice's coat in a closet with a load of others, many of them child-sized. Then she led the way through into the apartment.

Beatrice couldn't suppress a gasp of amazement. The place was huge, the gleaming stretch of floor punctuated by leather and chrome Eames couches, silvery-cream rugs and a huge glass dining table. But all that was nothing compared to the view revealed by vast sheets of glass on two sides of the room. London lay spread out below her, countless golden and amber lights glowing in the darkness, tall buildings reaching up to pierce the night sky, the river a black ribbon snaking through it all.

'It's stunning,' she said.

Frances smiled. 'Isn't it? We lived on the Upper West Side before, and I never thought we'd get a view like that. But this comes close. Now the kitchen is through here, and Peter's office, our bedroom, the kids' playroom...'

She led the way around the apartment, softly opening and closing doors. The place was enormous – Beatrice figured it would take her almost as long to work out its geography as it was taking her to get her head around the subway (or, for that matter, remember that she was meant to call it the Tube).

'Slate and Parker's room is here.' Frances laid a palm on the flat white surface of a door. 'They're asleep already – Parker goes down at six thirty and Slate at seven thirty, although now he's dropped his nap he's often kind of cranky by then. So after that you'll be free to clear up anything that needs doing and relax until Peter or I get home.'

'I see.' Already, Beatrice was looking forward to seven thirty on her first day.

'And this is the guest suite.' Frances opened another door and flicked on a light. Inside was a spacious, comfortable room, doors leading off it to a bathroom and presumably a closet. 'I know you said you'd prefer to live out, but perhaps now you've seen the apartment...'

She gestured temptingly around her – *All these things I will give thee.*

'It's gorgeous,' Beatrice said. 'Honestly, you're so kind. And if you ever need to work late, if you're out or whatever, I'd be glad to stay over. But I'd love to have a place of my own and some independence.'

The threat of a lecherous husband she'd made up for her mother clearly couldn't be produced for her employer. Beatrice waited for a reaction, feeling her nails dig into her palms as she clenched her fists.

But Frances surprised her. 'I totally get it. You'll want to stay with people your own age, make friends, see the sights on your days off. Do you need some pointers on areas that might be suitable? Here in Canary Wharf there are plenty of apartments with young professionals looking for sharers. Many of them are from the US too, like us. Peter could ask around at work and help you find something affordable? I could too, only young people working in fashion tend to live in areas that are a bit... You know. Sketchy.'

Beatrice hesitated a moment, then said, 'Actually, I was thinking maybe Spitalfields. It's easy to get here by bus.'

'Spitalfields?' Frances's eyebrows rose so high they disappeared behind her smooth dark bangs. 'Now that is sketchy.'

Beatrice forced a laugh. 'More bohemian, right? I read it's kind of the fashion centre of London, like the Garment District. I'd love to be based right in the heart of all that.'

'I totally get that too.' Frances's smile was warm. 'So I will ask around at work, then. But you're all set for now, right? Until you find somewhere more permanent?'

Beatrice nodded. 'I'm in a hotel. Mom and Dad offered to sub my accommodation for the first couple of weeks. And it's right close by, so I'll be here at seven sharp tomorrow.'

'Great! Peter might already have left for the office by then, but I'm here until eight thirty most mornings, so I can give you a hand with the morning carnage. Slate's in preschool from nine – we can walk over there together. And our cleaning lady comes on Wednesdays, but she'll let herself in.'

'Sounds good.'

'Wonderful! So I'll see you tomorrow, then. Unless you have any more questions?'

'I think I'm all set.'

Gushing with thanks for Beatrice's time and enthusing

about how glad they were to have her on board, Frances showed Beatrice back to the lobby, handed her her coat and pressed the button to open the elevator. Beatrice accepted a final hug and stepped in, waiting for the doors to close before she allowed herself a long exhale of relief.

It had all gone smoothly. Her employer seemed to like her and with any luck the kids would too.

And most importantly, she had managed not to let on that despite her years of babysitting throughout high school, two summers working as a camp counsellor and weekends volunteering at Head Start while she was in college, Beatrice found children tedious at best and infuriating at worst.

SEVEN

10 APRIL 2005

The dream. It came again last night and even though I'm awake now, the warm weight of the cat on my feet alive and reassuring and true, I can still feel its shadow. It clings to me like cobwebs, or like the veil of a bride before her father lifts it.

It makes me feel sick, bereft, ashamed.

Never tell people about your dreams, Orla, my grandmother used to scold, it's boring and therefore rude. But no one except me will see this and why shouldn't I be rude to myself?

I can go months, perhaps even years, without dreaming it. Sometimes I imagine I'm free of it at last, and then it comes for me again, the same as ever, only the details changing. Always, in the dream, I see her somewhere – sometimes in a familiar place, such as my kitchen; sometimes in a random location like a street I walked down long ago and believed I'd forgotten. Sometimes in a place that must exist only in my imagination.

Last night, it was in Spitalfields Market. Its vibrancy and clutter – the teetering racks of clothes; the shouts of the stall-holders; the teeming tourists wielding cameras and students hunting for bargains; the smells of mothballs, incense, spicy food and stale sweat – were intensified in my sleeping mind into a frightening chaos, a dense thicket of sensation.

Then I saw her, just the back of her, same as always. I recognised her instantly even among the crowd, the shoulders of her coat and her flying dark hair as familiar as my own reflection in a mirror. That glimpse sent me hurrying after her, calling her name, desperate to catch her up this time, even though I never have before.

I shouldered desperately through the throng, my breath coming in gasps. I came close to her, then lost her again. The heel came off my shoe but I staggered on, her name rasping again and again in my throat.

I'm never in any doubt that it is her. I am always so sure that I would recognise her anywhere. And every time, I lose her. She slips away, lost to me in my dream just as she is in reality.

Every time, I wake feeling like this: achingly sad yet somehow purged, relieved that – at least until next time – it is over.

I can't write any more today. I could fill three thousand pages, never mind three, without being able to describe this sense of loss, but at the same time I have no more words.

I will get up and feed the cat. I have decided to name her Maud, because I love the pilgrim soul in her.

EIGHT

I didn't go to see the house with Orla that day. In fact, I didn't see it at all until two weeks later. I left her outside the newsagent, taking her number and the address on Damask Square, thanking her and saying that I'd give her a call.

But somehow I couldn't persuade myself to do that. Part of me – the sensible part, I suppose – told me that she could be crazy, she could be a fantasist, she could be a people trafficker and the next thing I knew I'd be imprisoned in some Soho walk-up servicing twenty men a day, guarded by a Maltese thug with a firearm, my passport hidden in a safe somewhere amid bundles of cash and cocaine.

But there was another part of me that felt differently – a bolder, more adventurous part that told me I was worth more than slinking around people who'd treated me badly, that if I flounced out leaving my deposit to cover one month of my remaining rental contract and Samantha to cover the other, it was no less than she deserved.

So, for two weeks I dithered. For the first week, I kept my head down, went to work, ate my meals in silence at the kitchen table, and went out with colleagues whenever anyone suggested a pint after work. I spent one Saturday night at Emily's, sharing her double bed after an evening of wine, box sets and pick and mix.

It was only the next morning, over boiled eggs and soldiers – Emily's hangover cure of choice – that I told her about Orla and the house on Damask Square.

'Oh my God, you should totally live there!' she said. 'It would be amazing! It would be an adventure. It would be so cheap.'

I explained my fears about the Soho walk-up and the sex slavery.

'What?' she laughed incredulously. 'Who are you and what have you done with my rational friend Livvie?'

'That's the whole point,' I countered. 'It's not rational. Staying where I am is the rational thing to do.'

'No, it's not. Sometimes the rational thing to do is to take a leap of faith. What's the worst that could happen? It doesn't work out and you move in here with me once Carl and Hannah have headed off to Thailand.'

The following Sunday morning, I got dressed and headed downstairs, hearing Samantha, Amanda and Gary's chatter and the clink of spoons on coffee mugs immediately silence when they heard my feet on the stairs. Their three pairs of eyes watched me with cold suspicion as I put on my coat, said a cheery goodbye and let myself out.

As the door was closing, I heard Gary say something and all of them giggle.

Feeling suddenly lighter, as if I was breathing different air from that inside the house, I walked to the end of the street and waited for a bus. I could have walked, as I had before, but this felt more appropriate, somehow – more normal. Less desperate.

Twenty minutes later, I stepped off at the intersection

where the two corner shops stood opposite each other. My A–Z was open in my hand, as it had been throughout my journey, although I'd already memorised the route to Damask Square. I turned off the main road into a side street lined with 1960s red-brick terraced houses, two newer grey concrete tower blocks looming above them. Then I turned again, following a path through a small park where children played on swings and slides in the spring sunshine and a group of teenage boys kicked a football over the muddy grass.

Another turn, and the square opened up in front of me. A graffiti-covered street sign confirmed that I'd reached my destination: Damask Square.

I could see how beautiful it must once have been. There were perhaps a dozen tall houses arranged on two of its sides, the third open to the park and the fourth taken up by yet another newer low-rise building. In the centre was a garden bordered by black iron railings, a plane tree laden with acid-green spring foliage shading the grass where daffodils and crocuses bloomed. It must once have been a full square, I realised – probably German bombs had destroyed the rest.

The older houses were tall and elegant, four or five storeys high, taller than the block of flats. Their roofs were grey slate, their fronts white stucco, mostly worn and flaking. Pillared porticos sheltered their front doors and sash windows overlooked the garden – or they would have done, except most of them were shaded with blinds, shutters or in one case sheets of curling newspaper.

Slowly, I made my way around the square, the garden proving inaccessible owing to a padlocked gate. Number five was identifiable only because it was between number four and number six – it was only when I reached it that I could see the faint ghost of less-faded red paint on its door where the brass numeral must once have been fixed.

The door knocker was long gone, too, and the letterbox was an empty gap in the wood, disconcerting as a toothless mouth.

I raised my hand and knocked, the wood hard and heavy enough to bruise my knuckles before they made any significant sound.

Then I waited, feeling the sunshine warm on my back. Behind me, somewhere up in the branches of the plane tree, I could hear a magpie's cackling call; the voices of the children playing were distant now and the hum of traffic on the main road almost inaudible.

I'd almost given up and decided to send a text when Orla opened the door.

She was wearing what I was almost sure were the same camel-coloured wide-legged trousers I'd seen below her coat the first time I met her, and a bright red jumper in fine wool. There were small gold hoops in her ears and her short hair was tousled, her face free of make-up.

She didn't seem at all surprised to see me.

'Livvie.' She smiled. 'I hoped you'd come and here you are.'

'Hello.' I felt an answering smile over my face. 'I thought – I wanted to come and see the room.'

'Of course. Come in. I'm glad you waited, because it's all ready for you now.'

She turned and I followed her into the long hallway. A flight of stairs rose above us at its end and I caught a glimpse of a black cat sitting watching us, before it darted away.

To my left, I could see a closed door; to my right, another door leading to a room that seemed to be little more than a building site – or a bomb site. Planks of wood were propped up against the walls, cans of paint littered the floor and a ladder stood in the centre of it all like a heron watching over a pond.

'Don't look,' Orla urged. 'It gets better.'

So I averted my eyes from the room that opened up ahead of us, focusing instead on the stairs – bare wood, scuffed and paint-stained, each one dipping in the centre where centuries of feet had trod.

'So when did you buy the house?' I asked as we began to climb.

'I didn't.' Orla's voice came back to me over the sound of a power tool whirring to life somewhere. 'I inherited it. It was my grandmother's. Well, my grandparents', but he's been dead more than fifty years. To be honest I barely knew it existed – my grandmother never mentioned it. I think she was distressed by its... by what happened here. I was abroad when she died and not expecting anything to come to me, anyway, so it took a while for her solicitors to...'

The noise increased and I couldn't catch what she said next, so I answered, 'I'm sorry for your loss.'

'Yes. Thank you.' Orla led the way on to a landing. More doors opened up off it, and I could see rooms that must once have been grand and spacious but were now poky, divided up by makeshift walls into little more than cubbyholes. There were curling carpet tiles on the floor and suspended tiles on the ceilings, many of them suspended only by a corner.

'Have you lived here long?' I asked as she turned and began climbing yet another flight of stairs.

'It's been several weeks now. To be honest, I was a bit overwhelmed when I first saw it – I didn't know where to begin. But then Luke came, and it feels – not achievable, exactly, but not entirely unachievable either.'

'It's quite the project,' I said, remembering the TV show Emily was addicted to watching. 'A real Grand Design.'

Orla laughed. 'That's what Luke said. But we're a long way from designing anything. Now, here's the bathroom – it's one of the better bits.'

She tapped on a closed door, presumably in case Luke – whoever he was – was inside, waited a second and then opened it. I gasped. The bathroom was bigger than my bedroom in the house in Mile End, but almost entirely empty. The floor was bare boards, the walls painted white. Sunlight poured in through a vast window that overlooked the garden – a tangle of brambles and trees, somewhere in which I could hear a blackbird singing. There was a vast claw-footed cast-iron bathtub in the middle of the room with a shower above it, rust staining its surface beneath the taps. Underneath the window was a porcelain washbasin on an ornate stand. Against the wall was a toilet with a wooden seat, a long flush chain hanging from its cistern.

Everything was spotlessly clean.

'We had to get the basics sorted first.' Hands on hips, Orla surveyed the room with satisfaction. 'You'd have to share this with Luke and me for the time being, until we get the next one done.'

'Is it just the two of you living here?' I asked, hoping the answer could shed some light on who Luke actually was.

But it didn't. 'Us and Maud, the cat. I heard her crying in the street one night and invited her in, and she hasn't left. Would you like to see your— the room that would be yours?'

'Yes, please.'

I turned and stepped aside, waiting for Orla to take the lead again. She climbed another half-flight of stairs, this time to a landing with four doors leading off it. All were ajar, but she pushed open the one that I worked out would be at the front of the house, on the right-hand side.

'Here you are.' There was satisfaction in her voice – pride, even.

And I could see why. Even bigger than the bathroom, this room had the same wide hardwood floorboards, but these had been polished as well as sanded. Their smooth golden surface reflected the blue sky visible through two more sash windows. The walls were white with cornice mouldings, the ceiling high with a plaster rose at its centre. The smells of sawdust and paint hung in the air.

'I love it,' I gasped. 'It's beautiful. You must be so proud.'

I could hardly get the words out. Downstairs, the glimpses of dirt and disorder I'd caught had made me decide that this was a non-starter – however intrigued I was by Orla, I couldn't live in such a place. But now I'd changed my mind completely.

This wasn't a house that was slowly succumbing to neglect and apathy, sinking into ruin under the weight of forces stronger than I could ever be. I knew what that looked like, and it wasn't this.

This was a home emerging from a long sleep like a butterfly from its chrysalis, not yet perfectly formed but on its way.

'You'll take it, then?' Orla looked startled, as if this was the last response she'd been expecting.

'Yes. Yes, I really will. If I can, that is. How much were you thinking...?'

Orla told me. The rent was lower than I'd expected – lower than I'd been paying before.

'And there's no deposit, of course,' she added. 'We couldn't charge you for damages – it's already damaged enough!'

'Yes,' I said again, without hesitation. 'Yes, please. I'll need to get my things and probably take a taxi over.'

I paused, my mind racing. It was Sunday, almost lunchtime. If I hurried, I could be here by evening, sleeping tonight in this room.

'Unless that's too soon?' I added.

'I could help.' A deep voice startled me and I turned around.

In the doorway stood a man who made my breath catch. He was tall and lean with olive skin, wearing paint-stained jeans that clung to his narrow hips. A grey sweatshirt with a hole below the neckline revealed a glimpse of his collarbone. But it was his eyes that held me – grey or palest blue, startling against his dark complexion. When he smiled, the warmth of it reached those eyes and his voice was warm too.

'I could take you back to your place in my van,' he went on. 'Help carry your stuff. Unless you travel light, that is.'

'I'd love some help,' I said. 'Thank you.'

Unusually for me, I didn't hesitate at all. And I didn't feel as if I was being rushed into something – quite the opposite. I felt as if I was rushing – hurrying eagerly towards a future that might hold anything at all.

Except it would definitely hold Orla – Orla and Luke.

At least, that's what I believed then.

NINE

'No, Bibi!' Her face scarlet and tear-streaked, Parker squirmed away from Beatrice and set off across the room as fast as her toddler legs could carry her, her whimpering turning to screaming. 'No, no, no!'

Beatrice watched her for a second, hands on hips, then set off in pursuit. It was Friday afternoon and she was more exhausted than she could ever remember being before – not when she'd been up all night studying for her final exams at college, not when she'd got back from three nights at Burning Man and couldn't let on to her parents that she hadn't spent the weekend chilling at a friend's place in the Hamptons, not after the first night she'd spent with – what was his name again? – and struggled through a day of lectures dazed with sex and lack of sleep.

In a little over two weeks working as Slate and Parker's nanny, she'd had one day off. Strictly speaking, her weekends were meant to be free unless she was accompanying the family on a trip out of town, which had happened the first weekend. On the second, Frances had pleaded with her to come and help out at Slate's fourth birthday party, offering to pay her so handsomely that Beatrice had been unable to refuse. After spending the morning blowing up balloons and making sandwiches, the afternoon wrangling twenty-five sugar-hyped pre-schoolers and the evening clearing up, she'd barely left her hotel bedroom the following day, only to have to get up at six on Monday morning and face another week of children.

In her worst nightmares, she couldn't have imagined it would be so full-on. From the moment Frances left for work until the moment she returned home, there was no let-up. Even after she'd dropped Slate off at preschool, there were Parker's tantrums and demands for play and snacks to deal with. Even when Parker was having her nap, there were countless tiny socks to be paired and put away, food splatters worthy of a Jackson Pollock painting to be wiped up, the next meal to be thought about before the kids became totally unmanageable with hanger.

Even her identity was no longer her own – it hadn't taken long to realise that Beatrice was too difficult a name for Parker's two-year-old tongue, and once she'd started calling Beatrice Bibi, her brother and even her parents had followed suit.

Thank God, she said to herself, *thank baby Jesus and all the angels I no longer believe in for a day off tomorrow and another the day after that.*

'Parker, honey,' she said. 'Come on. We've got to go get your brother from school and that means you've got to put on your coat.'

'Nooo!' Parker howled, flinging herself to the floor, her arms and legs thrashing. 'I don't want to!'

At least she, having no emotional connection to the children whatsoever, was able to deal with them as dispassionately as if she'd been charged with looking after someone's pet snake.

Still, it was already three thirty. Slate needed to be picked up by four, otherwise a hefty fine would be added to Frances and Peter's bill and – worse – Beatrice would look incompetent. It was time for some UN-level negotiation.

She squatted down next to Parker, who ignored her and kept screaming.

'Now, Parker,' Beatrice said calmly. 'We're going to get your brother. It's cold out, so you can't just wear your fairy dress. You can choose whether you want to put on your pink or your silver rain boots – how about that?'

Parker stopped screaming and opened her eyes. Beatrice's mind flashed to the tin of chocolate-chip cookies she and Parker had baked earlier that morning – more fucking splatters, not to mention Parker knocking over the jar of chocolate buttons, which had skidded across most of the apartment. But resorting to bribery was a high-risk strategy – next thing she knew, the kid would be refusing to get dressed at all without large doses of sugar. Which Beatrice didn't mind in principle, but would be liable to make Parker even more hyper.

Plus, she might tell her mother.

Then Beatrice had an idea.

'Tell you what,' she said conspiratorially. 'You can wear my scarf. Come on, up you get.'

Startled by the sudden change in Beatrice's tone, Parker stopped screaming and scrambled to her feet.

'Wait there.' Beatrice hurried to the entryway and snatched the scarf from the closet. It was Givenchy, a silk and wool blend with the designer's name woven in white on to a black background, and she'd picked it up in a thrift store in the Meatpacking District.

'Scarf,' Parker said, reaching out a hand to grab it.

'Scarf,' Beatrice confirmed. 'Only we're going to turn it into a coat. Now, let's play mannequins. Arms out like this. Stand very still.'

Beatrice hunkered down again, looking from scarf to child and back again. *This shouldn't be too hard.* She draped one corner over Parker's shoulder, wound the length around her body like a sash, crossed it over the other shoulder, wrapped it around her waist and knotted the ends securely together.

Then she stood up and surveyed the result. Not terrible. She looked like a papoose, but she'd be warm enough.

'Silver rain boots with that, I think,' she said firmly.

'Silver,' Parker agreed meekly, her hands pressing into the soft fabric like starfish half submerged in sand.

'Good girl. Come on then, let's make a move.'

Hurrying now, Beatrice pushed her arms into her own coat, slung her purse over her shoulder and pushed the button to summon the elevator. A minute later they emerged on to the street, Parker's small, sticky hand clasped tightly in Beatrice's.

'Four hours,' she breathed to herself, like an affirmation. 'Four hours, then I won't have to see them again for two whole days.'

On Sunday, Beatrice woke up feeling almost human, having slept for twelve hours straight. She'd spent the previous day in bed, sleeping and mindlessly watching old episodes of *Friends* on the small, flickering screen of her hotel room television. She'd ventured out at lunchtime with her sketchbook, thinking she'd explore the local area a bit, but got no further than McDonald's before returning to bed.

Was this what it was going to be like? Months and months of living in a country where she couldn't learn to feel at home and a city she was too shattered to even see, all her hopes and intentions coming to nothing because she was simply too tired to actually live?

The weather helped: a glorious, sunny day, full of the warmth that spring had so far failed to deliver. Dressed in jeans, sneakers and a sweater, Beatrice walked away from the cluster of glass high-rise towers, following the bend of the river towards the City. She wanted to explore: to find the neighbourhood where the old men in Clonmara had told her the family's house had been located. But also, she needed to find a place to live; two weeks in a hotel – even such a basic one – had eaten into her funds alarmingly, even with her parents' contributions.

She didn't get very far before hunger made her stop, and she went into a café and ordered a full English breakfast. Mopping up beans with her toast, adding three spoons of sugar to her tea – the only way to make it drinkable, she figured – and even sampling the scab-like disc of black pudding, she hoped she might be mistaken for a local.

But she wouldn't, of course – no local would have an *A–Z* map book and a *Rough Guide to London* open next to them, studying it closely as they ate.

She could quite easily walk as far as the Tower of London, and check that out. She could get the Tube into central London and wander round Topshop and Selfridges. She could visit an art gallery or even the Fashion and Textile Museum.

But she knew she would do none of those things. She'd come here with a purpose: everything – the job that her parents had arranged for her, her insistence on taking a gap year before finding a proper job or a grad school programme, her insistence on refusing Peter and Frances's offer of accommodation – had been for one thing.

Only now that she was here, she had no idea how to actually go about it.

She rooted in her purse, found her notebook and placed it on top of the open *A–Z*, flicking through the pages. She hadn't added anything since arriving in London; the final entry was still there, the four words, one crossed out and corrected: *Big house in Spitalfields.*

She cast her mind back to that dingy, low-ceilinged room, its walls still stained yellow from the tobacco no one had been permitted to smoke for over a year. It was practically a miracle she'd managed to write it down at all, given how thick the men's accents had been and how many glasses of peaty Irish whiskey they'd insisted on buying her.

They'd told her that, yes, there'd been a big house in the area, long ago, and that a wealthy family had lived there.

'More than ten years ago, it would have been, since the old woman was taken into care.'

'Her son died some twenty years ago and his wife had run off years before.'

'He was one for the drink, and the ladies.'

Beatrice had done some rapid mental arithmetic. If the old woman had been old enough to go into a care home ten years ago, her son and daughter-in-law would surely have been too old to be of any relevance to Beatrice.

'Did they have any children?' she asked. 'A daughter?'

'Sure there was a girl.' The speaker scratched his head. 'But she went off to college in Dublin and no one ever saw her again.'

'Fair broke the old lady's heart.'

'And the house was sold and torn down, and they built bungalows on the land.'

Beatrice hadn't been able to stop her disappointment from showing in her face. She half-stood, beginning to thank the men for their time.

'Ah, stay and have another drop of this good whiskey with us, do.'

'Wait, there was another house, wasn't there?'

'In London.' The old man's face brightened. His friend gestured to the bartender and more whiskey was poured. 'In the East End, I believe.'

'The Doyles were after buying big houses.' A phlegmy cackle. 'Before they lost all their money, that is.'

'It would've been the old woman and her husband that bought it. Some notion of family history, because it was in

Spitalfields that they first made their fortune, back when all the Irish weavers crossed the sea to work there.'

'But they never lived there, because the war came.'

That was all the information Beatrice had been able to glean. The name of a place – Spitalfields – and a family – Doyle.

The nib of her pen hovering over the notebook, she traced the area on the page of the map. The yellow and white lines of the roads, their names printed in black, gave her no clue as to what the place might actually be like. But there it was, Tower Bridge to its south, Whitechapel to its east, the City of London to the west and Shoreditch and Hackney to the north.

None of those names meant anything to her either, yet they felt somehow mysterious and full of promise. She could almost taste the words as she formed them silently with her tongue.

Leaving the dregs of her tea and most of her black pudding, Beatrice tucked a ten-pound note under her saucer, pushed back her chair and stood up, tucking her books back into her bag. Now that she was almost there, almost within touching distance of a goal of sorts, she felt newly apprehensive, tempted to return to the familiarity of her hotel and *Friends*, and sleep some more.

But she couldn't. She wouldn't get another chance until next weekend and she couldn't afford to waste another week with no longer-term home and all her questions still unanswered.

She pushed open the door of the café and headed out into the street, the sunshine dazzling her before she lowered her shades over her eyes and started walking.

TEN

I remember the time before Beatrice arrived as a kind of halcyon period – the calm before the storm. But that's not really how it was. It was only a week, after all, between me moving in and us meeting her, and the honeymoon phase continued for quite a while afterwards.

Still, that Sunday stands out in my mind like a kind of landmark – a full stop between before and after.

The 'before time' began when Luke drove me to Mile End to pick up my things. The drive wasn't long – only about fifteen minutes, because it was Sunday afternoon and the traffic on the Mile End Road was light. All the way, we chatted. He told me about his card in the newsagent's window, how he'd studied fine art at university, then briefly worked as a graphic designer.

'But I hated it,' he said. 'Stuck in front of a computer all day. No disrespect to graphic designers, but it didn't feel like art at all, really.'

So he had slipped back into doing the construction work he'd learned from his uncle. Orla's house, he said, had seemed like a golden opportunity: free accommodation and a wage that was enough to pay for his other needs, in return for work that didn't look likely to dry up any time soon.

'That place is a project and a half,' he said, his hand lifting from the steering wheel to push back his glossy hair. 'And I won't be able to leave her in the lurch before it's finished.'

'You'll be an expert in house restoration by then,' I remarked. 'You'll be able to start your own property development business and make a fortune.'

He laughed, and I saw the flash of his white teeth. 'God, no. I want to transform buildings in a different way.'

'What's that then?'

He hesitated, then said shyly, 'Street art. You know, like—'

'Banksy?'

'Banksy's a wanker. All that anonymity and secret squirrel bollocks.'

'His art's worth a fortune, though.'

'Maybe, but... I want to do different stuff. Stuff that properly transforms urban communities. Makes them more relevant and vibrant for the people that live there.'

I glanced sideways at him. His eyes were on the road but he was smiling, as if he was looking at something far more beautiful than the traffic on the Mile End Road.

'Now I'm sounding like a wanker myself.' He laughed. 'I told Orla all this when I first spoke to her – I reckon it's partly why she gave me the gig. Like she'd rather have a struggling artist working on her house than a proper builder. Anyway, what about you?'

I told him that my degree was in English literature, but because I didn't want to be an academic or a teacher, I'd taken the first job that was offered to me, which happened to be as a junior HR assistant in the head office of a high street bank.

'They've got me working on the staff newsletter,' I admitted. 'Not exactly Shakespeare. Especially as it's all outsourced to an agency, and all I seem to do is chase people for information, then chase them again to sign it off. We're still working on the March edition, although we'll be lucky to get it out before the end of May.'

We'd arrived at the road where the house – my old house, as I already thought of it – was by this point. I directed him to turn right and he found a parking spot.

'Want me to come in with you?' he asked.

I hesitated. It would only take a few minutes to pack my things – clothes, toiletries and books. I didn't particularly want him to see the dirty laundry I hadn't got around to washing – but also, I felt that he'd act as a kind of bodyguard, protecting me from Samantha's malice.

And so it proved. When I opened the door and Luke stepped in behind me, she and Gary emerged from the kitchen, saw him and watched in wide-eyed silence as we walked up the stairs together. No snide giggles followed us, and when we returned downstairs ten minutes later, Luke carrying the suitcase holding my clothes, me with already splitting supermarket carrier bags of books in each hand, they stayed silent.

'I'm moving out,' I said unnecessarily. 'You can keep my deposit, but I won't be paying next month's rent.'

They nodded mutely. Luke stepped out and I followed him, locking the door behind me then posting the keys back through the letterbox.

'Chatty pair,' Luke said, his mouth quirking into that half-smile I was already learning to watch for. 'Must've been a laugh riot living with them.'

'Like you won't believe,' I said, and the two of us burst out laughing.

I couldn't help wondering whether Samantha and Gary could hear our laughter through the closed door. I hoped they could.

After that, things fell into a routine quickly. When I left for work, Luke and Orla would already be up, Luke scraping away decades of old wallpaper, Orla tackling the forest of weeds outside, Maud the cat perched on what remained of the garden wall watching her.

By the time I returned home, there'd be progress to be shown and comment on: a struggling rose bush uncovered from a net of brambles, carpet tiles torn up from the floorboards in one of the first-floor rooms, a skip outside that had been organised by Luke and paid for by Orla.

We ate together in the evenings, vegetarian food cooked by Orla. The kitchen, as she'd warned me, was one of the worst rooms in the house, the cupboards sagging off the walls, an ancient cooker with spiral hotplates and a rusty fridge its only amenities. But Orla's cooking was delicious and it felt almost luxurious to sit together at the shabby, Formica-topped table on rickety wooden chairs, eating and talking, Orla or Luke or sometimes both of them with a sketchbook on the table next to their plate.

It felt right. It felt like being a family. It got so as five o'clock approached, I looked forward to leaving the office and coming home.

When Saturday came, I was woken by the sound of Luke's feet on the stairs – already, I knew his heavy tread, quite distinct from Orla's lighter footsteps and Maud's almost inaudible padding. Then I heard him whistling and a low crunching sound as he connected a power tool to a plug socket.

Then the whirr of his drill started up.

For a moment, I was annoyed – *I never signed up for this! It's eight thirty on a Saturday, for God's sake.* But my irritation was short-lived and I found myself unable to get back to sleep, not because of the noise but because I wanted to get up and see what was going on.

I pulled on faded jeans and a T-shirt and left my room. Orla's and Luke's bedroom doors were open, both their beds neatly made. I could smell eggs frying and hear the sizzle of a pan when the drilling noise paused.

I descended the stairs to the first floor and found Luke wrestling with a large panel of dry-walling even taller than he was.

'Need a hand?' I asked.

'I'm all good. It's not heavy.' His voice was muffled, his face invisible. I could only see his strong, paint-stained hands gripping the edges of the board.

'Yeah, right. It's just awkward. That's what they all say.'

He put the board down and laughed. 'Go on then. If you could grab the other side, we'll get this downstairs and into the skip.'

I obeyed, and together we managed to do as he'd suggested, heaving the board up and hearing it crash on to the pile of rubble that already half-filled the skip.

I dusted off my hands. 'What's next?'

'You don't have to do this, Livvie.' He smiled at me. 'Unlike me, you're paying full whack.'

'But I want to help.'

'Are you sure?'

'Course. I've done my manual handling training at work. I can carry boxes of photocopy paper without putting my back out, and everything.'

'Sold.' He pushed his hair back from his eyes. It was dark brown with lighter streaks that I assumed had been left by the sun, not by a hairdresser. 'Let's grab some breakfast first, though. Orla said it would be ten minutes, about ten minutes ago.'

So we ate and then returned to work, and on Sunday I found myself up early, ready to start all over again. That day we spent stripping wallpaper and removing floor tiles, because Luke said he didn't want to do anything too noisy that would annoy the neighbours. Instead of fried eggs on toast, Orla produced a huge vat of minestrone soup for lunch, with home-made soda bread and butter. Then we began again.

And, at about half past three, I saw her.

I didn't pay much attention to her at first. All day, a steady trickle of people had been passing the house: the Hossain family, who rented one of the flats opposite; a group of students on their way to the park for a picnic, laden with cool boxes and blankets; a couple of chefs from one of the restaurants on nearby Brick Lane standing in the sun having a smoke break.

But this girl was different. She was walking like she didn't know where she was going – not strolling aimlessly or striding purposefully but pacing slowly, looking up at the tall houses and sideways at the railed-off square, then down at the map in her hand.

She looked about my age, but there the resemblance between us ended. I was tall and thin, cursed with the kind of boyish figure that was all knees and elbows. She was smaller and curvy, feminine even in her jeans and jumper. My hair was brown and not particularly clean, scraped back from my face with an old velvet scrunchie. Hers was blonde and in the sort of ponytail that involves tongs, back-combing and a tendril of hair wrapped and pinned to conceal the bobble.

Everything about her, from her glowing skin to her perfectly fitting jeans to the diamond stud I could see in her bellybutton between the waistband of her jeans and the hem of her spotless white jumper, spoke of money and time spent on her appearance.

I realised that instead of following Luke back inside the house, I was standing next to the skip, staring at her. As if she could feel my eyes on her, she stopped and looked back at me. Then the cadence of her steps changed and she came towards me, walking purposefully now, as if she knew where she was going when she hadn't before.

'Hi.' She walked up to me, pushing her sunglasses up to reveal china-blue eyes. 'This is Damask Square, right?'

She pronounced it differently from how I did, the 'a' drawn out to almost a drawl. *American?* I wondered.

'That's right,' I said. 'Can I help you?'

'I was just looking at the house. Are there any other big houses around here or are these the only ones?'

'The house?' I could feel sweat trickling down from my hairline and wiped it away, conscious of my grubby hands. 'There aren't any others like this that I know of. Not as big, anyway. But I've only lived here a week.'

'You're renovating it?' she asked, not that she needed to, given the skip and Luke emerging once more from the front door, lugging a rusty metal filing cabinet.

'Our landlady is,' I said. 'I'm just helping out. I rent a room here.'

'A room?' She took a step closer to me, her expression suddenly eager, as if she was about to push past me and dart up the stairs. 'As it happens, I'm looking for a room to rent.'

'Then maybe you should come in.' The words left my mouth, but for some reason, I felt reluctant to let her in – like I'd have any say in the matter. 'You could speak to Orla, our landlady.'

'Yes,' she said. 'Thank you.'

She paused, the look of avid curiosity passing over her face again. 'Orla who?'

'Orla Clifford.'

'Oh.' Briefly, her face fell. But then she smiled and walked past me and Luke, in through the front door.

And in that moment, everything changed for all of us.

ELEVEN

10 MAY 2005

How different the house feels now! I was woken this morning not by the sound of rain coming through the leaking roof – which still leaks; it's a specialist job to fix, according to Luke, who I have no reason to doubt – or even by the persistent kneading of Maud's paws on my chest, but by the sound of a hairdryer – an unpleasant reminder that the electrics, like the roof, will need fully replacing by an expert at vast expense.

Beatrice was up, getting ready to go off to her nannying job – incredible to me, since Beatrice seems little more than a child herself. How different she is to Livvie, who from the moment she moved in has also mucked in, helping Luke with tasks that need an extra pair of hands, pulling up weeds with me in the garden, even topping up Maud's water bowl if she's passing and sees it running low.

Beatrice – well. There is something about her that I find mysterious. It's not that she lacks maturity in contrast to the others: Luke is definitely an old head on young shoulders, and Livvie is clearly a girl who has had to grow up fast – when I ask her about her family, she answers as briefly as she can, and I sense that there is some deep hurt there she isn't willing or ready to share with me, so I back off and resolve not to meddle until the next time curiosity gets the better of me.

Beatrice is different. She chats openly about her parents: her doting, overprotective mom and dad in Philadelphia who reluctantly allowed her to go off on this adventure by herself, only insisting that she find a Nice Job with a Nice Family before paying for her open return ticket. But I can't help feeling that she is holding something back.

She says she needed a place to live, and I daresay she did. But why here? Why this wreck of a house with its damaged occupants, when she could be living literally anywhere? Anywhere within commuting distance of her employers' luxury penthouse, at least. She seems to be fascinated by the house and its history and, by extension, curious about me.

Curious – but also disappointed. I can still feel as if it happened five minutes ago the cool pressure of her fingers in mine when we shook hands on meeting. I told her my name and she smiled, but her smile looked as if it was hiding something – disappointment? Incredulity? As if she was thinking, Orla Clifford? Really? Is that all?

And since then, there have been times when she has fixed me with those wide eyes – so innocent, but also not innocent at all – and asked me to tell her more about my grandparents. Go on, Orla, it must be such a fascinating story.

I have told her that my grandfather bought the house but never lived in it. That I never intended to live in it either, and don't know how long I will stay here now that I am. And that's as much as I am willing to disclose to her, or any of them – at least for now.

TWELVE

'I hate broccoli.' Slate poked morosely at the steamed florets on his plate. 'It's gross. It's like eating snot.'

'I hate broccoli too, Bibi,' announced Parker, who five seconds previously had been eating it with gusto.

Beatrice looked at the children's plates, still laden with grilled chicken, homemade potato wedges and – yes – broccoli. *Try and make sure they get at least five servings of fresh fruit and veggies a day*, Frances had requested back in the beginning. And back in the beginning, they had. But now Beatrice suspected that familiarity might be breeding contempt, because both the kids were pushing boundaries – and pushing her buttons.

Probably, the best thing for her to do would be to eat with them, wolfing down her own vitamin-packed brassicas with enthusiasm. At first, she'd tried – she really had. But watching the kids eat just grossed her out, taking away any appetite she might have had for her own dinner. Perhaps that was part of the problem – they'd seen her push her plate away untouched enough times to get the hang of it.

She thought longingly of the chicken nuggets and curly fries that were in the freezer, left over from Slate's birthday party. They'd eat those for sure. But that would be the beginning of a slippery slope – and besides, Frances would be sure to find out. Not that she wouldn't find out that Beatrice was failing in her five-a-day task when she saw the remains of the kids' dinner in the trash.

'You don't have to eat it all,' she cajoled. 'Just a taste. Tell you what – if I put some of your dad's special hot sauce on it, then will you try?'

'Special what?' Slate regarded her suspiciously. Beatrice sensed weakness: he was open to negotiation.

'Lao Gan Ma,' she said. 'It's only for grown-ups, really. I don't know if you're allowed it.'

This was true, at least – she'd spotted a stash of jars of the stuff in the larder; presumably Peter stocked up when he travelled to Hong Kong for work.

'I want some,' Slate decided.

'Me too,' agreed his sister.

'All right.' Beatrice got to her feet, fetching a teaspoon from the drawer and an opened jar of chilli oil from the larder. 'Just a tiny bit, mind.'

She drizzled a small amount on to Slate's broccoli and a homeopathic one on to Parker's.

Both the children tentatively lifted a piece of broccoli to their mouths and tasted it. Both their eyes widened. Beatrice could see an instant flush appear on Slate's pale cheeks and the beginning of tears in Parker's eyes.

Shit. I've only gone and done it now.

Then Slate said, 'This is good!'

'It's yummy,' agreed Parker, although Beatrice strongly suspected she would have burst into horrified tears without her brother's endorsement.

Suppressing a fist-pump of triumph, she said, 'Good. Now if

both of you eat your dinners, you can have more tomorrow. But as soon as you're done it's time for your baths, okay?'

Three hours later, she slotted her key into the door of the house on Damask Square. As ever, a day with the kids had left her limp with exhaustion – but, as ever, a fresh surge of energy hit her when she stepped over the threshold. She could hear laughter coming from the kitchen and smell cooking – lamb, maybe, its savoury fragrance making her realise how hungry she was.

With a tingle of satisfaction, she remembered the conversation she'd had with Orla the previous Sunday, when she'd put down her knife and fork, leaving her dinner half-eaten. When she'd first moved in, Orla had made it clear that an evening meal would be included with the rent – not least because the kitchen was too cramped for four people to cook separate dinners. Beatrice had accepted the offer readily, but it wasn't long before she had second thoughts.

'Are you not hungry, Beatrice?' Orla had asked, concerned. 'Or do you not like nut roast?'

Briefly, Beatrice had considered her options: politeness or honesty? She'd settled for the best balance she could think of. 'It's delicious. But I have to admit, I'm a committed carnivore.'

Orla had looked at her steadily, her head on one side. Beatrice could imagine her thoughts: *I'm not running a hotel. But actually, I kind of am.*

'I see,' she'd said at last, with a smile that was as easily charming as always. 'Well, I can't have you starving. I buy meat for the cat, so there's no harm in buying it for you as well.'

A hollow victory, perhaps, but a victory nonetheless – one that Slate and Parker wouldn't have been able to gain over Beatrice.

She made her way down the hallway, following the smell

and hum of voices, hanging her coat on the makeshift rack with the others. The one time she hadn't bothered and had just dumped it over the newel post at the bottom of the stairs, she'd found it covered in plaster dust the next morning. Lesson learned.

'Good evening,' she said.

'Hey, Beatrice.' Luke was just getting up out of his chair, stretching his arms up to the ceiling. 'I was just about to head to bed. I'm knackered.'

'How was your day?' Livvie asked, stacking plates and carrying them over to the sink, where the hot tap groaned and spluttered before letting out a reluctant stream of scalding water.

Why does she bother? Beatrice wondered. *If she leaves it, Orla will just clear up herself.*

'There's a couple of chops for you in the oven,' Orla said. 'I'm afraid they might be a bit dried out. Did they keep you late this evening?'

Beatrice nodded, perching on one of the hard wooden chairs. 'Peter's in New York and Frances was out at a McQueen launch.'

Lucky Frances. Out having fun while Beatrice had been reading *Oh, the Places You'll Go* to her offspring.

Orla opened the oven and took out a plate. On it were two lamb chops, the fat crisp round the edges, and a pile of some sort of potato and bean sludge, which Beatrice presumed had been the meat-free offering. Not that she cared – she was hungry enough to eat her own hair.

'There's some salad, too.' Orla pushed a bowl towards her. 'Help yourself. Hopefully we'll be able to grow our own later in the summer.'

What would be the point of that? Beatrice wondered, slicing into a chop. *All that hard work when there are perfectly good lettuces in Sainsbury's.*

While she ate, Livvie finished the washing up and Orla pottered around the kitchen in the way Beatrice had noticed she often did, picking things up and putting them down again, wiping worktops that were already clean – or as clean as they were going to get, given the chips and scratches that marred their surfaces – or just standing, hands on hips, looking at the house as if wondering what she was going to have to do to it next – or as if she was listening, waiting for it to tell her what it wanted.

The thing was, Beatrice had come to realise, she was never alone. Not during the day, certainly – that was to be expected, with either one or two kids constantly underfoot – but not here, either. In the mornings, she was constantly made aware of Orla's presence by the crack of light showing beneath her bedroom door, even though she only emerged just as Beatrice was leaving. And in the evenings, Livvie or Luke or both of them – and often Orla, too – were downstairs, drinking tea, playing music on the ancient boombox Orla had picked up from a market stall.

I could be wasting my time here, Beatrice thought. *I don't even know whether this is the right place.*

All she had to go on was a search of Wikipedia, which had informed her that Spitalfields' weaving industry, back in the eighteenth century, had been centred on the area around Christ Church. A further search had revealed the handful of streets with Georgian houses that hadn't been demolished by either German bombers or 1960s town planners.

Damask Square could be the place she'd been looking for – but so could about fifty other possible candidates. That was assuming it even still existed: there was every chance that the Doyle family's house in Spitalfields had been reduced to rubble decades ago.

And as for Orla – any number of women living here could have inherited properties from grandparents. The chances of

Orla being who Beatrice hoped she was – or even connected to that woman – were vanishingly small.

Still, the need to find out clawed at her as insistently as her hunger had a few moments before.

'There's no need to wait up for me,' she said. 'It's almost ten. I'll finish clearing up down here and head to bed.'

Livvie yawned, drying her hands on a tea towel. 'All right then. Goodnight, Beatrice. Night, Orla.'

To Beatrice's surprise, she leaned in and dropped a kiss on Orla's cheek before hanging up the tea towel and leaving. A moment later, Maud the cat appeared at the window, eyed Beatrice suspiciously and jumped in via the sink, twining herself around Orla's legs.

'Come on then, madam.' Orla picked her up and Beatrice could hear the cat begin to purr. 'Sleep well, lovey.'

Beatrice only nodded, her mouth full of lamb.

She finished her meal, hastily washed her plate and cutlery and then sat down again, listening. She could hear the thud of the pipes as someone ran hot water, the whoosh of the toilet flushing, the creak of floorboards and the rattle of a window being closed.

She waited some more, until she was sure there would be no more sounds from the house until morning.

Then she got up, switched off the kitchen light and crept upstairs – not to her bedroom on the second floor but to the first.

The floor that used to be offices, where all the drawers and filing cabinets and folders full of dusty yellowing paper were.

The problem was, Luke was clearing it all out faster than she could investigate it. Each evening when she returned from work, the skip outside had grown fuller and fuller with swathes of stripped wallpaper, battered lever arch files, some empty and some not, and falling-apart cardboard boxes full of God knew what.

The other problem was she had no idea what she was actually looking for. But she couldn't shake the idea that, somewhere in the house, she would find the answer she needed – or even a clue to where the answer might be. She knew she had to start somewhere – and it had to be there, before all the junk and accumulated history was removed and Luke started sanding the floors, plastering the walls and painting over any secrets that remained.

So, by the light of the street lamp outside the window and the tiny torch she kept in her handbag, Beatrice began searching. She found nothing of interest – only the accounts of long-defunct sari importers, piles of back issues of *The Draper* magazine and folder after folder of typewritten minutes of meetings.

At almost three in the morning, her hair full of cobwebs and her hands black with dust, tiredness drove her to give up and head upstairs to bed. On the landing she paused, checking that all the lights were switched off in the bedrooms and she could hear no sound other than the almost inaudible breathing of the sleeping occupants of the second floor.

Then she saw it. A frame that hadn't been there before, hanging from the picture rail Luke had recently uncovered beneath layers of old dry-walling. He'd spent hours sanding and oiling the wood panelling, Beatrice remembered, and even she had had to admit that it looked beautiful, softly glowing and golden.

Clearly Orla had thought so too, and decided to grace it with a piece of art.

Beatrice shone her torch on it, peering intently. The narrow beam gave the wrong kind of light to appreciate the painting, glaring off the glass that covered it, but still Beatrice could see its quality. It was a watercolour landscape, showing a succession of hills bordering a valley, their slopes intersecting like the pleats of a dress. Above them stretched a twilit sky, the clouds painted in intense shades of pewter and violet. In the centre ground was the only warm colour: the glowing lights of windows.

Leaning in closer, Beatrice could just make out the fine lettering on the building's wall, between two of the windows and above a door that stood half open, revealing a slit of light so inviting Beatrice almost imagined she could shrink herself like Alice and step straight in.

Riordan O'Connell's.

It was the same name as the pub in Clonmara where she'd met the old men. Not only that – she'd have recognised it anywhere. It was the same pub.

THIRTEEN

I was woken by a noise. Probably not a very loud one but, as is always the way in the dark, small hours of the night, it felt that way – like a huge crash, as if a tile had fallen from the roof and shattered on the pavement outside my window or a door had slammed violently somewhere in the house.

I sat up, instantly fully alert, my heart pounding. And again – as is the way with sudden awakenings – I instantly forgot what exactly the noise had been. Perhaps it had only happened in a dream, because everything seemed silent now. I glanced at my watch and saw that it was half past three in the morning, and remembered that it was Friday. I needed to be up in a few hours – if I didn't go back to sleep soon, I'd be kept awake by the persistent trilling of blackbirds.

Then I heard another sound – the scrape of footsteps on the landing outside my door.

I froze, imagining an intruder having broken into the house, creeping up to murder us all in our beds – what other motivation could they have? There was nothing here worth stealing.

Perhaps Luke would wake up and deal with it. But I knew Luke was a heavy sleeper – often, I was disturbed in the mornings by his alarm clock going off for ages before he finally got up.

And then I detected another noise – the almost inaudible squeak of a doorknob turning. Not mine.

It was nothing, I rationalised – just one of the others getting up to use the bathroom, perhaps dropping something while they were in there, then letting themself back into their room as quietly as they could, hoping they hadn't disturbed the sleepers.

Except they had, and for me sleep wasn't going to return until I knew everything was all right. I pushed my feet into my slippers – knowing from experience that going barefoot in the house meant the soles of my feet would be coated in dust and grit that would transfer to my bedsheets – and pulled my towelling dressing gown on over the T-shirt and pants I wore to sleep in.

Then I walked across the room and carefully opened the door. The landing was in darkness, but I could see a crack of light below the door of Beatrice's room. I stepped across to it and knocked gently.

She didn't answer, but seconds later she opened the door. Her eyes were wide and she was fully dressed in the jeans and lilac linen shirt she'd been wearing at dinner that evening. The shirt was no longer clean – I could see greyish-brown streaks on the front that I could have sworn hadn't been there yesterday.

'Are you okay?' I whispered. 'I heard something and I wondered...'

'I... I heard something too. I went downstairs to see what it was but it... it was just the cat. And then when I was coming back up I tripped and fell over on the stairs.'

'You poor thing. Did you hurt yourself?'

She smiled. 'I'm okay. But I gave myself a fright. You know what it's like.'

I nodded. 'I do now.'

Beatrice giggled, then yawned hugely. 'I'm so tired but I don't think I'll get back to sleep now.'

'Me neither. Do you want tea?'

She shook her head. 'But I've got chocolate. Come in?'

Conscious that by standing around on the landing we were more likely to disturb Orla, if not Luke, I nodded again. Beatrice opened the door fully and I stepped inside, then she closed it silently behind me and sat down on her bed. It was made, I noticed, puzzled. Why would she make the bed before going to investigate a mysterious sound downstairs?

I couldn't think of a way to ask, so I joined her, kicking off my slippers and sitting cross-legged opposite her. She rummaged in the suitcase that stood open next to the bed, clothes spilling out of it, and produced a pack of Reese's Peanut Butter Cups.

'The crack of the candy world,' she said, ripping open the pack and handing it to me.

'Thanks.' I took one and bit into it, the chocolate sweetening my sleep-soured mouth.

'So what are you doing here, Livvie?' Her question surprised me; until now, we'd exchanged only barest details of what our lives were now – work, the house, what Orla had made for dinner – and none about what they'd been before. But I knew that was what she meant – she wasn't asking why I was sitting in her bedroom before dawn, that was for sure.

'I needed a place to live,' I said. 'Kind of urgently.'

Beatrice raised an eyebrow, nibbled round the edges of a chocolate before putting the middle bit in her mouth all at once, and waited for me to continue.

There was something about that moment – the horribly early hour, the intimacy of the bedroom, the dim light of the small lamp next to Beatrice's bed, my feet tucked warmly under my dressing gown – that made me let my guard down. I found myself spilling out the story of Samantha and Gary, their party, Gary's kiss, Samantha's rage and my abrupt departure.

'And then I saw Orla's ad in the newsagent,' I finished. 'And she was right there looking at it, and it just felt right, somehow.'

'So you never knew her before?' Beatrice asked. 'Or the house? You literally knew nothing about her?'

'Nothing.' Thinking about it now, it seemed like a mad decision – but who cared? It had all worked out fine.

'And it's all worked out great.' Echoing my thoughts, she smiled again. 'That's cool.'

I remembered the word Orla had used, and smiled back. 'Serendipitous.'

Beatrice yawned hugely. 'Looks like we're safe for tonight, anyway. We ought to try and get some sleep.'

'Yeah, I suppose.' Reluctantly, I stood up, feeling a wave of tiredness sweep over me. Then a thought struck me. 'We should go to the pub. You know, for a drink.'

Beatrice hesitated for a second. 'Why not? Tomorrow? Today, that is?'

'Let's do it. And... shall we ask Luke?'

'Roommates night out!'

I stood up, moved towards the door and then stopped. 'What about Orla?'

'What about her? She wouldn't want to come. It would be weird.'

'I suppose so. Okay, then. It's a date. See you later.'

'Sleep well, Livvie.'

To my surprise, although too briefly, I did.

That evening, I left work on time and hurried back home. I showered, washing my hair and shaving my legs, and put on some of the expensive face cream Emily had given me for Christmas, which I'd been illogically saving for best.

When I emerged from the bathroom, Beatrice was hovering on the landing in her dressing gown.

'I spoke to Luke,' she said. 'He's up for it.'

'Awesome! See you downstairs.'

I spent longer than usual doing my make-up and straightening my hair, and dressed in baggy combat trousers, a cropped vest top and high heels. Passing Beatrice's door, I could hear her hairdryer going and smell hairspray and perfume; the bathroom door was closed and the shower running again, so evidently Luke was getting ready too.

But my excitement faded and I felt a pang of guilt when I stepped into the kitchen and saw Orla there alone, opening the oven to check on the progress of a lasagne.

'You look nice, Livvie,' she said. 'Off out?'

'Just down to the pub. Beatrice and Luke and me. We thought, since it's Friday...'

'And since it's Friday' – Orla seemed unruffled by my news – 'I've opened a bottle of wine. It's only supermarket plonk. Would you like a glass?'

Half an hour later, Beatrice, Luke and I left the house. Any worries I might have had about overdoing my outfit for what was after all just a casual drink had been dispelled by Beatrice's appearance – she was wearing a short summer dress that showed loads of cleavage, and shoes even higher than mine. Luke was wearing his usual jeans and T-shirt, but they were free of paint splatters and he smelled of lavender and mint.

'We scrub up okay, don't we?' He grinned.

'You look amazing,' I told Beatrice. 'I love your dress.'

'Where are we going, anyway?' she asked without returning the compliment. 'You said "the pub", but which one? I totally don't understand pubs.'

I realised I had no idea.

But Luke said, 'The Crooked Billet does happy hour on Fridays, and there's a DJ later.'

'Sold,' Beatrice and I said together.

Walking past the square and towards the main road, I felt a sense of heady excitement. The sun was still out, the air warm against my bare arms. It was the weekend and I was out with two people who might be going to become my friends. Or more than friends? I caught the scent of Luke's skin again and felt his arm brush against mine as we walked, and I shivered in spite of the warmth of the evening. My excitement increased when the pub came into view, people spilling out on the pavement around wooden tables, drinks and cigarettes in their hands.

'You two grab a spot out here,' Luke suggested. 'I'll get the first round in.'

Beatrice and I found a place at one of the picnic tables, facing away from the group who were already there. A few minutes later, Luke reappeared, carefully balancing three plastic cups of Pimm's – ice, cucumber and strawberries bobbing on their surfaces. He handed one to Beatrice and one to me, then sat next to me on the narrow bench.

I felt the long, warm strength of his thigh pressing against mine and something inside my mind – or maybe my body – went, *Oh*.

Then I glanced at Beatrice on my other side. Beatrice, in her sexy dress, her long, corn-coloured hair flowing loose down her back. Beatrice, who'd been the one to invite Luke to join us in the first place.

I didn't want to tread on anyone's toes – especially not hers.

But she wasn't looking at Luke, or at me. She was gazing around her, taking in the throng of people.

'Look at those two,' she said. 'Reckon he's her boyfriend or her dad?'

I could tell right away who she meant. The man was at least forty, paunchy and balding, the girl about our age. As we watched, he put his hand on her bum and steered her inside.

'Eeuw,' I said. 'Her boss, I reckon. Having a crack at her after work on a Friday.'

'I mean, at least then there might be something in it for her.' Beatrice fished a piece of cucumber out of her drink and nibbled it.

'Oh my God,' I laughed. 'You wouldn't, would you? With Peter, your boss?'

'Peter? Hell no. Then if Frances found out and ditched him, I'd be stuck with those kids.'

I laughed, but her words unsettled me for some reason I couldn't quite grasp.

Then Luke said, 'See those guys over there? I think they're in a band. What're they called? The Mudlarks? Sort of indie rock. They played at Glastonbury.'

'Now in that case, I totally would,' Beatrice said. 'Having a rock star boyfriend would be great.'

'Apart from him sleeping with millions of fans every time your back was turned,' I pointed out.

The direction the conversation had taken made me feel weird, somehow. Like I wasn't ready to talk about sex with Luke sitting right there next to me. Or maybe like I did want to, to see how he'd react, what his view was on rock stars cheating on their girlfriends – or anyone cheating on anyone, really.

Looking at him now, away from the house, I appreciated for the first time how handsome he was – not just my type, taller than me and lean, with broad shoulders and elegant, long-fingered hands, but anyone's type.

My drink was empty, so I offered to get another round. The pub was busy inside, a press of people around the bar and others crowded around small tables holding shouted conversations over the blare of football on multiple television screens. I queued for our drinks and paid for them, then began to make my way carefully outside.

As I reached the door I saw something that made me stop,

then hurry out, pushing the door open so violently I slopped Pimm's over my wrists.

Beatrice and Luke were still sitting on the bench, the me-sized space still between them.

'Shit,' I said. 'You won't believe this.'

'What?' Luke asked.

'My old flatmate and her boyfriend are here. Remember, Beatrice, I was telling you about them yest— this morning?'

'They're here? That bitch and Mr Sleaze? Where?'

'Just inside.' I turned my face away from the window, which meant turning away from Luke. 'You can see them from here. She's wearing a red top, long dark hair.'

Beatrice peered past me. 'And he's the guy with the tattoo and acne scars? Nice.'

Luke looked bewildered. 'Are you okay, Livvie? Do you want to go somewhere else?'

'I—' I began.

But Beatrice spoke over me. 'No way. Come on, Livvie, you did nothing wrong.'

'What happened?' Luke asked. 'Did you fall out with them?'

Reluctantly, I repeated the story I'd told Beatrice that morning, conscious that while it didn't make me look that bad, it didn't make me look good, either. I should have done something different. I could have handled it better.

'I'm sorry, Livvie,' Luke said. 'I'm sorry that happened to you. So that's why they were weird when we picked up your stuff. They can't do anything to you now, you know.'

'I know.' I took a sip of my drink, the Pimm's dulling the edge of my anxiety. 'And you two will protect me if they come over, right? Pretend I'm someone else – my doppelganger.'

'I'd offer to fight him and protect your honour,' Luke joked, 'only he's the type to glass me and I don't want my beauty ruined.'

'Nothing could ruin your beauty,' I teased, feeling that – thing – pass between us again, a small jolt of electricity between our touching thighs.

'My turn to get a drink,' Beatrice said. 'Same again?'

She disappeared inside. It was getting dark now, but the evening was still warm. The air was heavy with the smells of cigarette smoke and women's perfume, mingling with diesel fumes from the main road. Inside, music began to play – the DJ starting his set.

'So that guy your old roommate's with,' Beatrice said, bringing over our fresh drinks. 'He spoke to me.'

'Gary did? What the— what did he say?'

'He was next to me at the bar. He said, "Nice tits." What a prince.' Beatrice made a being-sick gesture with her index finger in her mouth.

'Jesus.' Luke grimaced, rolling his eyes.

Chatting and laughing, we finished our drinks and then Luke bought another round. The alcohol was going to my head – I felt relaxed and giddy. Luke's shoulder was touching mine now, as well as our legs pressing together. As the night cooled, the warmth of his body felt more and more welcome.

'I have to pee,' Beatrice said. 'Be right back.'

'And then we should probably go,' I told Luke reluctantly. 'It's getting late.'

'We could stop on the way at the off-licence,' he said. 'Have a glass of wine in the garden.'

I imagined the two of us sitting under the stars, the smell of green, growing things surrounding us.

'That would be nice.'

'Are you warm enough?' he asked.

'Just about. It's getting chilly.'

I edged even closer to him, and felt his warm arm slip around my shoulder. Goosebumps sprang up on my skin, and not from the cold. I leaned my head against his shoulder, feeling the rise and fall of his breathing, inhaling the clean smell of his T-shirt.

After a while, I said, 'I should go and find Beatrice. She's been ages.'

'Don't get lost in there.' Luke grinned, and I said I wouldn't.

I couldn't see Beatrice inside, so I made my way to the toilet and had a wee. As I was washing my hands, Samantha came in. Taking a deep breath, imagining Luke's arm around me, Luke's presence protecting me, I ignored her and left.

And then I saw them. Gary and Beatrice, on the dance floor. Their bodies were pressed close together, and their mouths were, too. His hand was high on her bare leg, snaking beneath her dress. I stopped, the music and my own blood pounding in my head. Behind me, I heard the toilet door slam.

I saw Beatrice break away from the kiss, glancing towards me. I knew she'd seen me, and seen Samantha behind me – and I knew Samantha must have seen her.

Beatrice raised a hand to me in a thumbs-up gesture, then she broke away from Gary and headed towards the exit, laughing. Samantha pushed past me, through the throng of people towards her boyfriend, shouting something, her voice shrill with rage.

And I realised that Beatrice had done that for me. For me – but also maybe for fun, and just because she could.

FOURTEEN

9 JUNE 2005

Something has changed between the girls. And between them and Luke too – or more specifically between Livvie and Luke. I can sense it when they are in the room with me – which Livvie and Luke increasingly are not. I notice the two of them going out into the garden together after dinner, having hastily and dutifully done the washing up, and on weekends Livvie ostensibly helps Luke with his work, but I hear drifts of laughter coming from them where before there were only the busy sounds of honest toil: questions, instructions and occasional obscenities.

With Livvie and Luke I sense a romance could be on the cards; between Beatrice and Livvie it is something else – a power play, perhaps? They talk to each other like friends, they disappear into one or the other's bedroom at times, emerging wearing each other's clothes or make-up, and yet there's a crackle of tension between them that is quite different from the magnetism I can see Luke and Livvie beginning to feel for each other.

Could Beatrice be jealous of Livvie and Luke? It would not surprise me – not that she would want Luke in particular, but that she wouldn't want someone else to have what she cannot. She is a young woman who is used to getting her own way – I remember the casual fashion in which she asked me to cook meat for her evening meals, as if there was no question of me refusing because it is against my principles.

Also, she makes very little effort to help around the house. Not that I'd expect her to, exactly – but the others do. When she sees them hoovering or tidying or taking a load of washing to the launderette, she'll reluctantly put the clean dishes away in the cupboard or flick a duster around – the most pointless chore ever, in this building site where dust breeds like the rabbits did on the hills around my grandmother's house – before sitting down again with her magazine or going to lie outside in the sun, basking among the weeds like Maud does.

Well – I can't object to it. I signed up for this when I had the idea of taking lodgers, even though part of me bristles and longs to snap that I am her landlady, not her servant.

And there's something else I have just signed up to. Today I'll be attending a meeting of the Spitalfields Preservation Trust, a bunch of local do-gooders intent on conserving the architectural heritage of the area. I think they imagined I might have plans to knock the house down and replace it with flats, and sometimes I wish I could! But in return for my turning up in smart clothes and sitting before a committee like some kind of dancing monkey, they may 'offer me a grant' to assist with the renovations. And God knows I need all the assistance I can get, so turn up and dance I will.

I suppose I will have to go out and buy an ironing board and an iron – which will probably result in Beatrice asking me to press her blouses for her.

My God. Writing that has brought back a memory of my grandmother overhearing me asking our maid to do just that. She exploded with rage. Don't you think Colleen has better things to do, with this entire house to sweep and the beds to make? What did your last slave die of? You'll iron that yourself, young lady – it's time you learned.

Colleen left us shortly afterwards, because we could no longer afford to pay her, so my grandmother was right – it was indeed time I learned.

That has made me realise why I resent Beatrice sometimes, with her entitlement and her indolence. She is like I was at that age. Just like me.

FIFTEEN

As soon as she opened the door, Beatrice could hear laughter. She paused in the hallway, listening. She couldn't detect Luke's voice at all, only Orla's and Livvie's. Slowly, she walked towards the kitchen. Every muscle in her body felt leaden with tiredness; the previous night, she'd been up until three in the morning going through the last filing cabinet of papers on the first floor, but had found nothing of any value to her.

The house on Damask Square, it appeared, had once been home to a firm of accountants that had done the books for various local businesses, and Beatrice had spent a fruitless three hours looking through the ledgers of an Indian restaurant, a company that imported silk fabric from Vietnam – she'd felt a leap of excitement when she saw this, but it had subsided almost immediately; the names were wrong, the dates were wrong, everything was wrong – and a law firm that appeared to specialise in defending local gangsters.

The papers might have been interesting, but Beatrice had been able to make little sense of the endless columns of credit and debit, especially by the dim light of her tiny torch. At last, her head drooping and her eyes burning with fatigue and dust, she'd abandoned her search and gone to bed.

That was it, now. There was nothing left on that floor for her to investigate. She'd wasted whole nights – almost three weeks' worth of nights – and found nothing, and now she didn't know where to go next.

Nothing but the painting. She'd looked at it again and again, in daylight, admiring its quality and confirming – not that she needed to confirm – that it was indeed the pub in Clonmara. The hills were different now, their sides scarred with houses and small industrial estates. But the pub was still there, unmistakable. Beatrice wondered whether the painting showed the view from the big house where the Doyle family had once lived, now demolished.

She could, of course, ask Orla. The painting was unsigned – had it been in the house when Orla moved in? Had she bought it from one of the market stalls? Had she even – the thought made goosebumps rise on Beatrice's neck – painted it herself? But Orla had never mentioned art to Beatrice, even though she'd seen her out in the garden with her own sketchbook, drawing the cat as she lay sprawled in the sun.

Besides, she never saw Orla alone. Beatrice left the house in the mornings before anyone was up, and by the time she got home at night Livvie was almost always there, chatting to Orla in the kitchen as she was now.

Silently, Beatrice walked through the dark hallway. Next to her was what had once been the dining room – a cavernous space, littered now with cans of paint, a pasting table, bags of plaster and Luke's power tools. She hadn't been in there yet; there was nothing to see. Then she felt a draught on her arm, a current of cool air in the otherwise warm house.

She stopped and looked. A door beneath the stairs, which had always been closed before, almost invisible against the layers of paint that covered the panelling, was standing ajar. She nudged it, stopping almost immediately when its hinges let out a creak of protest.

But it had opened wide enough for her to see that behind it, a steep flight of wooden stairs led downwards.

There must be a cellar. Of course, a house this age would have one – coal would have been stored there, probably, back in the day. Beatrice shuddered, imagining the grimy darkness beneath her feet. Searching the first floor had been bad enough; down there it would be horrible. There'd be rats and Beatrice had a terror of rats.

A sudden thump on the floor behind her made her jump and she spun around, but it was only Maud, hopping down the final stair from the first floor on to the bare boards.

Her mind made a snap connection: cat, rats. She remembered overhearing Orla, half-laughing and half-revolted, telling Luke she'd found the head of a squirrel on the landing outside her bedroom. If Maud was capable of that, rats would be a piece of cake in comparison.

But before she could formulate the fleeting thought into anything approaching an idea, the sound of water running into the sink in the kitchen stopped and she could hear Livvie's voice quite clearly.

'I mean, it's not a *date* date, obviously.'

'Really?' Beatrice couldn't see Orla, but she could picture the smile on her face. 'What is it, then?'

'It's a... it's just a pizza, or maybe a movie. On Friday night.'

'Call me old-fashioned,' Orla said, the smile still there in her voice, 'but that sounds awfully like a date to me.'

Livvie laughed. 'Okay. You're right. It does sound like a date. But what if it isn't? What if Luke just wants to hang out with me, like as friends?'

'Then he'd be asking Beatrice to join you and hang out as friends, too,' Orla pointed out.

Beatrice flinched at the mention of her name. She remembered reading somewhere that eavesdroppers never hear anything good about themselves. She knew she should walk away – go upstairs to her room, come down later and see if anyone had left any food for her. But she didn't.

'Well... maybe.' Livvie's voice was almost drowned out by the clatter of plates. 'When we went to the pub a couple of weeks ago that was all of us, as friends. And maybe he has asked Beatrice to come too. I don't know.'

But I know he hasn't, Beatrice thought.

'If it looks like a date, walks like a date and quacks like a date...' Orla said.

Livvie laughed again. 'Which leaves me with the question – what do I wear? I mean, I don't want to look too try-hard, just in case it turns out not to be a date, and he's got a girlfriend or something, and he just really fancies a pizza.'

'He's never mentioned any girlfriend to me,' Orla said slowly. 'Let me think. It's been – what, almost three months since Luke moved in. And in all that time, I've never seen him going off looking like he's going to meet up with someone special, or heard him sounding all lovey-dovey on the phone, or anything.'

'Really? Are you sure?'

'Not that it would be any of my business if he did,' Orla continued. 'And it's not like this place is somewhere you'd want to bring someone for a night of passion. Though I can't help feeling... he needed a place to live, quite suddenly. Perhaps there was someone before. But there isn't now – I'm as sure of that as I can be.'

Beatrice heard the snap of a switch and the roar of the kettle starting up.

'So I dress like it's a date, then,' Livvie said, as if she was thinking aloud. 'But not fancy. Effortlessly stylish. How do you even do effortlessly stylish?'

'With your figure, you can wear anything,' Orla said.

'There's a reason fashion models are always tall and slender – clothes just hang better. There's a stall at the market that has some great second-hand designer pieces for bargain prices. I saw a Nicole Farhi dress there last week. Which would be too much for Pizza Express, of course, but if you fancied a browse, I'm sure you'd find something.'

'Which stall?' Livvie asked. 'I might go and have a look – maybe take an afternoon off work.'

'I'll show you,' Orla suggested. 'We could go together, maybe?'

'Really? That would be great. Because you totally know how to dress. You always look amazing.'

Really? Beatrice echoed silently. *Orla?* With her unfashionably short hair that she didn't even bother covering the greys in, and her clothes that, while admittedly well cut, were all clearly decades old? Why hadn't Livvie asked her, Beatrice, what she should wear on this date – if it was a date – with Luke?

Eavesdroppers never hear anything good about themselves. She hadn't actually heard anything at all, but she felt as if she had. She was queasy and resentful and – yes – hurt.

There was something about the way Livvie and Orla had been talking that told her this wasn't the first cosy chat they'd had while washing up the dishes from dinner. There was a kind of casual intimacy about their conversation that Beatrice could never imagine there being between her and her landlady – and nor would she want there to be.

Or would she? Livvie and Orla sounded like friends – or more than friends. Like sisters, or even like a mother and adult daughter: affectionate, familiar, respectful.

Beatrice didn't need a mother; she only wanted the truth. She had a perfectly good mother already, back home in Philadelphia. Although, somehow, she couldn't imagine asking her own mother for advice on what to wear on a date – she almost laughed aloud at the thought, but stopped herself just in time.

Her mother would probably suggest she wear a chastity belt, not some vintage designer treasure from a market stall.

I don't care, she told herself. *Let them go off on their girls' shopping trip. I don't care about Livvie and I don't care about Orla and I certainly don't care about Luke.*

She was fairly certain that the last bit was true.

She crept back into the hallway, eased the front door open and then closed it again, more loudly than she had before, almost slamming it. Then she walked back towards the kitchen again, this time letting her feet thud noisily on the floorboards.

She stepped into the bright warmth of the kitchen. 'Good evening.'

Livvie and Orla were sitting at the table, the teapot between them, the fragrance of the lapsang souchong tea Orla drank filling the air.

'Beatrice.' Orla smiled a greeting. 'They've kept you late again. Are you hungry? There are sausages and potatoes.'

'How was your day?' Livvie asked.

Beatrice didn't answer her. 'I'm not hungry. I'll go straight up to bed.'

Then she turned and made her way upstairs to her room.

SIXTEEN

11 JUNE 2005

I woke to see her looking at me. Not in the flesh, of course, but it took me a moment or two to realise that, befuddled as I was by sleep and the dim light filtering through the shutters, which are the solid kind, installed God knows how long ago by God knows who.

As soon as I switched on the light I realised that my mind had been playing tricks on me – it wasn't her at all. It was only the portrait I painted of her yesterday, as I do every year. And every year it leaves me feeling like I do today: hollowed out, as if something that was inside me before is there no longer, because it has been transferred on to my canvas. Like I'm the husk in which some sort of fruit once grew, or the shed skin of a snake.

It is the first thing I have painted since I came to this house, and more than three months overdue. All my life, I've harboured a dream of becoming a professional artist and all my life it has remained just that – a dream. This place was intended to be the turning point: I'd have a stable home of my own and all the time in the world, plus of course the glorious natural light that floods the top floor through the extravagant glazing, installed so that the weavers who worked there could see every intricate thread of the fine silk damasks taking shape on their looms.

If only I'd known that all there is to be found now up there is clutter, puddles and a nest of squirrels that is gradually being decimated by Maud, who presents me with a limp, forlorn body after many of her excursions upstairs.

I couldn't wait any longer before I painted it – I'd already delayed long enough. So I had to make do with my bedroom as a studio and my legs as an easel, closing the door because I didn't want anyone to see what I was doing.

No one has ever seen the portraits, not even Adrian, in the two years I was married to him. They have always been my secret. The previous ones – all twenty-one of them – are down in the cellar, stacked in one of my tea chests. Normally when I begin, I leaf through them, seeing the face growing older each year, changing: sometimes smiling, sometimes serious; sometimes framed by a scarf or hat; sometimes laughing and once thoughtful, her chin resting on her palm and her fingers half-covering her lips.

But this year I didn't have those reference points. I worked only from my mind's eye, lying on the bed as I am now, the sketchpad propped up on my knees and a jam jar of water next to me for my moulting brush.

I don't know how good a likeness it is – I never really do. Probably I never will. But I am fairly certain that when I allow the morning light in, it will show that I've captured the shape of this house in the background, the dappled shade of the plane tree mottling her skin, the fall of hair brushing her cheeks and my grandmother's eyes looking back at me.

SEVENTEEN

Before my date with Luke, I had a date with Orla. Not a *date* date, obviously – but something that felt almost as significant. She'd suggested that we go to Spitalfields Market to find me 'something a bit different' to wear and I'd enthusiastically agreed.

I had to admit to myself that part of me was sceptical about taking fashion advice from a woman so much older than me. But I instinctively felt that refusing would hurt her feelings and I sensed that, even with three of us living in the house with her, she was isolated among us. Also, I was curious to know more about her – what had compelled her to move into a ruin of a house she clearly could barely afford to live in? Where had she been before? How had her family come to own the property but never lived in it?

All those questions felt unaskable in the evenings in the kitchen or on weekends when Luke and Beatrice were so often there, their presence distracting in quite different ways.

So I booked an afternoon off work and hurried home, and Orla and I left the house, strolling through the sunny streets until we reached the market, where stall upon stall held rack upon rack of garments in rainbow-coloured profusion.

'My God,' I said. 'Where do we even start?'

Orla laughed. 'I know. When I first visited a night market in Hong Kong, I felt just like that. You get a sense for where the good stuff is.'

Another hint at her past – but there was no time to ask about her travels in East Asia now.

A rail of brightly coloured summer dresses caught my eye and I stopped, flipping through them. Next to me, Orla reached out and rubbed the fabric between her fingers.

'Polyester.' She glanced around, but the stallholder was a few steps away, his back to us. 'It's terrible for the planet, of course, but takes dye well, and obviously it's cheap. Look at the seams though.'

Obediently, I looked. They seemed like perfectly ordinary seams to me.

'Everything's laser-cut now, so the seam allowance is tiny,' Orla went on. 'Plus they use a really tiny, busy print, so they don't need to pattern match. It all saves the manufacturer money.'

'They're pretty, though,' I argued.

She smiled. 'They are. And perfectly all right if that's what you want. But you can do better. Come on.'

She led me on through the maze of stalls, pausing occasionally to remark on something. 'The trouble is, that trim could be real fur. Dog, maybe... That's a knock-off of a Pucci print... They've done a decent job... This might look and feel like silk, but it's actually rayon.'

I followed her, looking and listening and touching, occasionally asking a question which she was instantly able to answer. Sometimes she'd remove a garment from a rack and hold it up against my body, telling me at a glance whether it was my size without needing to consult the label.

'Now,' she said at last, 'here we might find you something.'

We'd reached the far end of the market now, where the clothing stalls ended and food outlets began. My stomach rumbled at the aroma of smoke and spices, but Orla wasn't thinking about lunch. She led me into one of the permanent shops that stood on the edges of the space and I looked around, blinking in the dim light.

Nothing here was new. The rails lining the shop were full of random garments in tweed, leather, denim and velvet, the musty smell of used clothes hanging over everything. I fought down disappointment – I hadn't wanted to hurt Orla's feelings, but I could have just gone to Oxford Street after work and found half a dozen dresses in the time we'd spent here already.

Orla didn't seem to notice my dismay. She rifled through a rail of garments, her hands swift and sure, and pulled out a dress on a wooden hanger.

'Vivienne Westwood.' She smiled in satisfaction. 'Silk, too. And it's your size.'

I looked at it doubtfully. It was a drab olive green, almost grey, sleeveless and apparently shapeless. But even in the dim light, I could see the sheen of the fabric, and when I touched it, it slipped beneath my fingers like water.

'It's cut on the bias,' Orla said encouragingly. 'Go on, try it.'

I had no idea what she meant, but I was intrigued. Out of hundreds of dresses, she'd picked this one for me. Everything she had said made me think she knew what she was talking about. And there was the feel of that silk – heavy yet soft, supple yet somehow structured.

'Okay,' I said, ducking nervously into the curtained corner that was the shop's only fitting room, tugging off the cotton skirt and T-shirt I'd worn to work, then standing nervously in my bra and pants for a moment before pulling the dress over my head.

It was as if, among the thousands of people browsing the market, the dress had been waiting just for me. It gave me curves where I didn't have any naturally. It made my legs look endless and elegant. It made my eyes look dark green instead of sludgy hazel.

I pushed the curtain aside and stepped out. Orla looked at me, her head on one side, smiling.

'That'll do,' she said. 'Maybe just a tiny dart there below the bust...'

She stepped forward and adjusted the fabric above my waist. I caught the scent of her perfume, clear and bright amid the smell of old clothes.

'How much is it?' I asked. 'I don't actually know if I can—'

'Fifty pounds.' The shopkeeper appeared at my elbow, sensing a sale.

'We'll give you thirty,' Orla countered instantly.

'Oh no, madam. Not possible. I'd be making a loss.'

'Thirty-five.'

'Forty.'

'Done.'

Moments later, we were leaving the market, the dress clutched like a treasure in a paper bag in my hand.

'How do you know?' I asked. 'I mean, where did you learn so much about clothes?'

Orla laughed. 'You could say it's in my blood.'

'In your... How?' I fell into step next to her.

'My family were in the rag trade,' she said. 'Weavers, originally. Back in the eighteenth century, when silk-making was a huge industry in this part of the world. That all changed, of course, when the Industrial Revolution happened. They didn't stay in London for long. But the business was built on silk.'

'So your mother is a bit of a fashionista?' I guessed.

'My mother? I suppose she is, in her way. But it was my grandmother who taught me about clothes. She used to say it's not about your figure, or how much money you spend – it's about caring. Noticing quality and craftsmanship, knowing what suits you and how to alter it so it's perfect. Looking after your clothes and your shoes so they last. But mostly about caring.'

'And it was your grandmother who left you the house in her will?' I asked, trying to make sense of the glimpses of Orla's past I was getting amid the homily about laundry and needlework. 'You must miss her.'

'Oh, no.' Orla's face was still now, the delighted smile gone. 'Not really. I hadn't seen her for over twenty years before her death.'

Questions wheeled in my brain. How could she have been so close to a relative as to have been left a whole house, yet gone half a lifetime without seeing her? How could she talk about her grandmother with such fondness, yet not miss her? But the look on Orla's face – not sad, not angry, just sort of closed off – prevented me from asking her anything more.

'Well, thank you,' I said. 'Thank you so much. I love the dress. And this afternoon – it's been an education. It's been fun. I feel like you've been my fairy godmother.'

The smile returned and Orla laughed delightedly. 'You know, Livvie, that's one of the nicest things anyone has ever said to me. And you shall go to the ball – or at least to Pizza Express.'

EIGHTEEN

Beatrice was woken by sunlight. The nights had grown almost as short as they were going to be and walking to the bus stop in the dark was a distant memory, but this was different – even brighter than usual. Blearily, she turned over in bed and looked at her watch.

Shit. It was quarter to seven. She'd overslept – her alarm was set for six but she must have turned it off in her sleep after sitting up late the previous night working on a drawing of Orla and Livvie in the kitchen, their heads together and their faces alight with laughter. The space around them was in darkness, heavy cross-hatching giving way to brightness at the table where they sat.

She'd tried to make them look like witches in a coven, but it hadn't worked – neither artistically nor as a way to relieve her feelings.

And now she was late for work – too late even to have a shower.

She sprang out of bed and pulled on yesterday's jeans and an old T-shirt from a Met exhibition of John Singer Sargent's early work, which was the only clean garment she had left.

Livvie had offered the previous day to take some of Beatrice's stuff to the launderette with her own, but Beatrice had forgotten and Livvie hadn't reminded her.

If she'd bothered, I'd have clean clothes, Beatrice thought resentfully.

After hastily cleaning her teeth and pulling her hair back into a ponytail, Beatrice hurried downstairs. Orla was already up; she could hear the back door opening then slamming shut again. Well, she had no time for chit-chat over coffee – or any coffee at all, come to that. Never mind breakfast.

'Beatrice?' Orla must have recognised the sound of her sneakers on the stairs.

'I'm just heading out.'

Orla emerged into the hallway. She was in her bathrobe, her hair unbrushed and slippers on her feet. There was an open notebook in her hand; Beatrice glanced at it curiously but it appeared to hold only writing – line after line of Orla's careful script. In her other hand was a cotton drawstring bag.

'Just one thing before you go,' Orla said. Her voice was calm and patient as always, but Beatrice could see tight lines around her mouth. 'Would you mind, when you make your breakfast in the mornings, putting the bread back in this bag and in the breadbin?'

'The what? Oh, the bread. Did I leave it out?'

Distractedly hunting for her keys, Beatrice cast her mind back. Yes, she'd probably made toast the previous morning, from the heavy wholemeal bread Orla for some reason insisted on baking. Had she forgotten to put it away when she was done? Maybe. Probably.

'Yes,' Orla said. 'Livvie gets a pastry on her way to work, Luke was up before you, and I don't eat breakfast. It was all stale this morning. I had to put it out for the birds.'

A spark of annoyance ignited inside Beatrice. 'Sorry. But I mean, come on. It's only bread.'

'Bread that takes time, ingredients and effort to make.' Orla's voice didn't sound quite so calm now.

'So don't make it. Go to the grocery store and buy it, like everyone else.'

'Beatrice. It's not just about the bread. Everyone else here prefers homemade to supermarket bread, and I think it's better for us and for the planet. If you don't like it, you're free to buy your own, but don't leave it to spoil for other people. And actually, I'd feel the same if it was Sainsbury's sliced white you were wasting.'

'Think of all the starving children in Ethiopia,' Beatrice said mockingly.

'As a matter of fact,' Orla countered, and Beatrice sensed she was becoming properly angry now, 'I do think of them. I think of the impact food waste has on everything – the fuel that's used to transport it, the depletion of global resources, the packaging it comes in.'

'God.' Beatrice rolled her eyes. 'It's one loaf of fucking bread.'

'If you don't want to think about those things, you don't have to. But have some consideration for the people who share this house with you.'

'Why didn't you tell that to Livvie when she went to do washing yesterday and couldn't be bothered to take my stuff?' Beatrice demanded, properly on the defensive now.

'Livvie said she'd asked you, and you hadn't given her anything to take.'

Success – Beatrice thought – *I've got Orla off the subject of the stupid bread.* But she'd inadvertently got her on to one Beatrice didn't like any better.

'Oh, so now Livvie's been tattle-taling about me? And she's your favourite so she's right and I'm wrong – obviously.'

Orla sighed, as if she was releasing all her anger. 'Beatrice. This is silly. Hear me out for a moment. I've never done this before. I'm trying my best to make this house a home for you all and to try and keep things working smoothly and fairly but I'm making it up as I go along. Sometimes things won't go right and I have to address them. But try and work with me, not against me. That's all I ask.'

'Ask away,' Beatrice snapped. 'But there's no need for you to lecture me like I'm a child. I pay to live here. You're my landlady, not my mother. And I'm late for work, so goodbye. Good chat.'

Orla didn't say anything more. Beatrice watched as she turned and went back into the kitchen, and heard the scrape of Orla's chair on the flagstones as she sat down.

Maybe she's going to cry, Beatrice thought triumphantly, slinging her purse over her shoulder and stepping out of the front door.

But as soon as the fresh morning air hit her face, she regretted everything she had said. She'd behaved like a spoiled brat – a little madam, as her mom used to call her on the rare occasions when she received a telling-off.

She'd come here searching for something – someone. She'd even, fleetingly, thought she might have found it in Orla. But the words hung between them now, impossible to take back.

You're not my mother.

The truth of what she'd lost – might never find – settled heavily on her as she composed her apologetic text to Frances.

NINETEEN

Orla was wrong – Luke didn't take me to Pizza Express. I suppose I should have known already that Luke wasn't a bog-standard date sort of person – but then, logically, it only took one not-bog-standard date for me to find out.

It didn't start exactly conventionally, either, because it began with him knocking on my bedroom door at seven on that Friday evening, as we'd arranged. Dating someone I lived with already felt strange, but not in a bad way. There were so many things about each other that were already familiar: he'd seen me first thing in the morning, my hair a mess and my eyes bleary with sleep. I'd seen him swearing, tears of pain leaping involuntarily to his eyes, when he hit his thumb with a hammer.

I'd seen him in his underwear, emerging from the bathroom rubbing his hair with a towel. He'd seen me emerging from the bathroom only wearing a towel. I'd liked what I'd seen and I hoped he did too.

Now here it was: the appointed night, the new dress – even better this evening than it had looked in the shop, thanks to Orla's pins and stitches – the knock on my door.

Shyly, I opened it.

'Hi,' Luke said. 'You look lovely.'

'So do you.' I smiled.

He was wearing jeans, not new but not the battered, paint-splattered ones he wore to work, and a grey T-shirt so new it still bore the fold marks from the shop. I could smell his aftershave – the lavender and mint scent I recognised from that night in the pub.

'Shall we go?' he asked.

'I'm ready. Are you going to tell me where we're going? Or shall we just walk and decide?'

'I thought' – his smile wavered and become almost shy – 'I wondered if you like spicy food?'

'Love it,' I confirmed.

'Then we'll go for a curry.'

I followed him downstairs, the soles of my wedge sandals loud on the bare wood. It was almost the shortest night of the year, and still bright and sunny, the daylight highlighting the new paint on the first-floor doorframes and the glossy, newly sanded floorboards, as well as the imperfections of the house: the stain on the ceiling where the damp had soaked through from above, the haze of dust motes hanging in the air, the cavernous, cluttered rooms on the ground floor, untouched as yet.

He opened the front door and we stepped out into the warm evening, turning to walk the familiar route around the square.

'What'll she do when it's finished?' Luke wondered, glancing back at the house. 'Sell it?'

'I don't know. I don't think so.' I remembered what Orla had told me about her grandmother. 'I think she feels kind of responsible for it – attached to it. I suppose she'll live in it, and paint, like she said she wanted to.'

'And rent out rooms for a hell of a lot more than she can charge in a building site.'

The idea jolted me. Although I'd only been living at Damask Square for a short time, it felt like longer. It felt like home. I didn't want to live anywhere else and – almost more – I didn't want anyone to live there except me, Luke and Orla. And Beatrice, of course. Maybe.

'What are you thinking?' Luke asked. 'You've gone all – gloomy? Pensive, anyway.'

'I was thinking about having to move.' I sighed. 'When it's finished.'

He laughed. 'We'll probably be about ninety before that happens. Stop worrying.'

To my surprise, I found that easy. The evening was so perfect, the sense of something good beginning so strong within me, that endings felt impossibly distant.

'So where are we going?' I asked.

'I thought...' His pace had increased slightly as we left the square behind us. 'Brick Lane.'

Really? I'd been in London long enough to know that the street, lined from end to end with a plethora of Indian restaurants whose owners stood outside their doors, competing fiercely with one another for custom, didn't exactly scream romance.

But I said, 'Cool. I've been there before, on a work night out. Two of my colleagues got seriously drunk and ended up playing frisbee with a poppadom. So we probably shouldn't go to the Imperial Palace.'

He laughed. 'We won't go to the Imperial Palace. Trust me.'

Before we arrived at our destination, the scent of spices reached me. I could hear music and raised voices, and as soon as we turned the corner we found ourselves in a press of people. Tourists wandered, bewildered, from restaurant to restaurant, pausing to read the menus displayed in the windows until they either chose at random or were accosted by a proprietor and ushered inside, like it or not. A group of young men who looked like they were on a stag night pushed boisterously through one of the doorways, demanding a table – poppadom-throwing was in their future, I reckoned.

'Free wine with your meal,' offered a bearded man in a white kurta. 'Best food on Brick Lane.'

Luke smiled, shaking his head politely. 'Not tonight, thanks, mate.'

'How do you know?' I asked. 'How do you know where to choose?'

'I just do.'

A few seconds later, he stopped outside the doorway of an unassuming-looking restaurant. There were no neon lights above its door, no menu pasted in the window. The interior was simple: tables with paper cloths covering them and small wooden chairs arranged on bare floorboards.

He nodded, then pushed open the door and I followed him inside. The room was full, but there were no stag parties here, no work nights out and no tourists with camera bags. There were couples, family groups, even a few men in kufi hats eating alone, bent intently over their food.

A waiter showed us to a table with brisk efficiency and brought a jug of iced water and two menus. They weren't the huge laminated sheets I remembered from my work dinner but printed simply on A4 paper, just a few items on each.

Luke nodded approvingly. 'Are you hungry?'

'Starving.' I realised I was.

'Then we'll have everything.'

A few minutes later, food began to arrive. There were little fritters stuffed with potato and herbs, crisply rustling deep-fried whitebait that was like nothing I'd ever eaten in a pub, skewers of tender chicken in a sauce Luke said was made with cashew nuts and melon seeds, and finally a lamb biriyani, fragrant with saffron.

I found myself almost too immersed in the deliciousness of

the food to talk much, other than exclaiming over each new flavour. Luke didn't seem to mind – he smiled happily at my enthusiasm, answering my questions about what the spice was on the chicken, how the rice got its tender crust and whether it was all right for me to eat the whitebait with my fingers.

'Okay,' I said at last, unable to eat another thing. 'Now you've got to tell me how you're such an expert on Indian food.'

He laughed. 'Must be because I am South Asian. Well – Bangladeshi. Half Bangladeshi.'

'What?' I looked across the table at him. His skin was dark, but no darker than mine would have been after a holiday in the sun, and his eyes were that clear, pale blue. 'Really?'

'Sure. Mum's British, but my dad's from Dhaka.'

'I'd never have known,' I said. 'I mean – not that it matters, obviously.'

'Of course it matters.' He smiled, but there was something else in his face – sadness or perhaps anger. 'I know I can pass as white, but it means I hear things people would never say in front of me if they knew. Horrible, racist comments.'

'I'm sorry. That must be – well, I can't really imagine.'

'It's okay.' He shrugged. 'You get used to it. I call people out on it sometimes, just to see them squirm.'

'And I guess every time you go home to your mum and dad you get to eat delicious food like this,' I joked.

He grimaced. 'Sadly not. My parents aren't together any more, and I don't really see my dad.'

'That's so hard.' I was torn between wanting to know more about him and not wanting to pry into something I sensed had caused him deep hurt. 'Did they separate a long time ago?'

'They didn't separate. They were separated. Dad came out here on a student visa, to study law. He and Mum got together at uni and I was – well, I was a mistake. They never got married, because Dad knew he'd struggle to get that past his family. But they were happy together, I think, until I was about four.'

'Then what happened?'

He poured more water into our glasses. '1988 happened. Massive crackdown on illegal migrants. Dad had to go back to Bangladesh, and I guess at first they both thought he'd be able to come back. But he never did.'

'You never saw him again?'

'I did at first. They both tried. Mum took me out there to visit him and when I was a bit older I went on my own. But he – I wasn't enough to make him want to jump through hoops to come back here. He never forgave the British government for what had happened. And when I was twelve he got married to someone else.'

I could just about imagine it. The effort to keep a little unit of three together, even across such a distance, a chasm widened by time and politics and family pressures. And Luke, stuck in the middle until he drifted inexorably to one side.

'That's so sad,' I said.

'Hey, it's all in the past now.' He gestured for the bill. 'And I'm bringing the mood right down, rambling about myself. What about your family, anyway? You go back home and see them often?'

'Hardly ever.' I hesitated. 'I don't... I don't really like where they live.'

'Nottingham?' He looked puzzled.

'Nottingham's all right. It's more – it's their house. I don't like going there much.'

'But you're cool with living in a building site?'

I laughed. 'Trust me, Damask Square's a palace compared to what I'm used to. Why don't we go on somewhere and have a drink?'

He agreed and I thanked him profusely for the meal, which he insisted on paying for. We found a nearby bar and shared a bottle of red wine, talking about things that weren't sad at all. Listening to his voice and the joyful sound of his laughter, admiring his strong hands as he lifted his glass, discovering the way his smile was slightly lopsided, I found myself hoping – longing, even – for him to kiss me.

And, just before we arrived home, he did. In the shadow cast by the plane tree, the street lamp obscured, he took me in his arms and I turned my face up to his. Our lips met, tentatively at first and then more urgently, our bodies pressing together in the cooling evening.

Then we unlocked the door of Orla's house and went upstairs to our separate bedrooms.

TWENTY

'"I thought I could, I thought I could, I thought I could,"' Beatrice read, before closing the book with relief. Parker was asleep, her thumb in her mouth, her long eyelashes fanned over her plump, flushed cheeks. Slate's eyes were closed, too.

Thank fuck. She allowed her lips to form the words but no sound to emerge. Another day was done – now all she had to do was sneak out of the kids' bedroom without waking them, stack their dinner plates in the dishwasher, mop the floor, put a load of washing on – and then she would be able to sit. Sit alone, in blissful silence, until Frances arrived home and she was free to leave.

But before she even stood, she noticed tears trickling down Slate's face. He wasn't crying like he normally did – the outraged bawl of a four-year-old – but silently, his eyelids squeezed tightly shut as if trying to prevent the tears from falling.

He was crying the way Beatrice used to when she was a child and didn't want her mother to hear.

'Honey?' she whispered. 'What's the matter?'

With any luck, he was actually asleep and just having some

weird *Little Engine That Could*-induced nightmare. Beatrice could relate to that – she often felt that if she had to read that stupid story one more time, she'd weep herself.

Then his eyes opened, his mouth turned downwards in an almost absurdly exaggerated expression of sadness, and he rolled over, burying his face in the pillow, his shoulders shaking.

For God's sake, don't wake your sister, Beatrice thought.

But she reached out a hand and stroked his shoulder gently. 'Slate? What's wrong?'

The little boy's shoulders heaved and a thin wail emerged, muffled by the pillow.

Shit, Beatrice thought. *He's properly upset about something. But what?* She was used to coping with skinned knees, devastation when cucumber was cut into rounds instead of sticks, and plain overtired grouchiness.

This felt different – like real sadness. She couldn't begin to guess what in the inner life of a four-year-old could have brought it on. She lay down next to him and pulled him into a cuddle, not knowing whether it was the right or appropriate thing to do but acting on pure instinct.

'My mommy isn't coming back,' Slate sobbed, turning over and looking at Beatrice with wide, swimming eyes.

What the fuck? she thought. But she said, 'Slate. Of course your mommy's coming back. She texted me just an hour ago. She'll be home just after eight o'clock. She's just late at work.'

Slate shook his head, not buying it. 'Mommy isn't coming back.'

'Honey.' Beatrice kept her voice as calm as she could. 'What makes you think that?'

'It's Dylan,' Slate managed between sobs.

'Dylan at pre-school? The new boy who you were going to be friends with? Did he say something to you about your mommy?'

If he did, I'll give the little bastard the telling-off of his life, she vowed, although she had no idea what she would actually do.

'His mommy gave him away and now he's adopted.' It took Slate a few goes, but eventually he got the words out.

Oh God. Not this. Beatrice felt as if cold water was being dripped down her spine.

'Slate,' she said calmly. 'You know how that works, right? Sometimes a mommy and daddy can't have babies of their own, so they have to—'

She stopped, her mind racing. There was a right thing to say here, appropriate words to use – she just had to remember them.

'They get to be mommy and daddy to someone else's baby. Someone who loved their baby very much but couldn't look after them. That's what happened to Dylan. But it won't happen to you.'

'Why, Bibi?' He looked at her, his eyes wide and doubtful. 'Our mommy can't look after me and Parker and that's why we've got you.'

'Slate, that's completely different!' She paused. *I've got to get this right or I'm screwed.*

'Your mommy and daddy both have big, important jobs. That's so you can all have nice things, and also so they can do things they love, that make a difference in the world.'

Quite how marketing two-thousand-dollar handbags or betting on the yen versus peso exchange rate made the world a better place, Beatrice wasn't sure. But that was definitely not an issue that needed covering in Adoption 101.

Slate was looking at her intently as she continued. 'And so that they can do that, they have to have someone looking after you when you're not at school,' she went on. 'And that someone is me. And I'm so blessed to have such great kids to be a nanny to, but you'll never be my kids. Not the way Dylan is his mommy's, or you your mommy's.'

Slate looked unconvinced. But at least he'd stopped crying – for now.

'When a baby's adopted, it's different,' she carried on, now totally feeling as if she was making it up as she went along. 'Grown-ups know – often before the baby's even born – that their mommy won't be able to keep them. Sometimes they don't have a daddy, or the daddy's not around. Not like yours, who's around every single day. Right?'

Slate nodded slowly. Then he asked, 'What if their real mommy does want to keep them though?'

She doesn't, Beatrice thought. *Not really. Not enough, anyway. She just wants a problem dealt with.*

But she thrust the thought aside.

'All mothers love their babies,' she said as brightly as she could. 'They always want to keep them, but sometimes they just can't. Maybe they try and it doesn't work out. But everyone's looking out for what's best for the baby, so they can grow up with a family that loves them, the way you and Parker are.'

'So I'm not going to be adopted?' Slate asked.

Beatrice felt tension she hadn't realised was there slacken across her shoulders. 'You are not. I one hundred per cent guarantee it.'

Please let this be the end of it, she pleaded silently.

But Slate wasn't done with her yet. 'How do you know?'

Beatrice pulled him closer, squeezing his small body against hers. Her hand had gone to sleep from his weight on her arm.

I've got one card left to play, she thought, *then I'm damn well giving him chocolate buttons and hoping he forgets all about this nonsense.* Only she really, really didn't want to play it.

What does it matter? He can only tell Frances, and she knows anyway. Or say something to this Dylan kid, and who cares what he thinks?

It was only the household at Damask Square she needed to

keep her secret from: Livvie and Luke and especially Orla. At least for now.

Right. I'm going in, she decided.

'I know because I know all about babies being adopted,' she said. 'I know because I was. My mother – the lady who had me, in Ireland where I was born – couldn't look after me, even though she loved me. And so my mom and dad, who couldn't have a baby of their own, adopted me, and took me home to live with them, and when they moved back home to America I went with them, because I was their baby now. And they loved me just the same as your mom and dad love you and Parker, and just the same as Dylan's parents love him.'

'What happened to the lady who had you?' Slate asked, his eyes growing sleepy.

'I don't know. She was very sad but she got over it, because she was young and beautiful like a princess.'

And then she got married and had lots of other babies and she kept all of them.

But Beatrice managed not to say that out loud. She never had – not to anyone.

'So you see,' she said, 'I understand how it works. You can trust me. And any time you're worried about this again, make sure you tell me or your teacher or Mommy or Daddy, right?'

'Okay.' Slate sniffed. His head was drooping now – he'd be asleep in a few minutes.

Beatrice sat up, pulled the covers up to his chin and smoothed his pillow. 'Want me to stay with you for a bit?'

Slate nodded. Beatrice took his hand in hers – it felt warm and clammy. His eyes were closing, the dim glow of the lamp making his and Parker's faces look peachy and luminous.

She waited, listening to the steady sound of her own breath. Then Slate made a noise that was half snore, half snuffle and turned over, his hand slipping out of hers.

Limp with relief, Beatrice stood up and crept out of the

room, closing the door gingerly behind her just as she heard the soft chime of the elevator. She spent twenty minutes explaining to Frances what had happened, amazed at how calm and professional her words sounded.

Then she said goodnight and went home.

In her bed at Damask Square, the silent darkness of the house surrounding her, she finally let the tears come.

TWENTY-ONE
12 JULY 2005

I was woken at four this morning by an unfamiliar sound – unfamiliar for that hour of the morning, at least: the click of a bedroom door opening and a brief ripple of laughter. Realising I needed the loo, I got up and stepped out on to the landing.

I don't know who was most startled – me or Livvie. She was just emerging from Luke's bedroom, wearing only pants and a T-shirt, and she was horrified when she saw me – as embarrassed as if I'd caught her trying to steal the silver. Not that there's any silver to steal.

Oh God, I'm so sorry, Orla. She blushed scarlet.

Not wanting to wake anyone else – although Luke was clearly already awake; I suppose it was Beatrice who I really didn't want to rouse – I tried to smile and make some kind of reassuring hand signal to her. But in the moment I doubt it did any good.

Poor girl – there's no need for her to feel embarrassed. If I hadn't known that she and Luke were sleeping together, I'd at least suspected it – and why would I mind them having sex under my roof? Even if I did, I'd have no business minding. They're grown adults and free to do as they please.

But don't break her heart, Luke. Please don't hurt her.

I couldn't get back to sleep when I returned to bed. The sheet beneath me felt uncomfortably ridged, my pillow too hot, my mind racing back to the past despite my best efforts to stop it.

Declan. It was him I was thinking of – him and me. That first time, stumbling from his study, my body thrumming with equal parts shame and desire.

I was barely older than Livvie then. He was old enough to be my father. So handsome, so charming and charismatic. So talented, we all thought – although now of course I can see his art was mediocre at best, amateurish and derivative. But I didn't think that then, and nor did my classmates – half of us were in love with him and not all that half were women. But it was me he singled out.

I couldn't quite believe it the first time he asked me to wait after a tutorial group. I felt myself blushing when he praised my talent and commented on my beauty. I felt like the most important person in the world when he offered me a whiskey. He didn't jump on me, or anything like that. Of course he didn't; he'd played the game before and he knew how to win it – win me.

He took his time, progressing over the course of a term from flattery to a touch of my hand, from there to a chaste kiss on the cheek then on to protestations of desire.

You're so beautiful, Orla. If only...

If only what? If only I wasn't his student? If only he wasn't married? If only I wanted him too?

And I did. More than I'd ever wanted anything, enough for the first two of those three things not to matter to me in the slightest.

I threw myself at him, that first time, telling him I was in love with him, believing him when he lied that he loved me back. Maybe he even believed it himself. It was only later, when the cool air of the Dublin night had banished the warmth of his hands from my skin, that my ecstasy turned to shame and dread.

Oh, Livvie – please don't feel that way, whatever you do. Please be careful.

TWENTY-TWO

When Beatrice was a little girl, most nights, her mom put her to bed and she'd read *Goodnight Moon* or *Where the Wild Things Are*. But on the evenings when her dad got home from work before she was asleep, he'd come into her room, sit in the armchair by the bed and tell her a special bedtime story. It wasn't read from a book; it was told from memory.

Beatrice couldn't remember when she'd heard it first. She was probably too young to remember anything. But she did know that it wasn't always the same; embellishments were added over time, words changed. Sometimes, if her dad was in a hurry, he'd try to short-change Beatrice by leaving out some of the detail.

Beatrice always knew when that happened, and it came to serve as a clue that her parents were going out for the evening and she'd be looked after by a sitter.

Once long ago, there lived a man and a woman. They had a big house in the city, with a big garden where a great maple tree grew. The maple tree was perfect for hanging a swing off of. Upstairs in the house was a charming little bedroom overlooking the garden, which would be perfect for a little girl's room. It had cosy pale-green carpet on the floor, and in the mornings the sun cast shadows from the maple tree through the window, falling where the little girl's bed would be.

From as early as she could recall, Beatrice knew the story well enough to say, 'Like my bedroom!'

Her dad would nod, stroking Beatrice's hair back from her face.

Just like your bedroom. But this man and woman had no children, and this made them very sad. Every day they dreamed of having a baby. Every Sunday they prayed to God to send them a child. They went to many physicians for help, but still no baby came. Some nights the woman would weep with longing, feeling as if her heart would burst from all the love she had there with no one to give it to, and the man's head would hang in sorrow because there was nothing he could do to help.

Even though she knew the story had a happy ending, Beatrice always felt her own heart ache when she imagined the man and the woman feeling so sad.

Then one day, the man came home from work with joyful news. He told the woman that they were going across the sea, to the country where he was born, where he would spend two years working. And he had an idea. The reverend at their church had told him that in that country, they might be able to find a baby they could bring home to live with them always. The baby would be theirs just as if it had been born to them, and they'd be able to give it all the love they had in their hearts to give.

'So they got on an airplane,' Beatrice would prompt.

So they got on an airplane and they flew across the sea. The man was happy to be back in the country he'd left as a child, and the woman was excited because she had never been there before. But both of them were thinking most about one thing: that by the time they returned home, they might have their baby with them.

'What happened then?' Beatrice would demand, although she knew the answer.

They found a place to live, an apartment in the heart of the city with big windows that looked out over the river. The man went to work each morning, and each night when he returned the woman would tell him about all the things she'd seen and done that day. And each night when they went to bed, she would ask, 'Have you...?' and he'd tell her, 'Not yet.' This went on for almost two whole years, and the man could tell the woman was losing faith. Until one day, when she asked the usual question and the man answered, 'Yes. Tomorrow.' The next day, they went to meet a priest: an old man in a long black robe, a gold crucifix hanging down the front. He had the kindest blue eyes the man had ever seen.

Beatrice's own eyes would open wider at this point. She knew the best bit of the story was coming.

The padre took them to a large, grey building surrounded by green lawns, a little way out of the city where they were living. A sister met them there – a beautiful young nun who smiled all the time. The man and the woman knew that the babies she cared for would have known nothing but kindness.

Beatrice would snuggle down into her pillow, listening and waiting.

The nun was holding a baby. The most perfect wee baby the man could have imagined, with golden hair and pink cheeks. He knew that this little girl would always be happy and smiling, always tell the truth, and that she'd grow up to be kind and smart as well as beautiful. The woman took her in her arms and held her close. The baby gurgled contentedly and the woman wept tears of joy.

By the time the story got around to her, Beatrice would generally be dozing off.

The baby slept at the woman's side that night and for thirty nights afterwards, and then it was time for them to go back on the plane to fly home. The baby girl was as good as gold – she didn't cry once, all through that long journey.

By now, Beatrice's father's words would become indistinct, blurred by sleep. Still, they were as comforting as the rustle of leaves on the maple tree outside or the Aramis cologne her father always wore.

The man carried the baby in through the front door for the first time, and upstairs to the little room that had been waiting for her all those years. The woman selected a cuddly toy from the shelf above her crib – a tawny-coloured bear with a gingham bow around his neck – and tucked him up in bed next to her new daughter.

Even in sleep, Beatrice's hand would reach out for Harold the teddy bear, her thumb rubbing the special place behind his ear where by now the fur was almost worn away.

Then the man leaned over and kissed his child goodnight. All of his dreams had come true and his heart was full. He said, 'I love you, my Beatrice.'

Beatrice couldn't remember the last time her dad had told her that story, any more than she could remember the first. At some point, it must have stopped: one or other of them deciding she had grown too old for it. Whenever that had been, though, it was some time before something even more important had changed: Beatrice had realised that in spite of all the detail in the story, someone was missing.

There was one character who never made any appearance, even though without her there would never have been a baby at all.

TWENTY-THREE

'I love your top,' Emily said, spreading our blanket out on the grass.

I put down the bag containing cans of lager and a pack of ice, which we'd picked up from the corner shop, and joined her, peeling off the T-shirt I had on over my bikini top and throwing it over for her to see.

It was the first time I'd properly caught up with Emily in a few weeks, and I'd missed her company, but at the same time being with her felt strange – almost as if the house on Damask Square was a different world, a kind of dreamland from which I emerged every morning for work and then returned to at night. It was a world where normal things like picnics in the park with friends somehow didn't happen.

'I picked it up in a second-hand shop,' I told her. 'Orla showed me how to cut off the sleeves and hem the edges, but I haven't got round to that yet.'

'Nice.' She opened two cans of beer and handed one to me, tearing open a packet of crisps. 'It suits you. This Orla's turning you into quite the fashion designer.'

'I don't know about that. But she found me a dress that I wore on my first date with Luke, and I—'

'Yes, come on,' Emily urged. 'Less of the *Vogue*, more of the *Just Seventeen*. How's it going with Luke?'

I turned over, propping myself up on my elbows, sipping Stella and feeling the sun on my back. It was a gorgeous summer Saturday, I was hanging out with my best friend and I felt perfectly happy.

'He's amazing,' I said. 'I mean, it's early days. We've only been... you know...'

'Shagging each other into early graves?'

I laughed. 'Yeah, that. Sleeping together for a couple of weeks and not every night, because it would be weird to almost move in together when we're already living in the same house. Kind of disrespectful to Orla, although she said she doesn't mind.'

'Not a lot she could do about it if she did, is there?'

'Well, no. But – you know. Even though I really like him – like, really, really like him – I feel like it's better if we still have some space. Did I tell you he's an artist? Or he wants to be. All the handyman stuff is just to make money while he builds a portfolio. He showed me some of his work and it's amazing.'

'Smitten.' Emily smiled. 'I knew it when you couldn't come to the Black Eyed Peas gig with me because you were "busy".'

'I'm sorry. I didn't want to let you down and it wasn't because of Luke. Just, I had an early meeting at work the next day and—'

'I'm only kidding. As it happens, you not wanting the spare ticket meant I could ask Josh from the office. I just gave you first dibs because you're my mate.'

'Josh from the office? Tell me more.'

She shook her head. 'Long-standing crush. But he was awful that night. He got absolutely shitfaced and tried to snog me on the Tube home then vomited on the platform when we got off. So I'm officially cured.'

I made sympathetic noises and opened two more cans of beer and a tube of Pringles.

'Doesn't matter,' she said. 'Better I find out now that he's a sleaze than six months down the line, right? But Luke – do you reckon it's serious? Or going to be serious?'

I turned over again, stretching my pale legs out to the sun.

'Depends what you mean by serious.'

'Taking him home for Christmas level serious?'

'Jesus, no. I've never taken anyone back to my parents' place, not even you.'

'Oh.' Emily's face fell. 'I'm sorry. I forgot.'

'Doesn't matter. I try and forget too, only it doesn't always work.'

'So...' she said, clearly trying to change the subject, 'what about the other girl? Bernice?'

'Beatrice.' I flattened my empty beer can and twisted it from side to side. 'She's an odd one.'

'Odd how?'

'She's all proper on the surface. Like she just stepped out of *Heathers*. But she's a loose cannon.'

I gave Emily a brief recap of the Gary story. Beatrice had never mentioned it afterwards and neither had I. At first, I'd assumed she was ashamed of what had happened – snogging a man she couldn't possibly fancy just because she was drunk and it seemed like a good idea.

But every time I remembered that evening – which I did often, because it had been the start of everything between Luke and me – it left me feeling strangely unsettled. It had shown me a side of Beatrice I hadn't realised was there – a kind of wanton destructiveness, like a child breaking something precious without thought for the consequences.

'So she gets pissed and snogs randoms with her beer goggles

on?' Emily offered by way of analysis. 'I don't see the problem – been there, done that.'

I grinned. 'Me three. But she – I'm not sure she likes me very much.'

'Do you think she fancied Luke too?'

'I don't think it's that. I think it's more – you know, like I said, Orla and I get along. And I think it's that that Beatrice doesn't like.'

'She's jealous of your landlady? Weird.'

'It's not like she even seems to like her. She just doesn't seem to like her liking me. If that makes any sense at all.'

'Not really.' Emily pushed her sunglasses back and frowned up at the sky. 'It all sounds a bit crush-on-the-games-mistress to me.'

'Maybe that's it,' I agreed. 'Beatrice is – well, she's kind of young in some ways.'

'Well, if she wants to sulk, let her sulk. And if she gets nasty, you can always sack the whole thing off and move in with me.'

'So long as Luke can stay over.' I grinned.

'Course he can.'

But, I realised, that wouldn't solve the problem, because it would mean leaving Orla behind with Beatrice. I couldn't begin to tell Emily how that made me feel – how I felt about Orla. It was unlike anything I could have imagined feeling about a woman so much older than me, seemingly so self-possessed.

I felt protective. And what I wanted to protect her from was Beatrice.

'The sun's going in,' Emily said. 'Typical English summer. Shall we decamp to a pub before it pisses it down?'

'Yeah, let's.' I stood up, pulling my top back on and rolling up the blanket. Strolling away through the park with my friend, I was able to put my unformed worries behind me for the moment.

TWENTY-FOUR

Back in the States, when Beatrice's mom had suggested she take a job as a nanny, it had seemed like a great idea: her mom would be happy because she wasn't working in a bar (dangerous) or in retail (tacky), and she'd be happy because – well, how hard could it be? She'd have loads of time, she'd thought, while the kids were at pre-school or napping or whatever. Investigating her past would be easy to do.

But the only downtime she ever seemed to get during the day was the all-too-brief window around lunchtime when Parker had her nap. At home in the evenings, now that her quest to sift through the papers and files on the first floor of the house had ended fruitlessly, she sometimes shut herself in her room and got on her laptop, but the dial-up internet connection was glacially slow and none of the websites she'd managed to find had yielded any useful information.

By the time she'd read some old lady's account of her experiences in the East End during the Blitz – respect to her, learning to use WordPress in her eighties, which was more than Beatrice could do at twenty-two – it was almost midnight and she could no longer keep her heavy, scratchy eyes open. An online forum dedicated to local history had proved similarly unhelpful, being full of misty-eyed nostalgia, recipes for fruitcake and in-fighting.

She'd been in London for almost four months, and she was no further in her quest than she'd been when she'd stepped off the plane at Heathrow. And what was more, her patience with the children, with the endless, grinding sameness of every day, was wearing thin. She didn't know how much longer she would be able to stick with this job before she gave up and headed off to Paris for the next leg of her gap year – but that would mean leaving unfinished business, abandoning the whole purpose that had brought her here in the first place.

She needed to try a different approach – perhaps a more analogue one.

'Are you not eating your sandwich, Parker?' she asked.

The little girl was poking without enthusiasm at the peanut butter and jelly, which had, until today, been her favourite thing.

'No.' Parker's bottom lip stuck out obstinately.

'Are you not hungry?'

'Don't like it. Don't want it.'

Feeling the familiar surge of annoyance, Beatrice eased the knots of tension from her shoulders and walked over to the window. It was raining and the view of London was obscured in a heavy, grey haze.

Barring the weather, every day was the same as the previous one, with only more of the same to look forward to.

'Right,' she said, forcing cheerfulness into her voice. 'You don't want it, don't eat it. Have a banana, then we'll go and fetch your brother. And then we're going on an adventure.'

Parker brightened, wolfed down the banana Beatrice peeled for her and happily put on her raincoat, which was clear plastic printed with yellow ducks. Pulling the zipper up under her chin, Beatrice felt her irritation subside: when Parker looked as adorable as she did now, it was hard to stay annoyed with her for long.

'What venture?' Parker asked as Beatrice helped her put on her yellow rubber boots.

'We're going to go to the library.'

Beatrice couldn't think why it had taken her so long to hit on this idea. Every day for weeks, she'd walked past the drab red-brick building, seeing but not really noticing the sign outside it, blandly official and bearing the tree logo of the local authority.

But now it seemed like the best plan ever. Libraries were great for kids – there was no way Frances would object to such an educational, enriching outing. There'd be story time, or crafts or something of that nature – she'd even seen a flyer on the noticeboard by the door that morning advertising 'Children's Hour – weekday afternoons'. Beatrice felt a rush of elation at the prospect of palming the kids off on another responsible adult. And then she'd be free to carry out her own research in a place that was, after all, built for that exact purpose.

'Come on,' she urged Parker. 'Let's go get your brother.'

Half an hour later, Beatrice had got the children settled down on two small plastic chairs that made up part of a circle of identical chairs. A grinning young man in shorts and a T-shirt – not at all the motherly, bespectacled lady Beatrice had been expecting – was introducing them to 'Rap and Rhyme Time'.

Could she leave them here and disappear for a few precious minutes on her own? She glanced around: the women who seemed to be in charge of the other children – mothers or nannies like herself – were dispersing, some heading for the café in chattering groups, others wandering off between the library shelves, doubtless craving peace and silence as Beatrice was herself.

'You're welcome to stay.' The young man, who'd introduced himself to the children as Neil, caught Beatrice's eye. 'But they'll be fine. I'm CRB checked, and the kids don't generally play up with me.'

'Sure?' she asked.

He nodded, his relaxed grin providing the reassurance Beatrice needed.

She backed away, slowly at first, but Slate and Parker were transfixed by Neil, who had taken out a guitar. Exhaling with relief, she returned to the main reception desk, which was staffed by a middle-aged woman with cornrow hair and glasses.

'May I help you?' she asked.

'I was hoping...' Now that she was here, Beatrice realised she wasn't sure what she had been hoping for. To have answers to her questions presented to her on a platter, possibly. 'I wanted to do some research into local history.'

'The history section's up on the first floor,' the woman said. 'But to be honest, we don't have as many books in it as we used to. They get damaged or borrowed and not returned, and we don't replace them because everyone wants to use the internet now.'

'Then how—' Beatrice began. 'What about old newspapers? From about the 1930s and 1940s?'

'Those I can help you with.' The woman smiled, stepping out from behind the desk. 'Again, it's all on computers now, but they're actually simpler to use than the old microfiche system we had before. Let me show you.'

She led Beatrice up a flight of stairs and over to a bank of computers, eight of them arranged in two rows of four, wooden screens around them, padded metal-framed chairs standing in front of them. A welcome screen invited her to create a username and password.

Beatrice sat down, pulled the chair in towards the desk and

typed in her email address, making up a random password she knew she'd forget straight away.

'Now if you just click over there...' The librarian's blunt, unmanicured finger pointed at the screen. 'And there, and again. That's the archive. I'd recommend starting with the *Evening News* – it had the largest circulation of any London paper at the time.'

'Okay,' Beatrice said. 'Thanks very much.'

Already, she felt daunted by the task ahead of her. The archive appeared on the screen as a list of years, bright blue Times Roman on a black screen. When she clicked on a year – might as well start with 1939 – a list of months dropped down, and those expanded into days. For each day, there was an early and a late edition of the paper, she discovered, clicking on a random date.

The front page of the newspaper appeared: a clear scan, which she realised she could zoom in and out of. The paper it had been printed on seemed to be an orangey-pink, the masthead an old-fashioned gothic typeface.

She scanned the headlines.

France Cancels All Army Leave

Mussolini Said to be Rushing Men to Spain

Gibraltar on Guard

And in the central column, which appeared to be devoted to lighter lifestyle stories, *Enjoy the Sun While You May*.

'Jesus,' she muttered. 'Dark, or what?'

An arrow to the right of the screen took her to the opening spread of the paper, and she zoomed in again, distracted by an advertisement for chocolate bars and a headline about minimum payments for boxers.

It was all so alien it might as well have been printed in another language – or another world. And, she realised quickly, the task was hopeless. There were hundreds of issues of the newspaper for every year, each running to more than forty pages. Even if she only flicked through them, even if she restricted herself to the years around the Second World War, it would take her days and days to go through them all.

She didn't have days and days. She had forty-five minutes each afternoon, and then only if she persuaded the children that 'Rap and Rhyme' was something they wanted to do every day – a long shot at best. Already, it had been half an hour since she'd left them.

Her chances of finding what she was hoping to find were about as good as they were of winning the lottery. And that was assuming she actually knew what she was looking for, which she didn't really – not beyond confirming whether the house she was living in was actually the same house that had been owned by the Doyle family from Clonmara.

She navigated out of the newspaper archive and logged out of her newly created account, knowing there was no need to remember the password because she would never use it again.

'Did you find what you were looking for?' the librarian asked, smiling, as Beatrice passed the reception desk again.

She shook her head. 'Not this time. But thank you for your help.'

When she returned to the children's section – the small tables and chairs and brightly coloured books reassuringly normal – Slate and Parker were the only kids left; Beatrice felt a stab of guilt as she hurried over. Neil was squatting down, talking to them, the cheerful grin still on his face.

'Here's your mum now,' he said.

'I'm not their mum – just the nanny. Sorry I was late collecting them. I got distracted by the newspaper archive upstairs. I was looking for articles about Spitalfields before the Second World War.'

Neil stood up. He was very tall, all lanky legs and arms, with a shaved head and a neatly trimmed goatee beard. Beatrice guessed he was a couple of years older than her and wondered fleetingly why a young guy like him would choose to spend a summer afternoon wrangling a bunch of kids in a library.

'You're into local history, then?' he asked. 'You'd love my grandpa. He grew up around there. Well, the whole family on my dad's side did, but he's the oldest one still around. He worked as a cobbler, back when those old houses were leather workshops.'

'He did?' Beatrice hesitated. She could think of nothing she'd enjoy doing less than listening to the meanderings of some senile old man. 'Actually, it's not so much local history, although that's part of it.'

'Oh?' Neil smiled. 'I'm intrigued. Tell me more.'

Beatrice glanced down at Slate and Parker and saw that they were still happily ensconced on their plastic chairs, their heads together as they paged through a Curious George picture book. If only she had the ability to make the two of them sit quietly and focus that Neil appeared to possess.

She looked back at him. There was no reason for her to entrust him with the details of her personal life – details she'd kept hidden from the people she lived with and saw every day. But at the same time – he was a stranger. She didn't ever have to bring the kids back here, ever see him again.

She lowered her voice and said, 'The thing is... I'm adopted. I was born in Ireland although I grew up in the States. My dad was working out there at the time. And now I'm trying to find out more about what happened.'

'To trace your birth parents?' he asked gently.

'That's... well, my mother, mostly.'

Her father had always felt like a shadowy figure, sidelined by her compulsion to find the woman who'd given birth to her.

'Why East London, though?' Neil asked.

Hastily, seeing that the children had finished the book and were beginning to bicker about what to look at next, Beatrice explained about her time in Clonmara, which had yielded only the fragment of information about a big house in Spitalfields.

'Wow,' Neil said. 'Sounds like you've got some detective work ahead of you. But hold on. There's something I remember reading recently – we get newspapers from all over the world here, every day. They all get laid out on a table upstairs. The ones in Bengali and Urdu are the most popular, and I can't read those but I love geeking out over the others.'

'Go on,' Beatrice urged impatiently.

'They all get recycled at the end of the week,' Neil continued, 'but centrally, they're digitised. I should be able to find the article, if you've got five minutes.'

'Yes, please.'

He hurried off, and Beatrice crouched down with the children, trying to get them engaged in another book and reassuring them that they could go to the playground on the way home, now that the rain had eased.

'Here you go.' Neil returned, proudly bearing an A4 printout.

Beatrice almost snatched it from his hand. It was a good-quality scan, but the columns of newsprint were slightly askew on the page. At the top, she saw the running head of the *Irish Times* and a date from a couple of weeks earlier.

But the headline told her all she needed to know: *National Adoption Contact Preference Register to Open.*

'Apparently you can write to them,' Neil explained, 'and tell them you'd like to make contact with your birth family. Only unless your birth family does the same thing, the request will just sit there on file. But it's a starting point.'

Beatrice gazed at the words, amazed. It hadn't occurred to her that something as prosaic as a change in the law, debated by a bunch of old people in whatever Congress was called over in Ireland, could hold the key to her past.

Seeing her face, Neil said, 'I can send you a link to the article, if you like. In case you lose that.'

'Yes. Yes, please.' She gave him her email address and he jotted it down. 'And it would be amazing to meet your grandfather, too, some time.'

She didn't really mean it. The house seemed secondary now that she had this far better new avenue to explore. But gratitude to Neil made her generous.

'I'll give you my number as well, then.' He smiled. 'Let's make a plan.'

She thanked him and said goodbye, then took the children's hands in hers and led them out of the library. The sky had cleared, the pavements were sparkling and a rainbow arched high over the glass towers of Canary Wharf.

It's a sign, Beatrice thought. *It's totally a sign.*

TWENTY-FIVE

I still remember the day everything changed. I can picture it as clearly as if it were a movie or a dream I'd just woken from, before the images my mind generated had time to fade. Of course, at the time I didn't see it as a seismic change – just an upsetting event, a blip that could be overcome with apologies, time, brushing beneath the carpet.

It was a Saturday morning in late July – one of the many days that were, in my memory at least, perfect: dry, sunny, still and happy. Luke and I were out in the garden, lying on the pair of deckchairs he'd recovered from a skip somewhere. Luke had his sketchpad on his knees and was drawing, from memory, a street scene – the bustling pavement of Brick Lane with its neon signs and crates of piled-up fruit and vegetables.

We'd placed the chairs on an island of cobblestones Orla had uncovered from the forest of weeds and brambles that had once filled the garden; she'd cleared some of the space, but not all of it, because she said that birds, bees and butterflies had thrived here for years and who was she to destroy their habitat?

Bees were everywhere that morning, I remember,

rummaging and fumbling in the blackberry bushes whose fruit Orla had talked about making into jam come autumn. Her promise had made me happy – I'd imagined us having jam on our toast, jam on the scones Orla would teach me how to make. Next time, I'd be able to make them myself; in future years, I might even make the jam.

I was confident, on that summer Saturday, that there'd be a future for us all in the house. I had no reason not to be. But at the same time, I was entirely immersed in the present – the heat on my bare skin as I stretched out in my deckchair in my bikini, the hum of the bees going about their business, the heavy scent of honeysuckle hanging in the air.

And Luke, of course. Luke's presence next to me, the occasional murmur of his voice over the music coming from Orla's tape player, the sun glinting off the fuzz of hair on his chest, the shiver that ran through me when he reached out a finger to brush my thigh.

We must have missed the first knock on the front door, because when the second came it was loud, impatient, almost aggressive. Maud, who'd been snoozing on the hot bricks next to us, raised her head, startled.

'Door,' Luke observed sleepily. 'I'll get it.'

'No, I'll go.' My feelings for him were at that early pitch of intensity where I wanted to give him everything, even the chance to lie in the sun for five minutes while I went inside. 'I need a glass of water, anyway.'

I stood up, pulling Luke's T-shirt on over my bikini, and hurried inside. The knock came again, even louder.

I opened the front door and saw a young man standing there, perspiring in the heat in his suit and tie.

'Sorry,' I said. 'We were outside and we didn't hear you knock at first.'

He didn't acknowledge my apology. 'May I ask if you're the homeowner?'

I shook my head, eager to get rid of him and return to Luke. 'Just a lodger.'

'Then is your landlord home?'

'Landlady,' I corrected. 'I'm not sure.' I looked behind me, half-expecting Orla to materialise in the hallway behind me, although I hadn't seen her all morning.

'Would it be possible to go inside and check?'

Although he was perfectly polite, something about his manner annoyed me.

'I don't think she wants satellite TV or to change energy provider,' I said. 'If that's why you're here.'

'It is not.' He drew his shoulders back, pompous in spite of his sweating face. 'I represent Digby Marchant real estate brokers. We've recently established an office in the area and are seeking to explore avenues of opportunity with potential vendors.'

An estate agent. That explained the suit – and the persistence. As far as I knew, Orla had no intention of putting the house on the market – even if it was in a saleable condition, which it wasn't – but it wasn't for me to decide. Anyway, Orla would be more likely to succeed in getting rid of him than I was.

'Hold on,' I said. 'I'll see if she's in.'

He grunted a response and I turned back into the house. Orla might be up on the top floor; she'd been spending time there when the weather was dry, painting, because she said the light was better than anywhere else in the house, better even than her bedroom.

I ran upstairs, past the empty first floor and on up to the second. The doors to my bedroom, Luke's and Beatrice's were all closed. Orla's was usually left ajar, so Maud could come and go as she pleased, but now it was closed too.

I knocked, but there was no reply.

'Orla?' I called, listening for the sound of footsteps coming from upstairs.

I listened but heard nothing.

Perhaps she was sleeping. I didn't want to disturb her if she was having a rare lie-in or a mid-morning nap. Then I heard a sound from inside the room, like something heavy being pushed or dragged across the floor.

I knocked again, then pushed open the door.

Beatrice was there. She was crouched down by the neatly made bed, an unfastened suitcase in front of her, which she'd been in the act of pushing back beneath the bed.

Bizarrely, my first reaction was to smile at her. I didn't even form the thought coherently, but I must have assumed that she'd overheard my conversation downstairs and come to look for Orla herself.

Almost immediately, I realised how absurd that was. Strange as she sometimes was, Beatrice would never have looked for our landlady under her bed – still less inside a suitcase that had been under it.

Even if the rational part of my mind hadn't dismissed the idea, one look at Beatrice's face would have done. She looked terrified. She looked embarrassed. She looked guilty as hell.

'What the fuck are you doing?' I heard myself burst out.

She sprang to her feet, kicking the suitcase under the bed. 'What the fuck are *you* doing? Snooping around like that?'

'Snooping? I wasn't snooping. I was looking for Orla. I knocked. If anyone was snooping, it was you. What were you looking for?'

I was still too surprised to be properly angry – still anticipating that Beatrice would be able to explain her behaviour, that I had somehow made a mistake.

So the fury of her response blindsided me.

'It's none of your fucking business what I'm looking for.' She stepped towards me, her face inches from mine. Her eyes were wide and her teeth literally bared, startling in the peachy smoothness of her face.

'It is my—' I began, then realised that, of course, it wasn't. 'You've got no business looking through Orla's stuff.'

'Right,' she sneered. 'Because you're Orla's – what? Her bodyguard? Her personal assistant? Her special pet? Only you get to decide what happens to her and her bedroom and her stuff?'

'I didn't decide anything,' I said, bewildered. 'No one has to decide that prying in someone's personal things is wrong. It just is wrong.'

'You think you're so special, don't you? With your sewing lessons and your paint roller and your boyfriend. I'll tell you something right now, Livvie – you don't own this house. You don't now and you never will. You don't get to make the rules here and tell me what I can and can't do. All these months you've been acting like the queen fucking bee – you think I haven't noticed?'

Unbidden, my mind flashed back to the actual bees I'd been watching just a few minutes ago, in the peaceful sunny garden where Luke was.

'I don't know what you're talking about. I never said I owned the house, or Orla – or anything. I just live here, same as you. There are hardly any rules – you know that. But there's just... I don't know. Common decency.'

'Common decency.' She mocked my accent, making it sound prissy and uptight. 'Is that what makes you use Orla like you've got some kind of right over her?'

'Beatrice, you're being daft. Of course I don't do that – I don't think that. I don't understand why you're so angry with me. I thought we were friends.'

She laughed – a hard, angry sound. 'So did I. But I know better now. You're just out for what you can get. Since you started fucking Luke and playing dressmakers with your precious Orla, you've barely bothered to speak to me.'

I felt my face flame. It wasn't true – and yet, in a way, it was.

Since before my first date with Luke – since going shopping with Orla, even before what had happened between Beatrice and Gary in the pub – I'd felt wary of Beatrice. Even though I'd barely acknowledged it even to myself, my growing relationship with Luke and my increasing fondness for Orla had allowed me to step back from her, and any gap I might have felt from doing that had closed over seamlessly.

'I'm sorry,' I said, regretting it immediately. 'I never meant to hurt your feelings. I want us to be friends – all of us.'

Again, I remembered the garden: how I'd allowed myself to imagine seasons and years elapsing in this house, everything peaceful, nothing changing.

'If you want me to be your friend,' Beatrice hissed, 'you'll stay out of my business. Got it?'

Before I could retaliate, saying again that it was Orla's business she'd been prying in, I heard footsteps on the stairs. Orla's tread was distinctive – brisk and light, always the tap of leather-soled shoes rather than the thump of trainers.

As if we were one person, Beatrice and I slipped out through the door and waited on the landing.

'Girls.' Orla rounded the corner of the first-floor landing and stood looking at us, perplexed. 'Is everything all right?'

'We were looking for you,' Beatrice said.

'There's an estate agent downstairs who wants to speak to you,' I explained.

But I realised that the man from Digby Marchant would have long since given up and continued to the next potential property listing. If he wanted to give Orla his sales pitch, he would have to try again another time. And Beatrice, by the simple use of that word 'we', had made me complicit in something – something harmful and wrong.

I knew, just as surely as Beatrice must have known, that I would never tell Orla what I'd seen that morning. I didn't want to betray Beatrice and I didn't want to hurt Orla, and therefore I would keep quiet.

Beatrice smiled and opened the door to her own bedroom, and I headed back to find Luke. As I turned to walk down the stairs, I saw Orla's gaze moving from me to Beatrice, puzzled and worried.

TWENTY-SIX

Beatrice expected to need her trusty *A–Z* map book to locate the address Neil had given her when he'd called to say his grandfather would be delighted to meet her, and asked whether she was free on Sunday. Her carefully worded email to the Irish National Adoption Contact Preference Register had left her Hotmail account several days before, but from what little she knew about bureaucracy she wasn't expecting a response any time soon, so she'd taken Neil up on his offer – she might as well continue with her own investigation in the meantime.

As it turned out, she did need the *A–Z* – but only to consult the index and flick through to the page it led her to.

It was the same page she'd consulted multiple times already, from the first time she'd used the map to find Damask Square. The paper was already dog-eared and smudged with the prints of her fingers, grimy after getting off the bus or Tube. Tracing her fingers over the grid from the top and right of the page, she found they met at a location just a couple of hundred yards from Damask Square.

It was one of the council estates just off the main road – Beatrice had walked past it almost every day. Past, but not through – there'd been no need for her to deviate from her accustomed route and, besides, part of her had felt apprehensive about venturing into the estate, as if she didn't belong there; it wasn't for the likes of her.

Well, all that was about to change.

Pulling back her hair and checking her reflection out of habit, Beatrice tucked the map into her purse and headed outside.

It was a hot summer day. She'd expected when she arrived in London that the city would be permanently shrouded in fog, either raining or about to rain. This spell of glorious weather had taken her by surprise, and she still never quite trusted it. Within a few feet of leaving the house, she realised she was dressed too warmly in her jeans, college sweater and sneakers, and could feel perspiration springing out on her top lip. It wasn't quite as stifling as New York at the height of summer, but it came close.

If she went back and changed, she'd be late. She'd always had it drummed into her by her mother that lateness was the height of rudeness, and she didn't want to be rude, so she carried on.

The council estate wasn't bordered by a high wall; one minute she was outside of it, the next she was there, surrounded by low buildings and taller ones, squares of unkempt grass and paved areas with children's play equipment in them.

She'd steeled herself to expect gangs of marauding youths, selling drugs or at least using them, and she found herself clutching her purse extra tightly by her side. But there were no gangs, either – just a group of women and children in their Sunday best, chattering as they strolled home from church; an old man walking a greyhound; three teenage girls in headscarves sitting on a bench, sharing a packet of sweets and giggling over their mobile phones.

The individual buildings weren't marked on Beatrice's map,

and the estate was larger in real life than it had looked on paper. She passed Osprey Court – a long, four-storey building – and Eagle Heights – one of the tall towers – and deduced that Hawk Heights must therefore also be a tower. So she lifted her eyes and headed for the two remaining towers that loomed over her, piercing the clear blue sky.

Then she heard the sound of running feet behind her and wheeled around in fright.

But it was only Neil, hurrying towards her, smiling. He was wearing either the same shorts he'd had on the day she met him or an identical faded camouflage-print pair, and a green-and-white striped T-shirt. Beatrice felt relieved – her decision to dress down, albeit too warmly for the weather, was vindicated.

'I thought it was you,' Neil said. 'I recognised your hair.'

Reflexively, Beatrice swished her ponytail – then wished she hadn't.

'How are you?' she asked. 'Thanks for meeting me.'

She held out her hand for Neil to shake. He looked taken aback, but did so.

'You're welcome. Gramps's flat is in that building over there – looks like you were headed in the right direction.'

'Is he ' Beatrice began, then stopped herself. All the questions she wanted to ask – Is he very old? Is he very poor? Why does he live here, of all places? – seemed even ruder than being late would have done. 'Has he lived here long?'

'Forty years,' Neil said. 'He and my nan moved here when it was built, with my dad and my aunties. The post-war housing boom, you know – loads of families got moved to places like this. They thought they'd really come up in the world – and not just literally.'

Wherever they were before must have been pretty bad, Beatrice thought.

'So he must know the area backwards,' she said.

'Like you won't believe. He can chatter on for hours about

old Mr Miggins whose wife ran off with the window cleaner and the Hassans' daughter who's a professor at Cambridge now and the two babies that were swapped at birth in the... Sorry.'

Beatrice looked at him, confused, then laughed. 'Don't be. I wasn't swapped at birth – I was just adopted.'

'Okay. I was worried I'd dropped a clanger there.' He smiled. 'But whether he'll know anything about this Doyle family I don't know. Not just that it was a long time ago – from what you said it sounds like they didn't really stick around here.'

'No, but if he could even remember that they were here at all, it'd help. I feel like the house I'm living in might just be the one my birth mother's family owned, but equally it might not. And if it's not, then maybe I could find the right house and maybe there'd be someone there who'd know something.'

'Well, I guess we're about to find out.'

She followed Neil up a few steps to the entrance of the building and watched as he pressed buttons on the metal panel by the door, his fingers moving swiftly and surely.

The intercom crackled and he said, 'It's me, Gramps. Me and Beatrice.'

There was another crackle and a buzz, and Neil pushed open the door.

'Let's hope the lift is working,' he said. 'It goes on the blink sometimes and then poor Gramps is stuck up there on the seventeenth floor until they get it fixed again. His legs aren't what they were and they've never been all that.'

'What if it goes on the blink when he's out?' Beatrice asked.

Neil laughed. 'Good question. Then he has to call the cavalry – that's me – and I take him to Mum and Dad's.'

But it turned out that the lift was working, and it bore them up to the seventeenth floor without incident. They emerged on to a concrete walkway bordered with metal railings, beyond which the ground looked very far away. Beatrice followed Neil along a row of doors, some a uniform dark red, others painted blue or yellow or stripped back to wood and varnished.

'Here we are.' He stopped and knocked on one of the red doors. 'He'd have come and waited for us, but Mum nags him to keep the door closed and use the peephole.'

'Because of burglars?'

'Because of Jehovah's Witnesses. He gets them in and argues with them and the poor buggers have to practically declare a hostage situation to get away.'

Whether the peephole was used or not, Beatrice couldn't tell, but the door opened almost immediately. In front of her stood an old man – at least, he was almost standing, bent nearly double over a walking frame. He was tiny, shrunken with age, his hands mottled and bony on the metal bars, the wrists protruding from his clean white shirt thin as a bird's legs. His hair was a shock of white, and his eyes when he peered up behind thick glasses were bright blue.

'Look what the cat dragged in,' he said, reaching out a hand to Neil as if he wanted to embrace him.

Neil leaned over the walking frame and hugged his grandfather. 'Good to see you, Gramps. This is Beatrice, who I was telling you about. My grandfather, Jack Isaacs.'

'Lovely to meet you, Mr Isaacs.' Beatrice gingerly took the fragile hand in hers. 'Thank you for inviting me over.'

'It's always good to see a new face. Especially a lady friend of Neil's – and come all this way to visit me.'

Beatrice glanced at Neil, her eyebrows raised. She lived less than a mile away. And surely he hadn't said...? Neil responded with a rueful grin and a shrug that could have meant anything.

'I'm living in London for now,' she explained. 'But I'm from Philadelphia originally – hence the accent, I guess.'

It was too late to correct him on the girlfriend front – Mr Isaacs was leading the way into the flat, moving confidently but painfully slowly, the wheels of his walking frame bumping over the linoleum floor and the dark Oriental rugs that covered most of it. Beatrice followed him down the hallway and into a living room.

It was like stepping into a time capsule. The sofas and armchairs had worn cushions on wooden frames, the fabric clean and the wood lovingly polished. The walls were papered in a floral print up to the picture rail and stripes above it, the colours long since blurred by the sunlight that flooded in through the window occupying an entire wall. Heavy mahogany bookcases were stacked with worn paperbacks and thick, cloth-bound non-fiction volumes, interspersed with framed photographs, also faded to ghostliness.

'Take a seat, my dear.' Mr Isaacs gestured towards the sofa. 'I'll put the kettle on.'

'Let me do it, Gramps,' Neil urged. 'You sit down and chat to Beatrice.'

Neil turned and left, and Beatrice found herself stepping towards the old man, gently taking his arm and helping him down into an armchair. She perched herself on the sofa at right angles to it, squinting against the light from the window.

'So you're a student of local history,' Mr Isaacs began.

'Um... not all local history,' Beatrice admitted. 'Although I'm sure it's all completely fascinating, of course. But I'm interested in the houses around where I live – Damask Square. Where the garment district used to be. The big, old houses. Especially the one I live in. And Neil said you might be able to help.'

'The family's lived here in the East End for ages.' Neil came back into the room carrying a tray holding a teapot, three cups and a plate of biscuits. 'I see Mrs Singh down the corridor's still baking for you, Gramps.'

'She thinks I'll starve if she doesn't,' the old man joked. 'I think I'll lose what I have left of my teeth if she does.'

Before the conversation could segue into chit-chat about the neighbours, Beatrice asked, 'So your family's lived here a long time?'

'We came here as refugees,' Mr Isaacs said.

Beatrice felt a chill of horror. 'From Nazi Germany?'

'Oh no.' The old man sighed. 'They weren't the first to persecute the Jewish people, and they won't be the last. My grandparents fled from Warsaw during the pogrom in 1881. They hoped they would be able to go on to America but they ran out of money. So they reached the East End and there they stayed.'

'And they worked here, in Spitalfields?' Beatrice asked.

'Worked and lived, four or five families to a house, all employed in the garment trade.'

'You'd call it a sweatshop, now, wouldn't you, Gramps?' Neil interjected.

'You probably would. In the beginning, they were just glad to have a roof over their heads and food on the table. The industrial unrest came later – the tailors' strike of 1889... but you're not here for a lecture on labour relations, are you?'

'It's fascinating,' Beatrice said. 'I'd love to know more. I had no idea – I mean, I knew garment workers lived in the area, but I thought they were mostly Irish.'

Mr Isaacs laughed. 'The Irish were long gone by the time we arrived. Most of them, at any rate. That's how it is – people flee one problem, they find another. Sometimes they stay, sometimes they move on. And when they move on, others come. Like waves on the seashore. After the Jews, the Bangladeshis came. Then the *Windrush* people, then others from Eastern Europe after the Cold War. That's how it goes.'

Beatrice felt a swell of frustration. Interesting as the old man's stories would no doubt be for her to listen to, they weren't leading her anywhere. She was reminded of the men in the Clonmara pub, with their meandering chatter, hoping she'd stay and drink with them so they could flirt gently with her and prove to themselves they'd still got it.

But they'd told her about the big house the Doyle couple had bought. They'd been quite definite about that.

'So there were no Irish people left when your family came?' she pressed.

'Barely any – or not so's you'd notice. Big Irish community up in Kilburn, if that's what you're interested in. But they came over to work on construction sites, not at sewing machines.'

The old man sipped his tea and crunched a biscuit, his palm beneath his chin to catch the crumbs.

Then his eyes seemed to clear as he remembered, and he laughed. 'There was one couple, though. One crazy Irish couple.'

'What happened?' Beatrice asked.

'It's not funny. Not really. But we laughed about it at the time. Young pair from Dublin, they were. His great-grandparents had worked in the area back in the day when there were Irish here, silk weavers. Then they went back home and made their fortune over there.'

'But this couple came back?' Neil prompted.

'They came back. Newlyweds, they were, wanting to buy a piece of their family history. More money than sense. And they bought the house where my family worked – lock, stock and barrel. Turfed us all out. But they never lived there.'

'Why not?' Beatrice leaned forward, her elbows on her knees, an untouched biscuit in her hand.

'Because the war came, see. You wouldn't want to stay in London with bombs falling round your ears when you could scarper back across the Irish Sea, would you?'

'But you stayed? You were here in London the whole time?'

'I was. I never got drafted because of my legs. Polio, it was, when I was a child. But I could still make boots, and I made them, from morning until night, first in that house and then in a factory nearby, once the Irish couple took it off the owner.'

'So after they bought it, what happened? They just left it?' Beatrice's heart quickened.

The old man cackled. 'I shouldn't laugh at others' misfortune. But it was a long time ago. The young man came over a couple of years later, to check on his investment. Never mind there was still a war on – like I told you, more money than sense. The house was still standing – but a couple of days later, he wasn't.'

'He was killed?' Beatrice asked.

'Killed by a German bomb. Leaving his young widow over in Dublin. I don't know what happened to her. I don't know anything more about it, really – just that. We laughed and laughed about it at the time – it was the talk of the neighbourhood. You had to get your laughs when you could in them days.'

'Can you remember anything else at all about them?' Beatrice urged. 'Their name, or where the house was?'

'Course I can,' the old man said. 'Doyle, they were called. He was Gerald Doyle. I don't recall the young lady's name, if I ever knew it. And the house was over on Damask Square, just a short walk from here. It's still standing today. Number five, Damask Square.'

TWENTY-SEVEN

I didn't speak to Beatrice for the rest of the day after our encounter in Orla's bedroom, and on Sunday, I went round to Emily's place and had a barbecue with her and her housemates, returning late in the evening. As usual, Beatrice had already left for work when I got up on the Monday morning.

But although our paths didn't cross, the sense of her presence in the house filled me with anxiety. The sound of her voice singing 'Don't Cry for Me Argentina' as she put on her make-up in the mornings woke me more reliably than my alarm clock. Only when I heard the front door click closed behind her at seven o'clock sharp could I feel myself breathe easily again.

I didn't know what to do. I'd felt that the house on Damask Square was a safe place, a refuge created by Orla's laughter, Luke's smile and even the patter of Maud's paws. Now, I didn't feel safe any longer. I felt the same hyper alertness, almost fear, that I'd felt back when I was living with Samantha and Amanda, and it was a sensation I'd believed I had left behind forever – left behind the day I'd closed the door of my parents' house to set off for university.

I'd been wrong then, and it seemed I was wrong again.

When I approached the house on Monday evening after work, I didn't feel the lift of my spirits, the eagerness to walk into a place where I was secure and welcome, which I'd always felt before. I felt tense, on edge, unwilling to discover what would be waiting for me when I opened the front door.

But as it turned out, I didn't need to open the door on that particular Monday – it was already open, held back against the wall by a brick, and Luke was emerging. He was shirtless, wearing a bright yellow safety helmet, his usual battered shorts and steel-capped work boots, carrying a sack of rubble in his arms.

The sight of him took my breath away, the longing to touch him sweeping over me.

His face lit up when he saw me. 'Evening, Liv.'

'Look at you,' I said. 'You look like the entertainment on a hen night. Sexy builder-o-gram.'

He laughed, tossing the sack into the skip as easily as if it was filled with feathers. 'Not so sexy if you could smell me.'

I moved in to hug him, but he stepped back, shaking his head. 'Seriously, Liv. I'm properly rancid.'

'Do you think I care?' But I only leaned in, kissing him gingerly without letting our bodies touch. I could taste the salt of his sweat on my lips, and to me he smelled delicious.

'I'm just about done here. The sparks knocked off at four – they've got another week, they reckon, and then the electrics will be sorted.'

'So we won't have to worry about Orla electrocuting herself every time she switches the cooker on?'

'Don't know about that. Wiring or no wiring, that thing's on its last legs. I'm going to grab a shower – want to sit out in the garden for a bit after?'

I hesitated. The thought of relaxing outside with him, the door to the kitchen standing open so I could wander in and out, helping Orla with dinner and chatting to her about my day, would normally have got my instant approval. But this evening I felt different. I wouldn't be able to relax around Orla, knowing I was hiding something from her. I'd be constantly alert to the sound of Beatrice's key in the door, the tap of her trainers on the floor, the rattle of the metal hardware on her handbag when she hung it up.

The silence that often followed before she entered the kitchen, when I knew she was waiting in the hallway, listening.

'Let's not go in just yet,' I suggested. 'Let's go for a walk.'

Luke opened his mouth as if to protest, then said, 'Okay. Guess I'd better put a shirt on.'

'No need to bother on my account,' I teased. 'Anyway, you look like you're wearing one already.'

He grinned, glancing at his bare arm, his bicep flexing in a way that made me long to touch it. 'Farmer's tan. Thought I'd get rid of it by stripping off today, but it's not shifting, is it?'

I shook my head, my heart fluttering with desire, and treated myself to a long look at his back view as he disappeared into the house.

Seconds later he emerged again, pulling his T-shirt over his head. 'I'm good to go. So long as you weren't suggesting we go to a fancy restaurant.'

'Just a walk. I wanted to talk to you.'

I led him around to the far side of the square, used my key to open the gate in the iron railings and guided him over to one of the metal benches that stood at intervals around its perimeter. The sun was beginning to sink, the heat of the day giving way to evening. The chestnut trees in the centre of the square cast long, cool shadows over us. Behind us was a long bed of roses, which had been tended carefully all summer by a volunteer from the preservation society. Their blooms were all shades from ivory to crimson, petals scattered on the path like fragments of a sunset.

Forgetting his alleged sweatiness, Luke laid his arm along

the back of the bench and I leaned back against it. We were alone in the garden and the noise of the city was muffled, the only distinct sound the trill of a robin somewhere in the branches.

'How was Emily?' he asked.

'Good. We had fun. She's excited to meet you sometime.'

I didn't tell him that Emily had said I was welcome to bring him to the barbecue, and I'd found myself saying it was too soon. It wasn't that I thought Luke wouldn't like Emily or Emily wouldn't like him – it was a kind of instinctive need to keep my life at Damask Square separate from my life outside of it, as if I was living in two distinct worlds.

'I'd like to meet her too,' Luke said. 'I'm sure I will soon. And your mate at work, the one with the cocker spaniel puppy...?'

'Kelly. Is it her you want to meet, really, or the puppy?'

He laughed. 'You got me. It's both – and neither, I guess. It's all the little bits of your life I want to get to know. Like, you hardly ever talk about your parents.'

'No,' I said slowly. 'I don't.'

'Do you want to? It's okay if you don't,' he said.

'It's nothing.' I looked down at Luke's hand, still grubby from working, resting on the leg of his jeans, and took it in mine. 'Nothing big, not like what happened with your dad. It's just... not right.'

'Not right how?' he asked gently.

'When I was little,' I said, 'I used to get invited round to friends' houses for playdates and birthday parties and stuff, like you do. I noticed their houses were different from ours but I didn't think anything of it because – you know – I was a kid and you don't notice stuff like that and anyway everyone's house is a bit different from everyone else's. But when I asked Mum if I could invite friends back to ours, she said no. Just a flat no, like that, every single time.'

'Blimey. Why not?'

'It took me a while to realise. By then, the other kids had stopped inviting me and I didn't have proper friends outside of school. I'd talk to people at lunch and stuff, and I was on the netball team. It's not like I was some kind of pariah. But after school and at weekends I'd go home and not see anyone except Mum and Dad.'

Luke put the arm that had been along the top of the bench around my shoulders and pulled me closer, a silent urging to continue.

'I was in the doctor's waiting room when I realised. I was fourteen and was sat waiting to be seen, reading *Eve* magazine, and I saw this story.'

'What was it about?'

I took a breath. I'd never told anyone except Emily this before.

'It was about hoarders. You know, living rooms so full of stuff you can't see the TV, the stairs a tripping hazard, the kitchen full of takeaway cartons that have been there for years. That.'

'I've seen stuff about that,' Luke said. 'It's some kind of – like a mental illness, right?'

'Right. So I read the article and I was like, that's Mum and Dad. That's our house. That's what's wrong.'

'How did it feel, when you realised?'

'Weird. I went from thinking the way we lived was just a bit different from other people to feeling ashamed, because now it had a name. I imagined our house being on TV one day and everyone thinking how disgusting it was.'

'What did you do?' he asked, his arm tightening around me.

'I tried to talk to them. I said, "Look, I know this is a thing now, let me help." But they didn't want to change. And besides, it was way more than one teenage girl could sort out, even if I'd worked every day for months and months.'

'I can imagine that.'

'So I gave up. I just focused on school and getting the best marks I could until I could leave and go to uni. And then I did.'

'I'm so sorry.'

His words sent me over the edge. I turned, burying my head in his bare chest, neither of us caring now what he smelled like, and I sobbed.

'I didn't go back to stay after that,' I managed to say. 'I took everything I cared about back to uni with me and now when I go back – which I don't often – I stay in a hotel. I hate it there. I hate... I don't hate them, not really. But I kind of do.'

Luke held me while I cried. After a while, he pulled a bit of blue paper towel from his pocket, checked it wasn't too dusty and wiped my eyes with it.

'Thanks for telling me,' he said. 'That must've been hard.'

I blew my nose. 'I bet when I said let's go for a walk, you weren't expecting that.'

'I've got to admit...' He grinned, and I half-laughed. 'But you did want to talk about something else. What's up?'

'There's something going on with Beatrice. Her and Orla. Something weird.'

Hesitantly, I spilled out the story of what had happened when I'd discovered Beatrice in Orla's bedroom going through her things. It had been impossible to tell him at the time, with Beatrice's open bedroom window overlooking the garden – she'd have heard everything. Besides, I'd been blindsided by guilt at my own unwitting complicity in what she'd done.

'So I felt like I couldn't say anything to her,' I finished. 'If I tell Orla, I'd be a snitch and also... I don't want to worry her. And I don't... I mean, what if there's some totally reasonable explanation?'

'Like what? She dropped an earring and it fell into a suitcase under the bed in a room that's not hers?'

'Okay, so there isn't a reasonable explanation,' I agreed. 'But what do I do? What if I tell her and she asks Beatrice to leave? Or I tell her and she doesn't ask her to leave, but Beatrice knows I grassed her up and hates me more than she already does?'

'She doesn't hate you. Come on, Liv, don't be overdramatic.'

'Sometimes,' I said tentatively, only realising the truth of what I was saying as the words came out, 'I feel like she hates all of us. But mostly Orla.'

'You know what I think?' Luke said slowly, as if he too was only just beginning to realise it himself, 'I think they're too similar, and that's why they get on each other's nerves.'

'Too what?' I asked, startled. Two people less similar than cool, steely Orla and spoiled, tempestuous Beatrice I could barely imagine.

'Yeah, I know. But there's things about them. They both like things their own way. They're both stubborn as hell. They've both got this way of holding their heads – I drew a thing yesterday, just a sketch, of Orla and I realised it could have been Beatrice, until I filled in the features. And there's another thing too.'

'What's that?'

'They're both hiding something,' he said. 'It's like that house is full of secrets and I sometimes wonder when I'll be clearing stuff out for the skip and I'll discover them.'

We sat in silence for a moment.

Then Luke said, 'And I can't say I'm looking forward to that happening.'

TWENTY-EIGHT

Beatrice was perched on the stairs that led up to the floor above her bedroom. Below, she could see right the way down through the house to the ground floor hallway, so she would know if anyone came in through the front door or up the stairs. And above – above were the attic rooms, with all the secrets they might hold.

She was reluctant to venture there for fear of broken glass, dead pigeons and spider webs. Sometimes, though, she wanted to. It felt almost as if the house was calling her, luring her, promising answers to her questions. Was she the great-grandchild of the mad Irish couple who'd bought this house back before the Second World War? Was Orla connected to them or had the house since been sold and bought by another couple, whose granddaughter Orla was? Would she ever find out the truth?

Not today. Today she was on the stairs for a more prosaic reason: this was the only spot in the house where the internet connection was even halfway decent and the call she was about to make would be difficult enough without it cutting out midway. She wasn't exactly looking forward to it but, after what she had learned from Neil's grandfather the previous week, she was determined to go ahead with it.

She checked the text messages on her phone, her fumbling fingers making her realise how much her hands were trembling. Then, taking a steadying breath, she opened Skype on her laptop. The familiar acoustic modem handshake buzzed from her speakers, followed by two familiar voices.

'Hello, honey.'

'Hello, sweetheart.'

The screen stayed blank for a second then flashed to life. Beatrice couldn't suppress a smile. Her mom and dad were sitting at the desk in her dad's study, beaming into the camera. Her dad was in his wheeled, high-backed leather chair, her mom presumably perched on a stool next to him, because her head was several inches lower than his.

Her mom's gleaming dark brown bob looked freshly styled and even though it was early Sunday morning and they wouldn't need to leave for church for another hour, she was wearing bright pink lipstick.

Her dad was wearing a pale blue and white striped button-down shirt and she could see his linen sport coat slung over the back of the chair. His smiling face was handsome as ever, the hair that had once been blond now silver and carefully brushed. It wasn't just the chairs that accounted for the difference in their height – Beatrice's mom was petite and birdlike while her dad was tall and stocky.

When Beatrice's friends at college noticed the photo of them on her nightstand, they'd invariably look at it and say, 'Wow, you take after your dad.' If she liked them, she'd smile and say, 'I know,' but if she didn't, she'd say, 'Actually, I'm adopted,' and wait for them to cringe.

'How are you, honey?' her mom asked. 'How's London?'

'Have you been to the National Gallery yet?' her dad asked.

'Is your landlady feeding you properly?'

'Are you coping okay with those two kids?'

Beatrice answered their questions patiently and honestly, and asked a few of her own – how was Sligo, the family Labrador? Were her parents going to spend their usual week in Florida in August? Had the Gilmores next door sold their house yet?

Then she said, 'Listen, Mom and Dad. There's something I want to tell you.'

'What is it, honey?' Her mother's brow creased anxiously. 'Are you all right? Do you need money? We can wire you some right away. You've not met some boy and fallen in love, have you? Because we'd—'

'Let Beatrice speak, Ruth,' her dad chided.

'Thanks, Dad.' Beatrice tried to laugh. 'Please don't worry, Mom. I'm fine. I just wanted to talk to you about this because it's important and I don't want to hurt your feelings, okay?'

'Go on then, honey.' Her dad rested his chin on his hand, leaning in close to the screen.

'First promise me you won't be hurt or angry.'

'If there's something troubling you, we'll do whatever we can to make it right,' her mom said – which didn't actually answer Beatrice's question.

Beatrice took a deep breath. 'Here's the thing. The reason I wanted to come out here – part of the reason, anyway – was because I... I want to know more about myself. My background. That's why I went to Ireland first.'

'I see.' Her dad's face was grave.

'It's not that you haven't been amazing parents,' Beatrice gabbled. 'You're the best. I love you and I always will. You'll always be my mommy and daddy. But I decided that I want to find my birth mother, if I can. I'm trying to do that and I wanted to ask if you'll help me.'

'Oh, sweetheart.' Her mother took a tissue from the box that always stood on the desk and wiped her eyes. 'We knew this might happen one day. We've talked about it often, haven't we, honey?'

'Now, don't upset yourself, Ruth.' Her dad slipped his arm round her mother's shoulder and pulled her close. 'Of course, we knew this time might come. But you know, it might very well not be possible to trace her.'

'I know,' Beatrice began. 'But—'

'It will probably be impossible,' her mom interjected. 'We want you to know that. We don't want you to be disappointed.'

'If I can't find her, so what?' Beatrice said. 'I'll just be in the same place I am now. No big deal.'

But she knew that wasn't true.

Her dad pushed his glasses up his nose. Beatrice knew this meant he was about to go into explaining mode, and he did.

'Things were different back then, especially in Ireland,' he said. 'There was a real culture of secrecy around unmarried mothers. It was believed to be for the best – for them and their babies. We were given almost no information ourselves.'

'I know,' Beatrice said.

'And there's another thing.' Her father sighed. 'We don't even know if that information was true. Often, what adoptive parents were told wasn't. They were given details about the baby's birth parents that had been falsified, in order to make...'

He hesitated, and Beatrice found herself listening intently.

'In order to make the baby seem more attractive,' her father finished with a heavy sigh.

'Not that you could have been anything other than attractive to us,' her mother cut in. 'We fell in love with you the moment we laid eyes on you. You know that.'

'I know,' Beatrice repeated.

Her father continued as if they hadn't spoken. 'The child of, say, a factory worker might have been harder to find adoptive parents for than the child of a university student, as we were told your birth mother was. The authorities knew that, and they wanted to give every baby the best chance. So sometimes...'

'They lied.' Beatrice tried to swallow the lump growing in her throat. What if that was the case? What if none of it was true – not the bit about being from a wealthy family in Clonmara, or even what she'd managed to glean about the big house in East London?

What if all her theories were wrong, and her birth mother was still somewhere in Ireland, cleaning floors or working on an assembly line in a factory somewhere?

Her father nodded. 'Sometimes they lied. With the best intentions, of course. Or sometimes incorrect information might just have been supplied in error. But that culture of secrecy is changing. It has changed. Now, adopted people can place themselves on a register, and if their birth family is on the register too, details can be exchanged.'

'I know.' Beatrice felt like screaming, but her voice came out quite calm. 'I did put myself on the register. I haven't heard back.'

'These things take time, honey,' her mother soothed. 'She may still—'

'Or she may not,' her father said. 'You have to keep that in mind, Beatrice. It may very well be that she... that her circumstances mean she's not in a position to reach out to you.'

She got married and had lots of other babies and she kept all of them.

'She may have passed away,' her mother said, as if that was the comforting conclusion.

'Is there anything else?' Beatrice pleaded. 'Anything else at all you can tell me about her that you haven't already?'

Her parents exchanged a glance. Her mom raised her eyebrows and her dad nodded almost imperceptibly.

'Not about her,' her dad said, 'but about you.'

Beatrice clenched her fists, her nails digging into her palms. 'Go on.'

'Before we brought you home to our apartment in Dublin,' her mom said, 'we'd already decided the name we wanted you to have. I wanted to name you after my best friend in college. She was the smartest, kindest, prettiest girl I've ever known, and she died in a car accident. I wanted to honour her – and you – with her name.'

Beatrice felt a lump come to her throat. 'I'm glad you did. I like my name.'

Her dad nodded. 'But they told us the name your... the name you were given at birth.'

'What is it?'

'It's an Irish name,' her mom said. 'We didn't want to take it away from you but we thought – it's hard to pronounce. We didn't want you growing up having to spell your name all the time. We thought it would make you different from other kids, and—'

'I was already different enough.'

'It's Aisling,' her dad said, and patiently spelled it out, the way Beatrice had never had to.

Not long after that, they ended the call. What was said in those last few minutes before they hung up was a blur to Beatrice, but she did remember how it felt to walk back down the stairs, through the silence of the house on Damask Square, the past unfurling like the wooden balustrade that curved gently downwards, thick with coat upon coat of paint at the top, then with the paint stripped away by Luke, then freshly sanded on the first floor and finally newly varnished at ground level.

When she'd walked up those stairs, she'd been Beatrice. Now, she was someone else.

TWENTY-NINE
5 AUGUST 2005

Somewhere in one of these notebooks, in one of the crates in the cellar where they are stored, are the pages I wrote after I discovered Adrian's affair. They were not easy to write – I felt as if my pen was vomiting out the words, so shuddering and ghastly was the process.

We'd barely been married two years. I felt everything anyone would have felt in the circumstances: shock, betrayal, devastation, helplessness. In hindsight, of course, I can see that we were never right for each other: he cared far more about his work in the struggle against Apartheid than he did for me, and I cared more for him than I did for the struggle, passionately though I'd thrown myself into both.

It was for the best, I can tell myself now, all these years later and miles away.

But I still remember the sick, churning fear I felt when I wrote down what I knew, as if writing would make it real.

That is how I feel today. Yesterday something happened and I have barely been able to think of anything else since, yet also until I put it down on paper, in black and white, I can allow myself to pretend – to deny – that it has happened at all.

It happened yesterday, in Imran's shop. Although of course it didn't – it has been happening over the course of months and years, across the sea in Ireland, in committee rooms and in the chamber of the Dáil Éireann, where Brian Lenihan and his colleagues have been discussing and debating, holding the fate of thousands of women like me in their hands.

Women like me and women like her – because she will be a woman now, an adult. My portraits over the years have charted her growth from babyhood through childhood and adolescence and now she is twenty-two, old enough to drive a car and vote and make decisions about the course her life will take.

A few years ago, they were proposing to make it a crime for adopted people to attempt to make contact with their birth parents. When I read that, I wondered whether she had read it too and how she felt. I felt fear for her, but for myself... relief, I suppose. But also a terrible, aching sense of loss.

Now it has all changed. I went into the shop to buy a copy of the Guardian, and I don't know what made me pick up the Irish Times as well. The story was tucked away on an inside page, because it is no longer new news. She can put her name on a register and so can I, and if we both do so we will be put in contact with each other.

It is a double lock: unless we both act, nothing will happen.

I can do nothing. Perhaps she will do nothing. And then nothing will change.

I am torn between hope and fear. Hope that I might see her at last, and everything will be wonderful. Fear of – well, everything else. Confronting my own weakness and failure. Coming face to face with someone who will surely hate me – how could she not hate me, after what I did to her? And fear, most of all, of raking up the past just when I have finally found myself somewhere I feel safe.

Am I, though? I'm almost certain that Beatrice has been in my room, going through my things. And weeks ago, before we cleared out the rooms on the first floor, I heard her there at night, searching. Searching for what? It can only be for secrets she believes this house holds – or the secret I myself hold.

THIRTY

'Slate had a nightmare last night' – Frances applied a careful curve of scarlet lipstick before snapping her compact mirror closed and tucking it in her purse – 'but he's all good now. Me, not so much. I'm shattered. And Parker's got a bit of a cold coming on, I think. She's been grouchy all morning.'

'Gotcha.' Beatrice's bus had been delayed, and she was only just stepping out of the elevator, rushed and flustered.

'I'm in meetings all day and I've got a product launch this evening,' Frances went on. 'Likely I'll only get in about nine. Peter might be back earlier, but I can't promise anything.'

'Okay.' Beatrice suppressed a sigh and forced a smile. It was going to be a long day.

Already, she could hear Parker grizzling from the kitchen island and Slate's feet kicking his stool in a way that set her teeth on edge. The summer holidays, which had started two weeks before, seemed never-ending, with both kids home all day – she wouldn't even have the respite of packing him off to preschool.

'I'm out of here.' Frances stepped into the elevator. It seemed to Beatrice that she might as well have been getting on a magic carpet that would take her away from the grind of motherhood, out into a world where everything was adult, stylish, clean and interesting.

'Right,' Beatrice said. 'Have a great day. Okay, Parker, I'm coming.'

She hurried into the kitchen in response to the little girl's whines, stepping on some abandoned Lego bricks on the way, skidding and almost going flying.

'Fuck.' She couldn't help the word slipping out as she fought to regain her balance on the treacherous polished floor.

'Bibi said a bad word,' Slate crowed. 'Did you hear, Parker? Bibi said fu—'

'That's enough, mister.' Beatrice fought to keep her tone light. If she made a drama out of it, he'd be chorusing fuck-based songs at her all day – and, worse, at his parents when they arrived home in the evening. 'Sometimes grown-ups say bad words when they've had a shock, but that doesn't mean it's okay for little kids to. So pardon me for my French.'

'What?' Distracted, Slate stopped kicking the island. 'You weren't talking French.'

'No, but I can.' Sensing an opportunity, Beatrice launched into a flood of schoolgirl French. *'Voici les chaises, et la fenêtre. Tu as joué avec les briques de Lego, mais maintenant tu vas manger le petit déjeuner avec ta petite soeur.'*

Slate gazed at her, impressed. Beatrice dropped a kiss on Parker's head. The little girl did look poorly, she reckoned – her cheeks were flushed, her eyes red-rimmed and her nose crusty.

Great, she thought. *One kid ill and the other bored shitless. Fun times.*

'What's for breakfast then, Parker?' she asked brightly. 'Toast and peanut butter? Oatmeal? Or I can make you an egg.'

'Pancakes?' Slate suggested hopefully.

'No.' Parker thumped down on the floor on her bottom. Beatrice sensed that the word was addressed to the world in general, rather than pancakes specifically. She conducted a rapid risk-reward analysis in her head. Pros of pancakes: tasty, easy, took a bit of time, could distract the kids by making shapes. Cons: utter pain in the ass to clean up, Frances wouldn't approve if she put cinnamon sugar and maple syrup on them, which, let's face it, she would, and if they liked them they'd start demanding them every day.

The lure of an easy win came up trumps.

'Pancakes it is, then.'

Slate jumped off his stool and did a victory dance round the kitchen island, but Parker stayed where she was, thumb in her mouth.

'Come on, Parker,' Beatrice cajoled, 'come help me and Slate make the batter. I'll show you how to put a hole in the eggshell so the witches can't sail away in it.'

Where the hell did that come from? she thought.

As she whisked the lumps out of the flour, helped Slate measure out a cup of milk and gave Parker an empty eggshell and a spoon, Beatrice fought to keep her mind from – not so much wandering as veering away. Away to Mr Isaacs' living room and the things he'd told her there. To Orla's bedroom, where she'd been hunting for the missing puzzle piece she knew must be there, somewhere in that house. To Livvie's outraged reaction to finding her there and Beatrice's success in deflecting her anger.

She didn't know what she was going to do next. If she'd asked anyone sensible, anyone she trusted, like Frances, say, or even Neil, she knew what they would say.

Talk to Orla.

It was the obvious thing to do. *Tell her what you know, and ask her for the truth – if she even knows it. If she doesn't, then you know you were on a wild goose chase.*

But that was the problem. The threat of denial, and not knowing whether that denial was true or a lie. The rejection that would compound every other rejection and leave Beatrice with nothing. And also – the thought hovered at the very fringes of her consciousness, too elusive to put properly into words – Beatrice wasn't sure she was ready to know the truth.

It was easier, safer, to pry around the house, have tea with an old man, go to the library, than it was to ask a simple question.

'Woah, steady there, Slate. You almost tipped that whole basin over, and then what would we have had for breakfast?'

'You'd have made more.' Cheekily, Slate stuck his tongue out at her.

'I would not, because there are no more eggs and besides I'd have been too mad at you. And if you carry on with that attitude, I could still change my mind.'

Meekly, Slate returned to stirring the batter and Beatrice set a pan on to heat, adding a fat slice of butter that soon began to sizzle.

After breakfast, the morning dragged on. She took the kids out for a walk, but Parker cried and said she hated the park and wanted to go home, and Slate slipped on a dog turd and fell over, getting it all over his jeans, so Beatrice did end up taking them home.

Then Slate wanted to do drawing, but lost interest as soon as he'd scattered his crayons all over the table. Parker wanted to blow bubbles, but cried inconsolably as soon as the first one popped. Slate spilled his juice on the sofa. Parker vomited up her pancakes.

At last, order temporarily restored, Beatrice resorted to switching on the telly, which provided a bit of peace at least. But she was concerned about Parker. She gave her Calpol, but that didn't seem to help. She offered her warm Ribena but she wouldn't drink it. She put her down for a nap but the little girl wouldn't settle, her nose too blocked and her lips too dry and the whole world too unpleasant for her to deal with.

By teatime, Beatrice's weary resignation was beginning to crystallise into worry. Parker's cold seemed to be settling in her chest. Her breathing was noisy and she gave occasional barking coughs. Her temperature remained stubbornly at almost a hundred degrees.

She fed the children mac and cheese and salad – one of their favourites – but Parker only picked unenthusiastically at it, chewing with her mouth open because she couldn't breathe through her nose and saying everything tasted funny.

'Okay, fine.' Beatrice gave up. 'You're not hungry. Let's have a bath and more Calpol and put you to bed, and I bet you feel better in the morning.'

But when Beatrice took Parker's clothes off, she was alarmed to see the little girl's belly hollowing as she struggled to get air into her lungs. Should she call Frances and tell her she was worried? But Frances had emphasised that she had a full-on day at work; it was Beatrice's literal job to take care of things at home.

Steam, she thought. *Hot water and steam will help. And plenty of fluids.*

Parker seemed calmer after her bath and so Beatrice put her to bed, read her a story and took Slate into the living room to watch a bit more television before his own bedtime. Although she'd left the children's bedroom door ajar, she and Slate were soon so engrossed in *Little Red Tractor* that she didn't hear Parker calling for her at first.

When she did, the sound was so alien she almost didn't recognise it – and then she did.

'I'll be back in a second,' she said, as calmly as she could. 'I'm just going to check on your sister.'

Parker was sitting up in bed, tears streaming down her cheeks. Her voice was so hoarse she could hardly get Beatrice's name out, and her lips were purply-pale.

'Bibi,' she gasped. 'Bibi!'

'Shhh. I'm here.' Beatrice sat down on the bed, panic coursing through her. She could hear the desperate whine of Parker's breathing; her body felt floppy and far, far too hot.

Shit. She can't breathe. She's going to suffocate, right here, with me in charge.

'It's okay, honey,' she soothed. 'We're going to get you to a doctor. You need to try and stay calm, okay? Slow breaths.'

The little girl's ribcage heaved as she fought to get air into her lungs and when it exited again she made that terrifying barking sound again, like a dying seal.

'Come on.' Beatrice scooped Parker up and carried her through to the living room.

'What's happening?' Slate asked, his eyes wide and frightened.

'Your sister's not well. I'm going to call your mommy.'

But Frances's phone rang out to voicemail, and Peter's went straight to voicemail without ringing at all. Beatrice left messages for them both, trying to sound calm, telling them their daughter had what she thought was croup – *Is it even croup? It could be an asthma attack. It could we whooping cough. It could be just about any-fucking-thing* – and Beatrice was going to get her seen by a doctor, just in case.

She couldn't bring herself to tell them that she was going to call 999, but that's what she did.

After an agonising twenty-minute wait – during which Beatrice veered between thinking that Parker was getting better and she'd been overdramatic and thinking that she was getting worse and was going to die – the ambulance arrived.

'It's croup,' a smiling paramedic confirmed after she'd checked the little girl over. 'Normally gets better on its own, but we'd better take her in. They'll want to give her steroids to ease her breathing. She might need to stay in hospital overnight.'

'I can't get hold of her parents.' Beatrice felt as if she could barely breathe herself, her chest tight with panic. 'And I can't leave her brother. We'll have to come and wait while she's seen.'

The paramedic agreed and soon Beatrice found herself in a taxi with Slate, creeping with agonising slowness through the traffic that the siren and flashing lights of the ambulance had been able to part with ease.

'Is she going to die?' Slate kept asking, and Beatrice had to keep answering that of course she wasn't, she was going to be fine, the doctors would make her better – over and over on repeat, praying that what she was saying was true.

As they were pulling up outside the hospital, her phone rang at last. But it wasn't Frances or Peter – it was Neil.

'Hey,' he said when she answered, his voice sounding so improbably calm and cheerful it might as well have come from another planet. 'How's it going?'

'I can't talk.' Beatrice bundled Slate out of the taxi, thrusting a twenty-pound note at the driver. 'I'm at the hospital. Parker's sick and I'm waiting for a call from her parents.'

There was silence for a moment, then Neil said, 'Mile End Hospital?'

'Yes.' Slate's hand in hers, Beatrice hurried through the revolving door and approached the reception desk.

'Want me to come and wait with you?'

Relief washed over her. Though it wasn't his responsibility to look after the children, the thought of having someone to look after her felt like a life buoy in a storm.

It took Neil just fifteen minutes to get there, and Frances arrived half an hour later. Although she'd received Beatrice's updates – Parker had been seen, she'd been medicated, she was going to be okay – she was still frantic with worry, more distressed than Beatrice had ever seen her. After pressing her son into a hug, she hurried straight through to the children's ward and left Beatrice playing tic-tac-toe with Slate on a notebook Neil had produced from his bag.

Peter arrived shortly after and, after checking in on his wife and daughter and thanking Beatrice profusely, said, 'Come on then, big guy, time for bed,' and set off home with Slate.

All at once, everything was calm. Beatrice found herself shaking all over, her teeth chattering even though the hospital was tropically warm.

'Hey,' Neil said. 'You've had a shock. I can't believe how well you held it together. Everything's going to be okay.'

Beatrice nodded, her hands clasped together in her lap.

'Can I get you a cup of tea? Or would you like a drink?'

'I don't think so. I should head home and get some rest. Thanks for coming – it means a lot.'

But she spoke automatically, barely conscious of Neil's words of reassurance as he walked with her through the warm night to the bus stop.

'I'll call you tomorrow, okay?' he said. 'Sleep well.'

'You too. Thanks again.'

She waited until he was out of sight, and then started walking. She didn't want to be on a bus with other people – she wanted to be alone. Throughout the evening, she'd remained calm, doing her job to the best of her ability. Now she was overwhelmed with emotions she didn't understand and, as she walked, she made an effort to process them.

Her feet found the sidewalk without feeling it. The balmy air dried the sweat on her palms without her noticing. A black cab blared its horn as she crossed a street without looking left or right.

It was only as she approached the house on Damask Square, its elegant white facade gleaming in the glow of a street lamp, that she was able to put a name to what she was feeling.

She hadn't just been worried about Parker because she was doing her job and responsible for the child's welfare.

She loved her.

In those terrifying moments when she'd thought Parker

might die, she'd felt as if her own heart would stop. The fierceness of her love was like nothing she'd ever experienced before, and with it came another emotion, almost as strong.

It was anger: a vast, overwhelming rage.

How could anyone abandon a child? How could Beatrice's mother have given her away?

Why had the woman who'd given birth to her not loved her like she loved the little girl who wasn't even hers?

THIRTY-ONE

It was Sunday morning and I was woken by Luke's kiss on the back of my neck. We were in my bed, the duvet tangled around our hips, the air around my body telling me that the day was already warm.

Luke's body was warmer. I shuffled closer to him, into the angle where his torso met his hips, feeling his arm wrap around me and pull me closer still. My eyes were still closed but I could see brightness against my eyelids.

Still half asleep, I let myself luxuriate in the promise of a long, lazy Sunday: perhaps going for a walk by the canal, finding a pub for a Sunday roast, maybe helping Orla bake bread or scones or gather the blackberries that were ripening in the warm August sun on the brambles in the garden.

But there was something else I wanted to do first – wanted to do more.

I turned around in Luke's arms, my eyes still closed, and my lips found his. His kiss was languorous, as if we had all the time in the world. In that moment, it felt as if we did – our relationship was still new, each kiss still full of promise of a future I was sure we could share. Whatever doubts I had about Beatrice, about what might happen to the life I'd hoped to build at Damask Square, vanished when I was alone with him like this.

He ran his hands over my bare shoulders. I could feel the roughness of his palms from manual work, the strength of his chest where it pressed against mine, his hair tickling my face. Like the first flicker of a candle flame, I felt desire ignite inside me, along with another, deeper feeling that was less familiar.

Is this love? Is this what love feels like?

Then all thoughts and emotions were swept away as his hands moved over my skin, his tongue teased mine and I moved on top of him, my body taking over so it felt as if he and I, the bedsheets and the sunshine, the room surrounding us and the house beyond it, were all just one living, gasping thing.

Afterwards, we flopped on our backs, sweat sheening our skin, holding hands and laughing.

'All right?' he asked.

'Nah,' I joked. 'Terrible. B minus, please see me.'

He squeezed my hand. 'Seriously, Liv. That was – you are – off the scale.'

I propped myself up on my elbow to look at him, suddenly serious too. 'What does the scale look like, then? Am I in the top fifty? Top ten? Top five?'

I'd never asked him about his past relationships before – or not-relationships, the numerous casual encounters I assumed a man like him must have had before me. He'd mentioned an ex-girlfriend casually in the past, apropos of nothing much: *My ex was obsessed with Coldplay; I never got what the fuss was about. My ex used to drink snakebite and black.* Once, when I'd commented on Beatrice's hair: *My ex is blonde but I've always liked brunettes best.*

'Top one, for sure. How about me?'

'Top one, too.' My body cooling, I moved closer, resting my head on his shoulder. 'But you haven't had that much competition, to be fair.'

'Really? You must've had loads of blokes before me.'

I shook my head, the hollow between his chest and bicep feeling like it had been made especially for me to lie in.

'I was a slow starter,' I admitted. 'At school I kind of didn't expect people to want to be with me, so I stood back and watched while everyone else snogged behind the bike sheds. Well, not exactly watched, but you know what I mean.'

'Yeah, I know what you mean.' His voice was teasing. 'There's a word for people like that, you know.'

'Stop it!' I laughed. 'Anyway, I had a serious-ish boyfriend at uni but it didn't work out. He cheated on me.'

'I'm sorry. That must've hurt.'

'Yeah, of course. But we weren't right for each other, no matter what I thought at the time. I'm over it now.'

He kissed my forehead. 'I should hope so.'

'And if I hadn't been, I would have got over it, like, five minutes ago. How about you?'

'Oh, I'm over him too.'

I dug my elbow into his ribs. 'I mean, what about your ex? The blonde one?'

'Caroline? She was years ago.'

'Okay, how about the one that was obsessed with Coldplay? Was that Caroline too?'

'Nope.' His voice was more serious now. 'That was Rachel. She was more recent.'

Rachel. Okay. I felt a brief stab of jealousy, even though I knew it was irrational and unnecessary.

'Right. Rachel, then. How recent, exactly?'

'Oh, about a hundred years ago. Back in the mists of time, before I met you.'

I smiled. It was like he'd known how I would feel and was giving me reassurance without me having to ask for it.

'Seriously, though. Were you together for long?' I asked.

'Two years. We met at uni, same as you and your bloke.'

Two years? 'That's a long time. When did you and her split up?'

He hesitated, then said, 'A week before I moved in here.'

I was jolted. I didn't expect Luke to have lived like some kind of monk for years and years, but that was recent. Like, *recent* recent. He'd split up with Rachel, moved into the house on Damask Square, and a few weeks later met me.

'So when you said you had nowhere to live and you were thinking of moving back to live at your mum's in Leicester, that was why?'

I felt the movement of his head as he nodded. 'Basically, yeah. I realised I couldn't live with Rachel any more.'

'So why... why couldn't you live with her any more?'

'Cos she kicked me out. Well, she didn't kick me out, but she gave me an ultimatum. She said, "You're not going to make a living painting pictures and trying to sell them on market stalls. You need to get a proper job and stop messing about, or get out."'

'And you decided to get out?'

I felt torn. Despite how I felt about Luke, I could see Rachel's point – I wouldn't want to be holding down a job and paying all the bills while the man I lived with haphazardly pursued a dream of being an artist. No one with a decent head on their shoulders would.

'It wasn't just that. Well, that was the catalyst. She was right – I'd stayed with her for too long without pulling my weight financially. I sold a painting here and there, did casual decorating labour, but it wasn't a steady income. And it brought home to me that we wanted different things.'

'What did she want?'

'To settle down. Buy a flat. Picket fence, the whole shebang.'

'Marriage and kids?'

'Eventually, yeah, I guess.'

'And you don't?' I felt as if I was feeling my way through a dark space, not afraid exactly, but not wanting to reach out and touch something that wasn't meant to be touched.

'Not right away. I probably will – I don't know – but it felt too soon.'

'I know what you mean. That stuff's for grown-ups, right?'

He stroked my hair. 'We are grown-ups. Just not like that.'

'There's so much other stuff to do first,' I said.

'Right. I'd love to go travelling, maybe to South East Asia, even Australia.'

'Like Orla?'

'Like Orla. Although maybe not for as long.'

I remembered what she'd told us – fragments, really, scattered through various conversations over dinner in the kitchen.

'She's been all over the place, right?' I said. 'Africa, Asia, South America. And now she's here.'

Luke nodded. 'I wonder if she would've come back. If it hadn't been for the house, I mean?'

A thought struck me. 'I wonder if she was running away from something. And the house was like – I don't know. An excuse to come back.'

'It was never her home, though. She's not even from London; she grew up in Ireland.'

'She did?' Orla had never told me that, but it would explain the ghost of an accent I'd noticed in her voice, long since overlaid, almost erased, by having spent time in other places with people who spoke differently.

'That's what she said. She studied fine art, same as me, only at Trinity College in Dublin.'

There was a note of something almost like reverence in Luke's voice and I wondered how he felt about having been so passionate about something and then having had to put it aside to paint walls instead of pictures.

'And now she's getting to be an artist again,' I said. 'Maybe you will, too.'

'Maybe I will. If I'm any good, I guess I'll have to find a way.'

I remembered the pictures he'd shown me: the bold, abstract canvases with their sweeps of brilliant colour, the way he could capture the essence of a person with a few strokes of a pen.

'You are good.'

'That's what you told me, like, ten minutes ago.'

I laughed. 'Not at that. Well, at that too.'

Luke stretched, releasing me from the cradle of his arm. 'Anyway, you'll get to meet Rachel, if you want.'

'What? When?'

'Her best mate Belinda's having a Halloween party. It's her thing – she's obsessed with it. Does it every year, plans it months in advance. She texted me and asked if I'd come and I said I'd think about it. She and I always got on well. She said Rachel wouldn't mind and I could bring someone if I wanted.'

'Wouldn't that be weird?' Meeting Luke's ex-girlfriend certainly felt like it would be weird. But even more than that – I had the sensation I'd had before, when I saw Emily or went to the pub after work, of a life outside of Damask Square that I almost ceased to be aware of when I was here. When I was with Luke.

'She'll have to meet you sooner or later. It wasn't a bad break-up and we've got loads of friends in common, and anyway – I mean, you're part of my life now, right?'

His words gave me such a thrill of pleasure that I forgot all about Orla and her past and even about Rachel – at least for the time being.

THIRTY-TWO
14 AUGUST 2005

Another morning, another sleepless night. I feel hollowed out with tiredness and unable to focus on anything. The words on this page are blurry and coming even more slowly than usual. I cannot paint – when I sit in front of a blank canvas there seems no point in marking it with a brushstroke or line of charcoal. When sweet Luke called me up to the first floor yesterday to show me the newly stripped panelling there, I could barely summon any enthusiasm, even though I could see how wonderful it looks.

Around me, the house is slowly coming back to life, the warmth of summer seeming to bring its blood rushing through its veins. The garden exploding in fruitfulness – the blackberries are ripening and the gnarled old apple tree is laden with fruit. Thanks to the Preservation Trust grant, I paid some electricians to do the rewiring, and I have a man coming next week to quote on repairing the roof.

But inside I am cold as ashes – as lifeless as this place was when I first moved in.

My thoughts return constantly to that contact register. The damn legislation. I don't even know what the register looks like

– I imagine it being a book, a heavy, dusty tome, although in reality it's probably a database on a server somewhere. Either way, it is a source of torment to me, like a cancer growing inside me. Like how I felt before she was born – as if I had been infected by some parasite.

All I wanted was to be rid of it – this thing that was growing inside me, threatening to destroy me. But I couldn't wish it away or even purge myself of it through violence – although God knows I tried; in a lifetime of riding horses, I never fell as often or as hard as in those few months.

That was how my grandmother found out – not through the changing shape of my body, which I hid beneath an old-fashioned girdle unearthed from a trunk of my mother's clothes, but because I appeared to have lost the ability to stick on a horse. And once she knew, it was all over – there was no escaping her and the help she promised me.

No one would know, she said. Only her and the nuns at the clinic. No one would ever find out. Once I had resigned myself to the fact that I would have to go through with it, something changed: I felt a kind of acceptance and then something almost like fascination. What was growing inside me was a person. I would never know her – thanks to the slow circling of my mother's wedding ring on a string over my belly, I was sure this would be a daughter – but I could see her, just briefly, hold her and then say goodbye.

But it didn't turn out like that. I tried so hard – I really did. Goaded by the midwives, who told me I was being a silly girl, weak and cowardly as well as sinful, I tried. Truly, I did. If my grandmother hadn't intervened and insisted a doctor be called, I would have died and so would she. As it was, we were both saved. Saved by the oblivion of a general anaesthetic and a knife through my skin.

Even then, I begged them not to operate, because I knew what would happen once I was unconscious. It did, of course.

By the time I came round, they had taken her away. Only my grandmother was there by my bed, holding my hand, saying, There, there, Orla. It's all over now.

I believed her – all these years, I thought that what she'd said was true.

But she was wrong. I have the means to make contact with her now and I can't stop asking myself the question: if I wanted so much to see her back then, why can't I bear to do so now?

THIRTY-THREE

Over the next couple of days, after the mercy of the weekend, Beatrice found herself bursting into tears at the slightest thing: when Slate gave her a picture he'd drawn of her, with long yellow hair, a bright red smile and hearts next to the wonky BIBI he had written underneath; when coffee spurted out of the sides of the cafetière as she was pushing down the plunger, scalding her hand; when Neil rang to check in and ask if she was okay.

'You've had a shock,' Frances, who had taken a rare two days off work to spend with Parker, told her. 'Me too. I haven't been able to sleep at all since it happened – I keep getting up and creeping in to check on them. And my sugar cravings are off the scale.'

Beatrice had found the opposite – whenever she tried to eat, she felt her throat closing, as if her body was echoing what Parker's had done when she'd been unable to breathe.

'I'll be okay,' she said. 'You're right, it was a shock. But it's my job to deal with things like that, right?'

'And you were marvellous. Peter and I will never, ever be able to thank you enough. You saved her life.' Frances lowered her voice so that Parker, contentedly bashing wooden pans in her play kitchen, couldn't hear.

'Don't.' Beatrice felt a fresh surge of the terror she'd felt that night. 'She'd have been fine. It was only croup.'

She pulled a tissue out of the box on the kitchen island and dabbed her eyes.

'Oh, honey.' Frances laid a comforting hand on her arm. 'Look – why don't you take the afternoon off? Get some rest. Have a break.'

'But what will the kids do this afternoon?'

Frances laughed. 'I will take care of that, of course. I don't know how we managed without you – even before I went back to work, the place was always chaos and the kids were feral. But I am their mother – I reckon I can cope without you for one afternoon.'

Reluctantly, Beatrice agreed. Frances was right – she needed to rest. She felt hollowed out with tiredness, but at the same time brimming with emotion, seesawing between tenderness and anger with such speed that she could barely put a name to her feelings from one minute to the next.

'If you take them out, Slate'll need his raincoat and I'm not sure where it is. I may have put it in the wash. And Parker's decided she doesn't like peas with her mac and cheese any more.'

'Beatrice.' Frances smiled, but there was a hint of steel in her eyes. 'I'll be fine.'

Beatrice felt herself flushing, tears prickling her eyes yet again. 'Sure. Great. Thanks. I'll see you tomorrow.'

Chastened, feeling as if her employer had segued from praising her to telling her off in the space of seconds, Beatrice left.

. . .

When she arrived back at Damask Square, the house was deserted. Livvie would be at work. Luke must have been out on some errand. And Orla – who knew? It would have been the perfect opportunity to do some more investigating, but Beatrice didn't have the energy.

She let herself into her room, took off her clothes, lay down in bed and fell asleep in seconds.

It was dark when she woke up and the house was as silent as it had been when she'd arrived home. She could see a full moon gleaming through the leaves of the birch tree outside her window; a glance at her watch told her it was two in the morning. She'd slept for twelve hours straight, and now she was wide awake, her mind humming with alertness.

She pulled on her pyjamas and thrust her feet into her sneakers, then sat for a few moments on the bed, listening keenly but hearing nothing. Then she stood up, picked up her torch and stole to the bathroom. She peed as silently as she could and crept downstairs, where she waited in the kitchen for a full five minutes, watching and listening.

She could hear the swish of the occasional car on the street outside. A moth, lured indoors by the light earlier, bashed against a windowpane somewhere. But no one stirred – it was so quiet Beatrice could hear her own breathing.

For a moment, she allowed herself to imagine that she lived here on her own – that the house was hers and hers alone. How beautiful she could make it! She'd put in a new kitchen and an en-suite bathroom with a power shower. She'd have her studio up on the top floor, where the light would be perfect. She'd have a little wrought-iron table and chairs out in the garden, and friends would come and sip rosé with her.

This house – she could see why Orla loved it. She could imagine loving it too. She felt in her bones that it partly belonged to her – or she belonged to it.

Then she heard movement and almost jumped out of her

skin. But it was only Maud padding downstairs, her eyes huge and luminous when Beatrice shone the beam of her torch on her face.

As ever the cat regarded her with wariness. She knew that Beatrice wouldn't feed her like Orla did, fuss her like Livvie did, or engage her in exciting games with discarded cable ties like Luke did.

Now, though, Beatrice had other plans for her. She had things to do, and Maud could help.

'Come on,' Beatrice whispered. 'We're going in.'

She stepped out of the kitchen and tiptoed to the door beneath the stairs that led down to the cellar. Since she'd discovered it, it had been in the back of her mind – something to be investigated, but not now. Later, when there was an opportunity.

And this was that opportunity.

She lifted the latch and eased the door open. The same breath of cool air she'd felt when she'd first noticed it greeted her now, along with the smell of cold dust and old things.

Through the opening, Beatrice could see a steep, narrow flight of bowed wooden stairs leading downwards.

She'd expected to have to manhandle the cat down with her, but that wasn't necessary. Maud approached the gap quite readily, her tail low and her whiskers bristling. She placed a paw on the top step, then another, then began to walk downwards, switching to bunny-hops as she neared the bottom.

'Good girl,' Beatrice whispered. 'Now don't let any rats near me, okay?'

She herself descended the stairs backwards, like a ladder. Each step was too shallow to fit the full length of her foot and worn so smooth with time that the wood was as slippery as glass. The air was cool and smelled horrible – musty and stale and just the way Beatrice imagined a place where rats lived would smell. The floor was flagstones, smooth but uneven beneath her feet, and the floorboards above just higher than her head.

A cobweb brushed her face and she suppressed a scream, forcing herself to take a steadying breath of the dank air and shining her torch cautiously around.

The space was huge – way larger than she'd expected. Probably, when the house had been built, it had been intended to store wine and perhaps even fresh meat and cheese, rather than coal. The walls were brick, gleaming damply in the beam of her torch.

Piled against one wall, Beatrice saw a stack of plastic tea crates, their sides black, their lids a brighter colour – orange or yellow; she wasn't able to tell in the pallid torchlight. She could no longer see the cat, who had padded off somewhere into the gloom.

She approached the stack of crates, holding her torch between her teeth, and reached for the top one. The plastic was rough beneath her fingers, embossed with an even, nubbly texture. The lid was made up of two halves, interlocking at the centre like fingers.

Carefully, she prised them apart and opened them. At once, she was met with a different smell – the smell of paint. Not the emulsion Luke used on the walls, which was so familiar to her now she barely noticed it when she stepped into the house, but oil paint, like an artist would use.

So Orla did paint, after all – it wasn't just talk.

The crate was stacked with canvases and sheets of cartridge paper that looked like they'd been torn from a pad, their edges serrated from the spiral binding. She leafed through them and picked one out at random, holding it up to the light of her torch.

She could see the outline of a girl's face, fine-boned and wide-eyed, dark hair falling to her shoulders, but the light was too bad for her to make out much more. Frustrated, she replaced the page and took out another, seeing the same face, this time painted in watercolour, smiling. The girl's cheeks were perhaps a little fuller, the hair shorter, the collar that framed her face rounded like a child's blouse. But it wasn't the identity of the sitter that caught Beatrice's eye – it was the style of the work.

There was real skill in the little painting. The areas where blank paper showed to indicate highlights were perfectly placed. The colour was intense in the background, yet as smooth as rose petals on the skin of the girl's face. Her eyes seemed to meet Beatrice's as she looked at them, as if she was saying, *Oh, it's you. Here I am, too.*

Beatrice would have bet her bottom dollar that it had been painted by the same artist whose landscape of Clonmara hung on the landing.

Then she heard a sound that made her drop the portrait to the floor. A scraping scurrying, like small, clawed legs, and then a high-pitched squeal.

Beatrice felt perspiration break out all over her body and adrenaline galvanising her. She didn't pause to close the crate – she simply bolted, her feet slipping on the damp floor, and clambered up the stairs on all fours, emerging gasping into the clear air of the ground floor.

Then she turned and pulled the door closed behind her, barely caring if it made a noise.

She stood in the silence, gasping and terrified. Only when her breath had settled back to normal did she creep back upstairs, shutting herself away in her bedroom again.

THIRTY-FOUR
17 AUGUST 2005

I am writing this at the kitchen table, my hands sweaty and trembling and my body still tingling with the aftermath of fear. I was woken this morning not by anything present, but by an absence. There was no Maud on my chest. No claws tentatively, then more persistently, pricking my face, the campaign for breakfast service getting started.

Once I realised she was not there, I knew there could be no more sleep this morning. Of course, she is a cat and like all cats she sets her own agenda, but also like all cats she is a creature of habit, her daily rituals varying only slightly depending on the weather, my movements and her mood. So I got up and came downstairs, calling her, but she was nowhere to be seen.

I looked out in the garden, but she wasn't slinking through the undergrowth or perched on the wall being taunted by squirrels. I looked outside the front door and walked around the square, terrified I would find her small, broken body hit by a car, but I saw nothing. Then I heard her muffled cries and knew, straight away, with absolute certainty, where she was and what had happened.

And I was right. As soon as I opened the door leading down

to the cellar, she dashed up the stairs, protesting furiously at her captivity although I dare say she'd had a wonderful time down there, decimating the mouse population. I fed her and then went down there myself, knowing full well what I would find. It was just as I'd anticipated: the topmost of my pile of storage boxes open, the portraits I've painted over the years scattered on the floor.

Beatrice. Beatrice's nocturnal exploration of the house inevitably led her downstairs, where she hunted through my things, discovering my secrets.

I didn't stop to think. I didn't consider what was the right thing to do – the mature, adult thing. I regret that now. I stormed upstairs and knocked on Beatrice's door, barely waiting for her muffled response before pushing it open and going in.

She was still in bed, sitting up under the covers, her eyes bleary with sleep. She looked so young – almost like a child – and I felt my anger fade slightly. Slightly, but not enough.

What were you doing? I demanded. Last night, down in the cellar?

Guilt flashed over her face. I could see her mind working as she tried to come up with an excuse – a lie.

I thought I heard someone down there. I woke up, I went to look. But I couldn't see anything. It must have been the cat.

Cats can't unlatch doors, Beatrice.

It was open. Someone must have left it open. Luke or Livvie.

And the box with my paintings in? I suppose that was open too?

I... Her eyes were wide and frightened. I hated her being afraid of me. I'm sorry, Orla. I could smell paint. I was curious and I opened the box.

I looked at her, saying nothing.

They're beautiful, Orla. You're an amazing artist. I paint a bit myself, but nothing like – nothing as good as that.

I see, I thought. Lies first, then apologies, now flattery.

I said, Beatrice, and then I stopped. There was no point launching into a lecture about respecting others' privacy. She knew all that – she knew she'd done wrong but she had chosen to do it anyway.

Please don't do that again. Please don't go down there and go through my things.

I'm sorry, Orla, she said again. Then, emboldened, realising I wasn't going to tell her to pack her bags and leave, she said, The painting on the landing. Is that yours, too?

I nodded.

I thought so. It's wonderful. Where is it? The scene, I mean?

A place in Ireland called Clonmara. You wouldn't know it.

She looked as if she might be about to ask me something else, but I was in no mood to answer her questions. I turned and left.

I shall have to get a lock for that door.

I wonder what her next question would have been, and whether she will ever find the courage to ask it.

THIRTY-FIVE

Beatrice waited and waited for Orla to say something more about her snooping in the cellar. On the first morning, after Orla had come into her room to speak to her about it, she came downstairs to find Orla sitting at the kitchen table, a few sheets of paper filled with dense, spidery handwriting in front of her and Maud the cat perched contentedly on her lap, and Beatrice's stomach lurched so violently with fear she thought she might be sick.

Now that Orla had had time to think about what Beatrice had done, she'd ask her to leave for sure.

'Good morning,' she managed, her mouth dry and her hands clasped behind her back.

Orla looked up at her serenely. 'Good morning. Cup of tea?'

'I'm okay, thanks.' Confusion and relief washed over Beatrice in equal measures. 'I have to go to work. I had the afternoon off yesterday, but I'm back in today.'

'Were you ill? I noticed you were in your room all evening.'

Beatrice shook her head, feeling a treacherous blush creep up her neck and over her face. 'I'm fine. It was – Parker, the little girl, had to be taken to hospital.'

She found herself spilling out the whole story. Orla listened in silence, her head on one side, rolling her pen from side to side over the pages she'd been writing on. Beatrice tried not to look too closely at them.

'That must have given you quite a scare,' she said, when Beatrice had finished. 'Is the child all right now?'

'She's fine.'

'And what about you?' Orla's eyes rested searchingly on Beatrice's face.

Maybe I could say that's what I was doing – the shock kept me awake and then I thought I heard something down there.

But there was something about Orla's steady gaze that told Beatrice she'd only be digging herself deeper if she tried that.

Instead, she heard herself saying, 'I'll be okay. It's strange though. I never realised how... how fond I've got of her. Of both the kids. I was quite calm at the time, but afterwards...'

'A delayed reaction. It's often the way. Maybe take it easy for a few days. Make sure you get plenty of rest.'

'Yes, I will. Thanks, Orla.'

More confused than ever, Beatrice picked up her bag and left. Had her unintentional display of vulnerability saved her? Or were those words – *Make sure you get plenty of rest* – a warning of some kind? Were the pages she'd seen Orla writing on – *A diary? A letter?* – some sort of trap intended to catch her out prying again, this time red-handed?

Beatrice had no idea.

All week she lived with a creeping dread, worse than waiting for a dentist appointment because this had no fixed time or date. She could step, unsuspecting, into an ambush at any moment.

When the letter she had been expecting finally arrived, her mouth went dry with fear. There it was, on the kitchen table, placed neatly on top of the pile of post that included leaflets from local Indian restaurants, a flyer from a gutter-clearing company and several bills for Orla. Furtively, her heart pounding, Beatrice shoved it into her purse.

If Orla had seen it, surely now she would say something.

Only Orla didn't pounce or ambush Beatrice. She treated her just the same as she always had, with the exception of those occasional long, searching stares which made Beatrice feel as if Orla was rummaging around inside her head the same way she'd rummaged through Orla's paintings. That, and a lock appeared on the door leading to the cellar one evening, the hasp surrounded by a dusting of fresh wood shavings, a bright new brass padlock securing it.

That settled it. Orla knew that Beatrice didn't plan to abandon her investigations, so she'd taken steps to prevent her.

But why wasn't she saying anything?

As the days passed, Beatrice's sense of anxiety heightened, but as a week went by and then a weekend, when she was off work and in the house most of the day, alone with Orla because Livvie and Luke were out and she couldn't, somehow, force herself to go out and do any of the London sightseeing she'd promised herself and her mother she would, it ebbed.

If Orla was going to ask her to leave, she would surely have done so by now.

So Beatrice went to work on the Monday morning feeling – not relieved, exactly, but as if a storm cloud had lifted without any rain having fallen. The cloud was still out there somewhere, the deluge might still come, but for now she was safe.

Except she still hadn't found the courage to open the letter. It was still there in her purse, sealed, the official logo on the envelope sending her heart pounding whenever she looked at it.

She also found herself approaching a new week of work with a sense of excitement and delight she'd never felt before. This could be the week when Slate signed his artwork without the 'S' being written backwards. It might be the week when Parker cracked putting on a T-shirt by herself. Now, when she stepped out of the elevator into the apartment, the day ahead felt replete with possibility, and she found herself dropping to her knees and pulling both the children into a hug when they came running to greet her.

'You're looking better, Bibi,' Frances observed, turning away from the remains of her and the children's breakfast on the kitchen island. 'Not as tired as you were a while ago. Good weekend?'

'Yes, thank you. I got plenty of rest.'

'And what are you planning to get up to today?'

Beatrice knew her employer's mind was already on her own working day, and that whatever she answered, the question would be repeated in the evening: *And what did you get up to today?*

But she said, 'I thought we could go to the new messy play session at the SureStart place this morning. And then maybe the park in the afternoon. You'd like that, wouldn't you, kids?'

'I want to go to the library,' Slate said.

'Do you now, my little bookworm?' Frances brushed a manicured hand over her son's head.

'I want to see Neil. Neil tells the best stories.'

'Are you sure?' Beatrice asked. 'It's going to be sunny. We could go on the slides in the park.'

'Stories,' Slate insisted.

'Then Bibi will take you to the library, honey.' Frances kissed each of her children on the head then stepped past Beatrice into the elevator. 'Won't you?'

'Sure,' Beatrice agreed. 'But first we need to get you two dressed.'

With any luck, she thought, Slate would have forgotten all about the library by the time that had happened. It wasn't that she didn't want to go – the prospect of sitting quietly by herself while someone else occupied the kids still had its appeal. But she knew there was no point looking through the newspaper archives any more – there was nothing more for her to find there.

And Neil – for some reason she couldn't quite name, she felt awkward about the prospect of seeing him.

Slate didn't forget. After persuading them to spend the morning in the park and then wrestling with them over their lunches, Beatrice – unable to face disappointing him – reluctantly gave in. She soon found herself sitting cross-legged on the fringes of the circle of children while Neil, glove puppets on both his hands, launched into an improbable tale about a lonely little boy who was befriended by a dragon.

He isn't a good-looking guy, she thought – nothing like the dark-haired, chiselled-featured boys she'd dated in college. But there was something cute about the total lack of inhibition with which he engaged with the children, the way his goofy grin flashed out when they laughed at the funny parts of the story, the way he held their attention, fascinated, through every pause.

'And so Ferdinand the dragon went to school every day with Jeremy,' he concluded, 'and soon, he found he had lots of friends. All of the other boys and girls wanted to play with him and his dragon, and Jeremy didn't feel lonely any more. But the funny thing was, none of the teachers ever asked him why he came to school riding on the back of a dragon.'

Neil got to his feet, laughing and shaking his head as the children crowded round him pleading for another story. Beatrice hung back, waiting for Parker and Slate to give up and accept that it was time for them to leave.

But Neil brought them over to her.

'That story was adorable,' she said. 'You had them in the palm of your hand. Did you make it up yourself?'

'I guess.' Neil smiled. 'My mum used to make up stories for me when I was a kid and I kind of got the taste for it.'

Beatrice thought of the story her father used to tell her at bedtime. Somehow, the memory no longer brought the nostalgic comfort it once had.

'Anyway, how's it going?' he asked. 'Have you found out anything more? About the house?'

Beatrice's hand moved involuntarily towards her purse. Her feelings of awkwardness – shyness, almost – about Neil had dissipated now she'd seen him behaving so naturally around the kids, greeting her so casually. She might as well open the letter now – if its contents were confusing, Neil could help her understand. And, more importantly, she could dispose of it here, in the public library, in the large cardboard bin with the recycling logo on its side. It would be safer here than in Frances and Peter's apartment, and certainly safer than in the house on Damask Square.

'I got the deeds to the house.' Her words came out in a rush. 'I sent off to the Land Registry for them. Apparently anyone can – it doesn't have to be your house or anything. You just pay a fee and they send them.'

'Wow. And what did they say?'

'I don't know yet. I've got them right here.'

She took out the envelope and showed him.

'Cool. So are you going to open it, or what?'

Now that the moment was upon her, Beatrice found it quite natural to slip her thumb into the corner of the envelope and slide it across, the paper tearing more or less evenly along its fold.

As easy as opening an envelope, she thought.

She took out the paper inside and looked at it. It was a photocopy, the blank areas pale grey and the printed ones darker, as if the original document had been yellowing or its print faded with age, or both.

Neil leaned in close to her shoulder and they both looked at it.

'The house hasn't been sold since 1938,' Neil said. 'So your landlady...'

'Her grandmother didn't buy it from the Doyles. She can't have done. She must be...'

Even though it was the information she'd been hoping for, now that it was there in front of her, she felt a sick sense of something like dread.

'What are you going to do?' Neil asked. 'Will you ask her if she's your birth mother?'

Beatrice's mouth was dry. 'I can't.'

'I get that. It's quite the conversation to have.'

'And we... we had an argument. Things aren't great between us. And anyway – I can't be sure. Not *sure* sure. I can't confront her if I'm not sure. She might say it isn't true. I'll have to think about it.'

'Bibi?' Parker appeared at Beatrice's side, her hand tugging at her skirt. 'I'm hungry.'

'Sorry, sweetie. We'll get you home.' She turned back to Neil. 'I should get going.'

'Before you go.' Neil had pulled the puppets off his hands and was looking down at them. 'I was going to ring you, but now you're here, I might as well...'

'Might as well what?' Beatrice asked.

All the confidence he'd shown in front of twenty boisterous children a few minutes ago seemed to have deserted him.

'Ask you in person. Ask you whether you'd like to go for a drink sometime.'

'A drink? With you?'

'Or a movie. Or a coffee or whatever. See an art exhibition somewhere.' He looked up from the puppets, met Beatrice's eyes, then looked down again.

'Like a date?' Beatrice asked, and he nodded.

Beatrice thought again of her mother's bedtime story: the same every time, apart from the minor differences and embellishments. Clearly, Neil's mom hadn't needed to tell just the one story, over and over again. She'd been able to give free rein to her creativity, knowing that her son had a family that was truly his.

Neil had roots: the grandfather he visited so often that he knew the ins and outs of his relationships with his neighbours. The Shabbat dinners the family no doubt had together every Friday. The lack of self-consciousness with which he was able to entertain a group of kids.

Beatrice longed for those things. All the material possessions her parents had given her, all the love they'd lavished on her, would never make up for that. And while Neil gave freely of himself, she was still learning who she herself might be.

Not Beatrice – the other girl. Aisling. The one who might have been Orla's daughter, except Orla hadn't wanted her and had given her away.

'I'm sorry,' she said. 'I'm not really looking to date anyone right now.'

She watched his face fall, then recover quickly. 'No worries. It was worth a try.'

'But maybe we could have lunch or something anyway,' she added hastily. 'You know, as friends.'

'I'd like that,' Neil replied. 'I'll ring you.'

Beatrice said goodbye and hurried away with the children. Later, while she cooked their dinner, her thoughts kept returning to him. Had she made a mistake, rebuffing him so abruptly? But he'd said he'd call her anyway. The thought made her smile, and she found herself hoping very much that he would.

THIRTY-SIX

15 SEPTEMBER 2005

Well. Beatrice has finally apologised to me. Last night, after dinner, she came up to my room and knocked softly on the door. I felt my senses prickle instantly to alertness and I pulled the cord of my dressing gown tight around my waist – as if it were armour, not a flimsy old cotton robe – before I opened the door.

Beatrice was freshly showered, her hair wet and hanging down her back. She wore no make-up and she looked young and vulnerable. To my surprise, I felt the urge to take her in my arms and assure her that I wasn't angry, not any more.

But I sensed that an embrace wouldn't be welcome, so I just waited, smiling encouragingly.

She politely asked to come in, and so I stepped aside and she entered, closing the door behind her. She was holding something in her arms – a pad of paper, close to her chest as if, like me, she felt the need for a shield.

I wanted to say sorry, she said. I've behaved terribly. I had no right to snoop through your things. There's no excuse. It won't happen again.

I said, Thank you, Beatrice. I appreciate your apology and I accept it. I shouldn't have reacted the way I did and I'm sorry for that.

And Maud, she went on. I shouldn't have left her down there. You must have been worried.

She was perfectly all right. She would've been hunting quite happily in the dark.

I thought I heard a rat, she said. And that's why I had to run away. I'd have tidied your paintings away otherwise.

Not out of respect, I thought, almost amused, but to conceal the fact that she'd been looking at them in the first place.

But I said, I'm frightened of rats, too. They horrify me.

Their scrabbly claws. She winced at the thought. And their tails – ugh!

Ugh, I agreed.

We looked at each other, grimacing, united in our distaste, and then we both laughed. It's the first time I think I have shared a laugh with Beatrice and it felt good – it felt healing.

Anyway, she said. I was going to buy you some flowers, to say sorry. But I thought of something better.

Shyly, she turned around the sketchbook she was holding so I could see the page that had been pressed against her chest. It was a painting of the roses that grow in the garden square. Late in their season now, they are overblown and fading but still beautiful, all the shades of a sunrise in their delicate petals. She'd captured them perfectly, and in watercolour – my favourite medium.

The painting is exquisite, and I told her so.

You have real talent, I said. Have you always painted?

I don't think I'm very good at it. My dad always tells me I am, but he loves me so of course he says nice things.

I laughed. That's what fathers are for, isn't it? But he is right. He's not just being kind.

She said, Thank you, Orla. It means a lot.

In return, I thanked her for the gift, told her I would treasure it, and that I appreciated her coming here tonight.

We said goodnight after that and she went off to bed. I hope she has slept well. I hope she understands that I've forgiven her and that whatever made her want to pry through my belongings has passed. I don't want to have to be angry with her again – I want to protect her.

THIRTY-SEVEN

'Something to wear to a Halloween party?' Orla smiled delightedly. 'Sure we can find something for you. What were you thinking? Are we talking sexy witch here or giant pumpkin?'

'Well, it's a month away so I've got lots of time to decide. But I'm definitely not leaning towards giant pumpkin – Luke's ex is going to be there,' I told her.

'Oh, she is? Well, in that case we're definitely on the sexy side of witchy, aren't we? Not too sexy, mind.'

'Why not?'

'Because I'm guessing these are Luke's friends you'll be meeting? And you don't know them.'

'Well, no, I don't. But...' I was surprised. I wouldn't have expected Orla to suggest I tone down my sexiness level – which would have reduced it to practically negative figures – just because I was going to be meeting Luke's friends.

'Remember Bridget Jones in the movie?' Orla folded her arms. 'When she turns up at the tarts and vicars party only no one else is a tart or a vicar? You don't know them, so you don't know how seriously they'll be taking this Halloween lark.'

'Oh. Yes, I see what you mean.'

'And if you're all got up as a sexy spider and they're in jeans, you'd feel just a bit foolish.'

'God – I'd be mortified.'

'You would. So you want to aim for something that could be a Halloween costume but could also be your normal clothes.'

'But how are they to know I don't go to work every day dressed as a sexy spider?'

Orla laughed and I saw a glimpse of what she must have been like when she was younger – a beautiful girl, full of silliness and fun. 'Well, don't say I didn't warn you.'

'You have. And I think you're right. I could just wear a black dress and do some zombie make-up or something.'

'A black dress?' She looked at me, her head on one side. 'You know, I think I might have just the thing for you.'

She glanced over her shoulder, silent for a moment as if she was listening. But she must have known – as I knew – that she and I were the only ones in the house. It was a Friday evening; Beatrice wouldn't be back from work for at least another half hour, and Luke had gone to see his mother in Leicester for the weekend.

'Hold on while I get my keys,' she said.

I watched her hurry out of the kitchen and run lightly up the stairs. I heard her tap across the landing, then resume climbing up to the second floor. There was silence for a few minutes before she returned, a bunch of keys jingling in her hand.

But they weren't the only keys she had. On a slim gold chain around her neck, I could see another, smaller key – one that must have been hidden by the neckline of her top until she'd taken it out, used it and forgotten in her haste to conceal it again.

The suitcase, I thought. *The suitcase I saw Beatrice going through – she's bought a lock for it, and she keeps her keys in there.*

So Orla was aware of what Beatrice had been doing – and yet Beatrice was still there, living in the house. She hadn't been asked to leave or even, as far as I knew, reprimanded for snooping through Orla's things.

Why not? What Beatrice had done was outrageous. Clearly Orla cared enough about her privacy to put stuff under lock and key – but not enough to say anything to the person responsible.

But before I could make sense of the questions racing through my mind, Orla led me towards the door beneath the stairs that I presumed led to the cellar, although I'd never had any reason to open it. She slipped a key into the padlock that held closed a hasp on the door – bright, new brass; surely that hadn't been there last time I looked? – and opened it.

'Come on down,' she said. 'Mind the stairs – they're steep and a bit slippery.'

Gingerly, I picked my way down the narrow flight of wooden stairs. The cellar was cavernous, stretching away beneath the whole of the ground floor. The grey flagstones on the floor were worn smooth with age, and the only light was what trickled in from a grating outside.

'It's kind of creepy down here,' Orla apologised. 'One of the first things I got Luke to do was clear out all the junk, because I was worried about rats. I'm mildly phobic of them. That's one of the reasons I was so happy when Maud decided to move in.'

I shivered; the air down here was noticeably cooler than the rest of the house.

'I can imagine,' I said. 'It's definitely spooky. Still – we were talking about Halloween, right?'

'We certainly were. Now, I've a whole load of old stuff down here. I never thought I'd accumulate possessions, but you do, don't you? They get so they have a kind of power over you.'

She led me over to a stack of storage boxes arranged along one of the walls – sturdy, plastic tea crates, their sides rough-textured black, their lids bright yellow. I could see sticky labels on their sides, the edges curling slightly in the damp air, each bearing Orla's neat cursive handwriting.

Art materials. Winter clothes. Party clothes. Portraits. Notebooks. Photographs.

It takes a special kind of pack rat, I thought, *to lug a crate full of notebooks around the world with them.* I remembered Orla's bedroom, almost minimalist in its tidiness. How strange that she should keep one part of her house like that, and yet have all these accumulated possessions down here.

The topmost crate was the one labelled 'Portraits'. Orla lifted it down easily – clearly whatever pictures it contained, there weren't very many of them. Then she reached for the one labelled 'Party clothes' and heaved it to the floor with more effort.

She levered open the interlocking halves of the plastic lid. The air filled with the smell of cedar and perfume, and she crouched down again, lifting off a layer of tissue paper.

'I haven't looked through these old things in ages,' she said. 'When I was packing up to come here, I just shoved everything in.'

Slowly, feeling like I was intruding on something private, I approached and squatted down next to her.

She lifted out a royal blue satin dress, a large, crumpled bow on its shoulder.

'Look at this horror. I wore it to a ball when I was eighteen. The 1980s had a lot to answer for.'

I laughed. 'It'll probably come back though, and be worth loads.'

'It certainly cost enough at the time.' She pushed back her hair. 'And this monstrosity was a bridesmaid's dress – at least I can't take the blame for choosing it.'

She laid a peach-coloured floral frock over my lap. I could hear the rustling of tulle beneath the stiff skirt.

'I should take the whole lot down to the market.' She sighed. 'I might get a few quid for them. Ah – this is what I was looking for.'

She stood up, a beaded black garment hanging from her arm. Even my inexpert eyes could see that it was in a different league from the other dresses, timeless and beautiful.

'Schiaparelli,' Orla said. 'It was my grandmother's. I think it would fit you.'

I stood too, placing the other dresses back in the chest, and Orla handed me the black one. I could feel the weight of it and see countless jet beads glinting in the dim light.

'Orla,' I said, 'I can't possibly wear this. Not to some random Halloween party. It's too precious – it must be worth a fortune.'

She tilted her head. 'It's only gathering dust down here, Livvie. Well, it would be if it weren't hidden away in a box. Clothes are meant to be worn.'

Before I could protest again, she reached out, placing a hand on each of my shoulders, her eyes fixed on my face. 'Please? Just try it?'

There was no way I could decline – even if I'd wanted to. And, looking at the dress, I realised that I didn't – not really. Seeing it had awoken something in me – a kind of covetousness that was almost lust. The Vivienne Westwood dress Orla had found for me in the market had made me feel the same, in a smaller way. It had, I realised, been a precursor to this, a gateway that had made me realise beautiful things – and even beauty itself – were not just for other people.

'I'd love to,' I said.

I was quite used to trying on clothes in front of Orla by now. Unselfconsciously, I kicked off my shoes and stepped out of my jeans, pulling off my T-shirt.

'Let me help you.' She located the few tiny buttons on the

back of the dress, unfastened them and eased it over my head, guiding my hands into the armholes.

Immediately, I could feel the weight of the embellishments, their surfaces scratching the skin inside my arms. From shoulders to hips, the dress was heavy, almost rigid – below that, the skirt felt weightless against my bare legs.

'It's above the knee on you,' Orla said, 'shorter than it was designed to be, but that doesn't matter. My grandmother was five foot five – she was considered a tall woman then. Turn round and let me button you up.'

I obeyed, feeling Orla's dexterous fingers skilfully fitting the tiny buttons into their places.

'I'll need someone to help me get into it,' I said nervously. 'I don't want to damage it.'

'You won't. It was made to last. But you're right – my grandmother still had a maid to help her dress, even then.'

I couldn't see Orla's face, but the tone of her voice had changed, from excitement to wistfulness.

'You must miss her,' I said tentatively. 'Your grandmother, I mean. She must have really loved you, to have wanted you to have the house.'

Orla moved in front of me, adjusting the straps of the dress over my shoulders.

'Your bra strap shows at the back,' she said, 'but you don't need to wear one.'

For a second I felt rebuffed, but then she went on, 'She did love me. And I loved her. She was like a mother to me. She never had a daughter, you see. Just one son – my father.'

She raised her eyes from the dress to my face, unsmiling. I didn't know what the right thing was to say – whether to ask her more, wait for her to volunteer, or move the conversation back to the safe territory of fashion.

'I'm sorry,' I said softly. 'Sorry for your loss.'

Orla sighed. 'I'd already lost her, in a sense. When I moved away. I left because I thought I didn't want to see her again and by the time I did, it was too late.'

Questions whirled through my mind. Why had Orla moved away? Where was her own mother in all this? What had happened to change things so drastically between her and the grandmother she'd clearly been so close to?

'I hated her at first,' Orla went on, almost as if I wasn't there. 'It's a strange thing, how love can turn into hatred. But it didn't take me long to realise that it was myself I hated, far more than her – myself and what I'd done. That was the thing. I didn't think she'd ever forgive me, and until she had I couldn't forgive myself.'

'I'm sorry,' I muttered again, wishing I could find more, better words to say.

Orla sighed. 'She thought she was doing the right thing for me. And she was, really – at least, as far as there was any right thing, after what I'd done. She was a remarkable woman. A strong woman.'

'So are you,' I said. 'You're amazing. I don't know what she was like, but I can imagine her being just like you. I bet she'd be really proud if she could see you now.'

Orla smiled. 'Thank you, Livvie. You're a sweet girl. She'd have loved to see you in that dress, I know that. Now come on – let's get you dressed again and go upstairs. It's too full of damp and memories down here.'

So we went up. I hung the dress away in my wardrobe and helped Orla make ratatouille for dinner. Orla didn't mention her grandmother again that night. But I couldn't help dwelling on what she'd told me, and wondering what could have happened to destroy their relationship. Whatever it was, Orla carried the legacy of it with her like a weight.

What kind of event could have torn a family apart like that? I could think of only one thing that could have led to such a rift, such shame and regret, such a need for secrecy and silence.

I believed I knew what it was. And, remembering Beatrice's spying through Orla's possessions, I became certain that she knew, too.

I just couldn't figure out how Beatrice might have guessed, nor why she seemed so desperate to find out the truth.

THIRTY-EIGHT

Her tongue pinched painfully between her front teeth, Beatrice piped the final rosette of pink icing on to the surface of the cake, then stepped back and surveyed her handiwork. It wasn't perfect – not by a long stretch. The sketches she'd done in her notebook had shown a cute yet graceful unicorn's head, complete with fluttery black eyelashes, a flowing lilac mane and a twirly horn.

What she'd actually produced looked more like the love child of a Shetland pony and a rhinoceros.

Still, for a first attempt at least, it was decent. Once she'd chucked some glittery shit over it to hide the worst of its flaws, it would definitely pass muster. Parker would be happy; Frances would be complimentary. And the cake-baking project had fulfilled its purpose: it had given her an outlet for the need she increasingly felt to express how she felt about the kids.

They're not your children, she kept reminding herself. *Don't overstep.*

But she found it hard to heed her own advice. The moment she stepped into the apartment in the mornings and heard Parker's feet tapping on the parquet as she ran to greet her; watching

Slate finish a plate of food she'd cooked; being able to give them cuddles when they cried and see their tears turn to smiles – all those moments now brought her indescribable happiness.

Just yesterday, as he was dropping off to sleep, Slate had murmured, 'I love you, Bibi.'

'I love you, too,' Beatrice had said, feeling tears prick her eyes.

She wasn't sure if that had been the right response, but surely there could have been no other? Nothing in the childcare course she'd done had covered this, and even if it had, nothing could have prepared her for it. She knew she was meant to meet the children's physical needs, stimulate them mentally, provide appropriate discipline consistent with what their parents requested.

But love them? That was something else entirely.

Beatrice stepped back from the kitchen worktop and reached for the canister of edible glitter. The piped bits of the cake were okay, but the areas of white frosting that were meant to be smooth weren't. Maybe unicorns had dapples. She used a teaspoon to apply careful splotches of glitter to the most uneven areas, aiming for crescent shapes but not quite achieving them.

It would have to do, she concluded after a few minutes of painstaking sprinkling. Parker would wake from her nap any moment and then it would be time to fetch Slate from pre-school, take the kids for a quick run round the park before it got dark, and give them their dinner.

Then it would be her favourite time of the day: watching them splash in the bath, emerging damp and fragrant, ready for their story and bedtime. She remembered how, just a few months before, she'd have been gritting her teeth, willing them to go the fuck to sleep so she could clock off and watch TV until Frances returned home.

Now, those moments felt precious. The children tucked up in bed, clean, fed and content. The random questions they asked: Did dinosaurs have willies? Where did the sun go at night? How long was it until Christmas?

And, just the other night, from Parker, 'Bibi, do you have a mommy and daddy?'

'Of course,' Beatrice had said. 'Everyone has a mommy and a daddy.'

'But you're adopted,' Slate had pointed out, as if Beatrice might have forgotten.

'That's right. So I have a mommy and daddy who I lived with when I was growing up, and another mommy and daddy somewhere else.'

'Where?'

'I don't know yet. But I'm trying to find out.'

Beatrice opened the kitchen cabinet, slid the cake on its board inside and closed the door. It was time to get Parker up.

First, she checked her phone. She'd almost forgotten to look at it while she was engrossed in the cake, and it had been on silent so as not to disturb Parker's nap.

And there it was – a missed call from Neil.

With each passing day, her hope that he would call warred with growing certainty that he wouldn't. Why should he? She'd been clear about not wanting to date. But his silence had left an unexpected ache.

Beatrice needed a friend. She'd thought at first that she and Livvie might become friends, but then Livvie had grown closer and closer to Orla, and that had made Beatrice push her away. And, of course, Livvie had Luke – who would want Beatrice's friendship when they had giddy loved-upness and sex on tap?

The more she thought about Neil, the more she felt herself drawn to him. All the qualities he had that had made her think he was wrong for her – the stable family, the history stretching back generations, his steady demeanour – now seemed increasingly desirable.

She hadn't wanted him, but him not calling had made her feel she needed him.

And now, at last, he'd called.

Hastily, her fingers fumbling on the keypad of her phone, she began to text.

Sorry I missed your call. Just about to dash off and fetch Slate from school. How's it going?

His response came gratifyingly quickly.

Not too bad. Fancy a drink when you knock off work?

Sounds great! Where?

He suggested a pub on the river, roughly equidistant between Frances and Peter's flat and Damask Square, and Beatrice – after hastily consulting her *A–Z* – agreed.

She had no time to change or top up her make-up. Fortunately Frances was home early – just as she was giving the children a goodnight kiss – and she hurried out, walking along the river in the darkness to Limehouse, chiding herself for how nervous she felt.

Neil was already there when she arrived, a pint of beer on the table in front of him.

'Hey.' To her pleasure, he looked delighted to see her. 'How was your day?'

She told him about the unicorn cake and he exclaimed over her preparatory sketches.

'That looks awesome. I bet Parker will be made up.'

'We'll find out tomorrow. The family are going away for a

few days for half term and I wanted her to have it before they leave, although her actual birthday's only on Sunday.'

'So you'll get a few days off? Or are you going with them?'

'Not this time. They're going to stay with some work colleague of Peter's in the Cotswolds. Sounds like it's a massive, fancy house – I'd have liked to see it but at the same time, I could do with a break.'

'That's good. Because I've had an idea. It's about finding your birth mother.'

Beatrice sipped her wine, frowning. 'I mean, what if I've already found her? Everything – it all points to it being Orla. But I've messed up so badly and anyway I'm just not quite sure enough. I mean – she could have a sister. Or her grandparents could have had other kids. Some Irish families are huge. I could be her niece or her second cousin or something.'

'Surely even then she'd want to know?' Neil said.

'But what if she didn't? What if I asked her and she didn't care? Or she thought I was just some scammer after the house? I need to know for sure before I can confront her. And if it's not her, then I'm wasting my time. It's my actual mother I need to find.'

'Well, I think I've found a way for you to do that.'

Beatrice looked at him, assessing. All her efforts, all her investigation, all the information her own parents had been able to give her – and somehow Neil had a solution? It didn't seem possible.

'Seriously?' she asked.

'Sure. I mean, you know your birth date, right? And you know you were born in Dublin?'

Beatrice nodded. 'The place my mother's meant to be from – Clonmara – is too small to have a hospital.'

'Well, then.' Neil smiled with satisfaction. 'It should be quite straightforward. I went on a genealogy forum online and I found out.'

'What is it?' she asked. 'What do I do?'

'Births – and marriages and deaths – are public records,' he said. 'In Ireland, same as here or in the United States or anywhere else. I could go and look up the Taoiseach's birth record if I wanted to.'

'The what?' Beatrice asked.

'The Irish prime minister,' he translated.

'You mean – the information's there for anyone to find?'

'Anyone with the time and patience to go to the General Register Office in Dublin and look for it,' he said.

'Oh.' Beatrice felt utterly deflated. All her detective work and this solution had been there all along? All she had to do was go through a list of names in a book?

'Sure. You know where you were born—'

'The hospital was called St Gerard Majella's, apparently.' Somehow, the name emerged from Beatrice's memory, even though she'd barely thought of it in years.

'And – I guess your parents told you the name you were given at birth.'

'It was Aisling.' For the first time, she spelled it out.

'That's a lovely name,' Neil said, 'but I still like Beatrice better.'

She smiled, feeling her face flush a little. 'Me too.'

'There we go, then.' Neil drained his pint. 'While you're off work, you can go to Dublin and head to the General Register Office and take a look at the records.'

'Seriously? It's that simple?'

'I mean, there are no guarantees. Something could have gone wrong somewhere. There could have been a mistake with the dates or something. But it's got to be worth a try.'

'Neil...' Gratitude and surprise made Beatrice feel vulnerable, and for once she couldn't prevent herself from showing it. 'I'm scared.'

He reached across the table and touched her hand – just a

brush of his fingers. 'I get that. Would it help to have some company?'

'Are you saying you'd come with me?'

'Sure.' He grinned. 'I've always wanted to see Dublin. I read *Finnegans Wake* at uni. Should have put me off the place for life, but it didn't.'

'That's – thank you, Neil. Let's do it.'

'Deal,' he said.

THIRTY-NINE
28 OCTOBER 2005

I wrote three pages this morning and I will write three tomorrow morning, but I am writing this now because I don't know what else to do. I feel I should put down what has happened, although I wish it hadn't – I wish I could just rewind the tape and erase my own weakness, my own stupidity.

I have told Livvie my secret, told her the truth.

She came into my room, about half an hour ago. She would never burst in without knocking, but she was excited and in a hurry – off to her party in the Schiaparelli dress, wanting me to see her in her white foundation and black lipstick, a ghost from the 1920s or some such idea, looking bizarre but beautiful, wanting me to approve and compliment her.

She tapped on the door and then opened it straight away, and came in before I had time to hide the photograph.

I don't look at it so often now, partly because it has become too fragile from being carried around in my wallet for twenty-two years. When I do, I usually cry, so I suppose I was crying when Livvie came in.

I must have been, because her face changed from radiant excitement to concern and she dashed over to the bed in her high heels and crouched down next to me, her hand on my knee, saying, Are you okay, Orla? Of course I wasn't okay, but what else could she say?

And then she saw the photograph. It's only just recognisable now – the colours, never bright, are faded and the edges are tattered. The focus was never particularly sharp, and now it is even more blurred from all the times when I caressed it with my fingers, over and over, not realising that I was rubbing away the emulsion. I've stopped doing that now, and I keep it in a little acetate sleeve so that it won't be completely destroyed.

But it is still clearly a baby. A newborn in a pink romper suit, eyes scrunched shut beneath a pink bonnet, the marks of the forceps still visible on either side of her poor wee head. You can see the arm and hand of the sister who was holding her, but not her face. I don't know which of them it was who held her and which of them took the photograph. I only found it when I left the clinic, tucked in my bag in an envelope with my name on it.

Livvie said, Is that your baby, Orla? like it was no surprise to her.

I said, Yes. They took her away before I came round from the anaesthetic, and so I never saw her. I never held her.

She said, I'm so sorry, Orla. What a terrible loss. She is beautiful.

That was kind, because in the photograph she looks like any other newborn baby.

I did not want Livvie to think that the baby had died, so I said, It was for the best. She got to live her life and I got to live mine.

Livvie said, She was adopted.

I simply said, Yes.

Livvie said, Do you want to talk about it?

I must have known by then I'd already said too much, because I said, No, thank you. I'll be all right.

She sat with me for a few minutes, brought me a cup of tea – after offering me whiskey, good girl that she is – and then she went off to her party. She would have stayed with me if I'd asked, but I wanted her to go. Most of all, I didn't want her to know that she is the first person I have ever told.

FORTY

I almost didn't go to the Halloween party with Luke. I stood on the landing outside Orla's bedroom, dithering, the black dress hanging heavily from my shoulders.

Mostly, I was longing to go: to be shown off by Luke in my glamorous dress and carefully done – spooky, but not ugly – make-up, to meet his friends, to party and sparkle. But I was filled with sadness and worry about Orla and what she had just revealed to me. After what she'd told me about her grandmother, I'd had an inkling about what had happened – that she'd done something an older, conservative woman would have found it impossible to forgive. But the reality of it – to have had a baby and be forced to give her up, to have lived for over two decades with that sacrifice and only a worn photograph to show for it – broke my heart.

But Orla had told me to go. She'd lived with her loss long before I'd known about it; tonight was just one more night to add to the thousands she had spent without her daughter, not knowing where she was, whether she was safe and happy, whether she longed for Orla the way Orla longed for her.

There was also a small, selfish, craven part of me that didn't want Luke to be alone the first time he saw his ex-girlfriend since their break-up.

His emergence from his room made up my mind for me. He was dressed as a vampire, a flowing cloak over his black jeans and jumper, a set of plastic fangs from a joke shop protruding over his lower lip. He looked utterly absurd and utterly gorgeous, and in that moment I realised I wanted to be with him more than I wanted anything else in the world.

'Raaaar,' he growled, embracing me, adding indistinctly, 'time to deflower some virgins. Oh, too late.'

I burst out laughing. 'Are you going to wear those teeth on the Tube?'

'No.' He spat the teeth out into his palm, wrapping them in a square of kitchen roll and putting them in his pocket. 'Sorry. That was kind of gross. But I can't keep them in after the big reveal – they make me lisp and drool. You'd make me drool, anyway, in that dress – you look beautiful.'

'Thank you.' I smiled up at him, for once secure in the knowledge that that was true. 'Let me get my coat, and I'll see you downstairs.'

But as soon as I was away from him, even just stepping through the door into my bedroom, my thoughts veered back to Orla. Had she known the baby would be taken away? Had she wanted that to happen? Could she have kept her? Why hadn't she married the father? Who even was the father? If she'd known she couldn't keep the baby, had she thought about terminating the pregnancy?

There were so many questions I couldn't imagine the answers to, and certainly couldn't imagine ever asking Orla, who'd always seemed so self-contained, so private in spite of her warmth and kindness to me.

Luke and I left the house and then got the Tube to a part of North London I didn't know. On the way, to distract myself from thoughts of Orla and prepare myself for my public debut as Luke's girlfriend, I asked him questions.

'So who's going to be there tonight?'

'Rachel, obviously. Her sister Becky, most likely, and Becky's fiancé, Rob, although they might have got married by now. Her best mate, Belinda, whose flat we're going to. Other friends of theirs – Anna, Lauren, Helen, Gemma, their boyfriends. I dunno, maybe twenty people?'

Thinking of this room full of strangers, I felt a stab of nerves. *Please don't let them hate me. Please don't let Luke look at Rachel and realise he still fancies her.*

As we approached our destination, I felt my spirits lift. From the street, I could see the balcony of the flat that must be Belinda's decked out in full Halloween regalia. Fake cobwebs were strung across the balustrade. Purple and orange lights framed the window, which bore cut-out silhouettes of witches on broomsticks, bats and black cats. An army of carved pumpkins peered down at us, their eyes gleaming from the candles within.

She's obsessed with Halloween, I remembered Luke saying, and I felt a spark of fondness for her – this was the kind of girl I could be friends with, and by extension perhaps that meant I could become friends with Rachel. I imagined us going for coffee together, Luke's ex-girlfriend and his current one – no acrimony between us, only shared affection for the same person.

Luke pressed the buzzer and, over the music that flooded down from the first floor, I heard a crackly voice answer. I followed him up the stairs and into the flat, which was noisy, hot and full of people.

A girl in a witch's outfit, green make-up caking her face, approached us and regarded us curiously.

'So you came,' she said.

'Hi, Anna,' Luke replied. 'This is Livvie. Belinda invited us.'

'Hi,' I muttered, all my misgivings returning.

'Well, you should get a drink. There's wine, beer, rum punch and soft stuff.' She hesitated, her eyes narrowing under their heavy make-up. 'Rachel is in here somewhere. She isn't drinking.'

I was briefly puzzled by this seemingly irrelevant detail, but then Luke took my hand and led me inside. I felt grateful for his presence – plenty of guys would have abandoned me and gone off to talk to other people, but not him.

'Wine, Liv?' he asked. 'Belinda's rum punch is notorious. She makes it every year and someone always ends up spewing in the bushes.'

'I'll play it safe, then,' I said.

I followed as he made his way with relaxed familiarity to the kitchen, where he poured me a paper cup of warm white wine and took a beer for himself from a washing-up bowl filled with melting ice.

'Want to mingle a bit?' he asked. 'I'm sure we'll find Rachel soon, and I'll introduce you. Don't worry – it's going to be fine.'

'I'm not worried,' I lied, smiling.

Then I saw her, and I realised just how worried I needed to be.

She was in the living room, standing by the open balcony door. As I had expected any girlfriend of Luke's to be, she was pretty. More than pretty – beautiful, even. Her hair was long, down to her bra strap, dark and shiny. She was petite, with the pert, clean-cut features of a china doll. She was wearing a costume that I supposed was meant to be a bride of Dracula – long, white and flowing, with dribbles of lipstick blood trickling down the smooth skin of her neck.

With a brief lurch of dread, I wondered whether Luke had planned this – him the vampire, her the former virgin. But it was impossible – Luke had told me just that morning that he had no clue what he was going to wear, and only after lunch dashed out to the market where he'd bought the plastic fangs.

Then I wondered if it was part of her costume – but the look on Luke's face told me that wasn't the case, either. It all made sense – why she'd been okay with him coming. She wanted this to be public, to have the support of her friends around her when Luke found out. To front it out, because she didn't know how he would react, so that if he was angry with her, there'd be waiting arms to comfort her, and if he wasn't, there'd be witnesses.

As for me – well, it turned out she *wasn't* delighted I was there and I couldn't blame her. But I was just collateral damage in the big reveal she'd planned.

Beneath the white dress, Rachel was clearly heavily pregnant.

FORTY-ONE

'This can't be it.' Beatrice stopped, looking at the roughly drawn map in her hand. 'It says number eight Lombard Street, but this looks all wrong.'

She gripped her umbrella, keeping the scrap of paper safely out of the rain. The owner of the pub with rooms where they were staying had seemed quite certain he was directing them to the right place, confidently sketching the streets on a piece of paper with the logo of a whiskey distillery at its top and including helpful arrows showing them which way to walk.

Clearly, he hadn't actually had a clue. That or he'd been playing some kind of elaborate joke on them.

'Let me see.' Neil held out his hand, but Beatrice's own was shaking so badly she almost dropped the paper on the wet cobblestone street.

Since their arrival the previous evening – even before that, since before they'd boarded their flight – she'd been wracked with nerves. She'd felt none of her usual excitement when the plane accelerated down the runway, its speed forcing Beatrice's back against her seat before the jolting of the wheels stopped and soaring weightlessness began. Her anxiety had lifted only briefly after the bus journey from the airport – the same as any bus journey from any airport to any city, she'd thought, watching the stretches of anonymous motorway and grey industrial buildings flashing past the windows – when she'd been able to show Neil some of the sights she remembered from her first visit.

'This is Trinity College, where Oscar Wilde studied.'

'This is Ha'penny Bridge – I'll show you the sketch I did of it sometime.'

'This is where I went for dinner – the beef and Guinness pie was insane.'

So they'd gone there for dinner, but when a plate of the identical beef and Guinness pie was placed in front of Beatrice, she'd suddenly felt as if her mouth had been filled with sawdust and was unable to eat a thing.

'Nervous?' Neil had asked gently.

She'd nodded. 'I feel like I'm going to spew.'

'Come on then.' Neil had pushed aside his own half-finished plate and gestured for the bill. 'The sooner we go to bed, the sooner it'll be tomorrow and you'll be able to stop worrying.'

They'd walked back to their lodgings and said goodnight outside their separate bedrooms. Beatrice had thought for a moment about pulling Neil into a hug or inviting him in, just to see where it would lead. But it wasn't right – she couldn't use him like that, for validation or to pass the time or as some kind of human Zopiclone.

It wouldn't be fair. He deserved better.

So she had slept alone – or rather, not slept, twisting in her bed in between being tormented by dreams in which the house on Damask Square burned to the ground, her father arrived in Dublin and bundled her off to the airport before she could fulfil the purpose of her visit, and she found a piece of paper with a name on it that should have been her birth mother's but was Livvie's.

Now, here they were, outside the General Register Office – or where the General Register Office should have been but wasn't. Beatrice had thought she'd known what to expect: a grand, official building with pillars at its front and a flight of stone steps leading up to an imposing wooden door, like something out of Harry Potter.

This wasn't that. It was a modern, double-storey building that looked more like a block of council housing or a government office than a wizard's bank or a storage vault for secrets.

'Look.' Neil gripped her wrist, steadying her hand so the paper didn't fall. 'It says over there, Research Room. This is the place.'

'Yes,' Beatrice said. 'I suppose it must be.'

She tucked the scrap of paper into the pocket of her jeans and stepped on to the cracked concrete path leading up to the unassuming door. She could feel her heart pounding; her head felt as if it was floating high above her shoulders – like she was watching herself from above. She was barely conscious that Neil had taken her hand in his.

He pushed the door open and they stepped inside. The room was warm, carpeted in hard-wearing grey tiles. At intervals around it were pods and banks of desks, padded chairs set in front of them and privacy screens dividing them.

It reminded Beatrice of nothing so much as the library where Neil worked, except instead of the rainbow profusion of books that filled the shelves there, here the books were in only three colours: red, green and black. They were stacked neatly, each colour together.

'I guess we go over there,' Neil whispered, pointing towards a window on the far wall marked 'Reception'.

Behind it stood a middle-aged woman in an olive-green cardigan that looked hand-knitted. Her greying hair was held back from her face by a tortoiseshell Alice band and she wore steel-framed glasses. She looked like a picture of a librarian in a children's book.

'May I help you?' she asked.

Beatrice felt suddenly furtive and ashamed, as if she was doing something that wasn't allowed.

'I'm adopted,' she began. 'I was hoping to—'

'Speak up, please,' the woman said, but her smile was friendly.

'Sorry.' Beatrice felt herself blushing. 'I wanted – I'm trying to find my birth records. I was adopted, and I—'

'Right.' The woman moved away from the window, pushed open a door next to it and stepped out. 'Come on, let me show you.'

She led them over to the shelves of books. Now, Beatrice could see that the red ones were marked 'Births', the green 'Marriages' and the black 'Deaths'.

'Do you know the year when you were born?' the woman asked.

Beatrice nodded. '1983.'

'And the date?'

'February the twenty-seventh.'

'That's a good start,' the woman said. 'Entries are categorised by when they're registered, you see. December birthdays are tricky, because they're often entered in the following year's volume. And do you know the name you were given at birth?'

'Aisling.'

'All right, so...' The woman reached out to a shelf of volumes, running a finger over their spines. 'Here we are. 1983.'

Beatrice looked at the volumes. There were four of them,

each about the thickness of a telephone directory. In gold lettering on their spines were printed *A–DOOL, DOON– KENT, KENZ–ODEA, ODEI–Z*.

The woman took down the first volume and placed it on a table, opening it at random. Beatrice could see columns of clear upper-case printing, not quite black against the not-quite-white paper. Centred at the top of the page, Beatrice read 'Index to Births'.

'Now, here's where you begin.' The woman pointed towards the fifth column, marked 'Date of Birth'. 'The index is alphabetical, so you'll need to go through each page until you find a date of birth that matches yours. There were about two hundred babies born each day in Ireland, so across these four volumes, that's roughly how many matches you'll find.'

'Gotcha,' Neil said.

The woman glanced at him, smiling, as if she was noticing him for the first time.

'It's good you're here to help,' she said. 'It can take a day or more to go through it all, especially if you're unlucky enough to have a mother whose name was Murphy, say. Or of course if...'

'If what?' Beatrice asked.

'Sometimes, the records aren't accurate. Sometimes it's just clerical error, but occasionally... well, they were difficult times. But we'll not worry about that just yet, will we?'

Mutely, Beatrice shook her head. The record of her birth would be there. It would be accurate. It had to be. She couldn't have come all this way to leave disappointed.

'Now, the next thing you'll do is you'll look in the third column.' Her accent made it sound like 'tird'. 'There it says M or F, see? So you get to eliminate about half the results right away, because you're not looking for a boy.'

'I see,' Beatrice said.

'Then,' the woman continued, with the patience of a teacher explaining fractions for the thousandth time, 'you look at the first column – "Surname" – and the fourth – "Mother's Maiden Name". If those two are the same, that means the baby wasn't registered with the father's surname, which means the parents weren't married, which almost certainly means an adoption.'

'Okay.' Beatrice managed to speak. Now that the scale of the task ahead was clear, her nerves had dissipated and she felt only a steely determination. 'So when we find a record that looks like an adoption, then we check the name.'

'Correct.' The woman smiled. 'And hopefully you'll find an Aisling with your birthday and unmarried parents.'

'It'll be like looking for a needle in a haystack,' Neil said. 'But we'll get there.'

'The pages are only printed on one side,' the woman pointed out encouragingly, 'so there's only half as much to go through as it looks like. You'll be grand. Call me if I can be of any more help.'

She bustled away and Beatrice watched as she pushed the door open and resumed her wait behind the reception window.

Neil picked up the first of the 1983 volumes. 'Right. Let's do this thing.'

He carried the book over to a table and set it down, pulling over a chair for Beatrice. They sat and Beatrice laid her hand on the red cover, feeling the slight roughness of the cloth beneath her fingers.

'Shall we skip straight to C and look for Clifford?' she found herself whispering even more quietly than she normally would in a library – almost as if she was suggesting cheating on an exam.

'Your landlady's last name?' Luke asked.

Beatrice nodded.

'But if we didn't find anything there, we'd only have to go back to the beginning,' Neil pointed out.

'Okay,' she agreed. 'Let's start together on this volume, then we won't miss anything. Once we've got the hang of it we can divide them up.'

'Deal,' he said. 'Ready when you are.'

Beatrice opened the book to the first page of names and dates.

Aadair, Mary P. 1983. 24/07/1983. F. Ryan. Dublin North. 1983/Q3, she read.

'What's the last column?' she asked Neil, terrified that they'd missed something vital.

'I guess it's the year and quarter when the birth was registered.' Neil touched the column header with his forefinger. 'It mustn't matter. She'd have told us if it did.'

'I guess so.'

Beatrice forced herself to keep her eyes on the third column, scanning it rapidly but – she hoped – thoroughly. None of the birth dates matched her own.

'Done?' Neil asked.

Beatrice nodded reluctantly, and he turned the page. Again, there were no babies born on 27 February – nor on the next page, nor the one after that.

It was about ten pages in when Beatrice heard Neil's voice say, 'Got one!'

Beatrice's heart leapt and her eyes jumped automatically to the right. But the letter in the 'Sex' column was 'M'.

'Sorry, Abberneaty, Padraig R,' Neil said, 'you're no good.'

'Poor Padraig.' Beatrice couldn't help giggling. 'Hope you have nice birthdays, anyway.'

They carried on. Beatrice tried to stop her attention wandering, but she couldn't help it. Occasionally an unusual name would catch her eye – a Zeta amid all the Christines and Pamelas, or two babies with the same date of birth, surname and mother's maiden name.

'Look.' She pointed to the entry. 'Twins.'

Neil nodded. 'Concentrate.'

It was twenty pages more before Beatrice spotted an entry that made her heart jump in her chest. When she looked at it again, she realised that the date was July, not February – the 7 and the 2 similar enough to confuse her already tiring eyes. But Neil's finger was pointing at the same name.

'Full name, Ackroyd, Elaine M. Mother's maiden name, Ackroyd,' he murmured. 'Elaine's mother wasn't married. She must have been adopted.'

Beatrice stared at the page. She wondered where Elaine was now; whether her adoptive parents loved her as much as Beatrice's own; whether she'd ever sat in this room, searching this book for her truth.

Neil turned the page and they continued to scan the columns rapidly in unison before turning the page and beginning again – but Beatrice found herself wanting to be quicker still.

'Steady on,' he cautioned. 'We don't want to miss anything.'
'Yes, but... Okay, you're right.'

Finally, Neil turned a page and the name at its top was Clide. Beatrice felt perspiration spring out on the palms of her hands and abandoned the 'Date of Birth' column altogether, scanning only down the list of names.

But they went straight from Clifferly to Cliggett. There hadn't been a single baby born in 1983 with the surname Clifford. Not on 27 February or any other day. Not adopted or born to married parents. None at all.

Beatrice looked up from the page, her eyes stinging from strain and the threat of tears. She felt as if all their patience had been rewarded only with failure. She looked back at the shelves of remaining books – the three volumes still to go through, along with the remaining quarter of this one, and she was overcome with despair.

'Come on,' Neil said. 'Chin up. You could still be in here somewhere.'

But Beatrice was already on her feet. 'I'm done with this. I'm going straight to look under Doyle.'

Leaving the *A–DOOL* volume open in front of Neil, she hurried to the shelves and pulled out the next red book, carrying it back with her arms outstretched like a waitress bearing a tray.

'Scoot over,' she said.

Neil closed the book and slid it to one side. Beatrice laid the other in its place and opened it at random near the beginning.

'Dracott,' Neil read. 'You're too far in.'

'I know.'

Not wanting to damage the pages, the impatience almost killing her, Beatrice leafed backwards.

'Doze,' Neil read, his finger on the bottom of the page. 'What a name.'

But Beatrice barely heard him. The name sprang out of the page as if it was printed in bright red instead of muted black.

Doyle.

There were three of them. Sebastian R, born in October to a woman whose name had formerly been Kelly. Roisin T, whose mother had been born an Irwin.

And *Doyle, Aisling. Date of birth: 27/02/1983. Sex: F. Mother's maiden name: Doyle.*

'There it is,' she said. 'That's me.'

'Does that mean your landlady...?'

'I don't know. She must've got married. Clifford must be her married name. The house never changed hands from when the Doyles bought it until she inherited it. It's got to be her.' Her voice sounded loud in the silent room. 'She must be. It's here, in the official record.'

'Hold on,' Neil said. 'What if she had a sister?'

The thought had crossed Beatrice's mind before, but now it made even more sense. 'You mean if there were two grand-daughters, but only one of them got the house, because...'

Her throat closed, imagining it. One daughter who'd done

everything right, inherited everything. The other cast out, stripped of her child, her home, her place in the family.

She stood abruptly, the chair scraping against the floor. 'I'm done searching through records. When we get back to London, I'm confronting Orla. I'm going to make her tell me the truth.'

FORTY-TWO

When I saw Luke's reaction to seeing Rachel, my first instinct was to comfort him. But I didn't get the chance: the two of us stood there, frozen, for just a few seconds, our drinks forgotten in our hands, before Luke moved away from me. Hesitantly at first and then more purposefully, he edged his way through the crowd towards the window where she was standing.

I could see Rachel's friends nudging one another, their whispers inaudible to me over the music. I knew what they were saying, though – *He's here. He's seen her. Shit, he's only turned up with his new girlfriend.*

As I watched, Luke put his hand on Rachel's shoulder. She turned to look at him, the purple and orange lights from the balcony illuminating her face. Whatever had been there before – the smile, the bravado – had vanished and she looked small and vulnerable, the swell of her belly beneath her white dress seeming almost too heavy for her slight frame to support.

She sketched a gesture with her hand – *Shall we go outside?* – and Luke nodded – *Sure.* Even from the back of the room, I could feel the blast of cold air as she opened the door and the two of them stepped out.

Then the wave of self-doubt that had been held back by shock overwhelmed me. Had he known all along – lied to me by omission to lure me into a relationship in spite of still having one with his pregnant ex-girlfriend?

But that didn't make sense. Luke wasn't like that – I didn't want to believe he could be like that. Nothing about the way he'd treated me or his reaction to seeing Rachel suggested anything other than total shock and disbelief. For those few long moments, I'd almost forgotten that I existed, but now I became conscious again of my own presence in the room, alone and superfluous, the eyes that weren't fixed on Luke and Rachel watching me curiously.

What's she going to do? Is she going to dump him?

I wasn't. But, pathetically, I felt as if I'd already been dumped: as if all the months of closeness and laughter and sex between Luke and me might as well never have happened.

There was no one there I could talk to. No way of fronting it out, having another drink, shrugging and saying they'd find a way to figure it out.

Luke and Rachel were still out on the balcony, still talking intently. His back was to me, so I couldn't see his face, read his reaction. Abruptly, my mind turned to self-preservation. There was no place for me here in this room full of strangers. Any moment, someone might come over to me and ask me if I'd known, how I felt, whether I was okay.

I wasn't able to deal with any of those questions – I didn't know the answers.

I turned, feeling as if I was in one of those dreams where however much you try to hurry, you're moving in slow motion, as if through water or syrup. I went into the kitchen and put my cup down among the litter of bottles and crisp packets. Then I let myself out of the flat and, as if released from the dream by the cold night air on my face, I almost ran down the stairs, out of the front door and into the street.

Clumsy in my high heels, which had felt perfectly comfortable when I'd left the house on Damask Square, I hurried back towards the Tube station, my feet skidding on the fallen leaves that blanketed the pavement, taking a wrong turn down an unfamiliar street before getting my bearings again.

Like an animal fleeing to its burrow, all I wanted was the safety of the house, the calm reassurance of Orla's presence, the hum of the kettle and the purring of the cat.

It was almost eleven when I reached Damask Square, but the light in the kitchen was still on. I could hear the clink of Orla's teaspoon in her saucer and her voice as she chatted nonsense to Maud.

Relieved, I stepped through the hallway, ready to make myself comfortable and unburden my worries to Orla. But then I stopped, paused in my tracks by a wave of horrified guilt.

Orla herself had had an unplanned pregnancy. She hadn't mentioned the child's father, but of course there had been one – perhaps a man who'd abandoned her, making it impossible for her to keep her baby. All these years later, she was still living with the trauma of that decision.

There was no way I could confide in her about what I'd learned tonight, or ask for her advice on what to do about it.

Praying that she hadn't heard me, I turned and crept up the stairs to my room. I took off Orla's grandmother's dress and placed it carefully on a hanger, feeling a pang of sadness as I remembered the giddy excitement with which I'd put it on earlier in the evening. I couldn't wash off my make-up without Orla hearing me in the bathroom and realising I was home, so I did my best with a handful of wet wipes, put on my pyjamas and got into bed.

Then I waited. I heard Orla coming up, the usual near-silent pad of her footsteps as she got ready for bed, the click of her light switch, and then the lighter, quicker tap of Maud's paws as she joined Orla on her bed.

It was another hour before Luke got back and I had almost given up hope, convincing myself that he was going to stay with Rachel in her North London flat. Relief washed over me when I heard his key in the lock, immediately replaced by a churning lurch of apprehension when he tapped softly on my bedroom door.

I got out of bed and opened it. 'Hi. Thank God you're back. Are you okay?'

'Hi.' He pulled off his absurd vampire cloak and sat down, reaching for my hands but not meeting my eyes. His shoulders were slumped beneath his black jumper. 'I'm fine. But... Liv, I'm sorry.'

'Sorry for what?' My mouth was dry.

'Sorry that happened to you. Sorry I didn't notice you leaving and come after you. Sorry I didn't text you.'

Not, *Sorry I'm going back to Rachel*. That was something. But the weary set of his shoulders and the look in his eyes – resignation or perhaps even defeat – told me he was anything but fine.

I said, 'Do you want to tell me about it?'

He half-shook his head, but it turned into a nod. 'First of all, I had no idea. Genuinely. Do you believe that?'

I had no reason to doubt him. 'Yeah, I guess so.'

'Rachel said – she told me that when she found out, she couldn't make up her mind what to do. She thought about – you know. Terminating the pregnancy. She had an appointment booked and everything. But she couldn't go through with it. And then she thought she'd just go ahead with having the baby on her own.'

If only she'd stuck to that, I thought. Then I realised how deeply selfish that wish was.

'So she waited until tonight for you to find out,' I said.

'I don't really get why.' Luke shrugged. 'But she was

nervous, I suppose. She's always had a bit of a sense of drama. And she wanted her mates there, in case I went off on one.'

Which was basically what I'd guessed, in those few moments before Luke had left my side and gone to her. 'But you didn't.'

'What would be the point? It's done now. There's no going back. She's having the baby. And I...'

'You what?'

'You know, Liv. It takes two to tango. It's not like she made this happen on her own. I've got to take some responsibility.'

I felt tears begin to spring up in my eyes and grabbed the handful of grubby make-up wipes, pretending I was dealing with a stray mascara smudge as I dabbed my lower lids.

'What are you going to do?' I asked.

'Rachel said it's up to me. She's going to want money – at least, the child's going to need it. This isn't his fault.'

'It's a boy?'

He nodded. 'She found out a while ago. Anyway – she says I can be involved or not.'

'And do you want to be?' My voice was calm, but the sick churning was back in my stomach. I didn't know what Luke's answer would be, but I knew that tonight had changed everything.

Or rather, not tonight. A night months ago, before I'd even met Luke, when he and Rachel had lain together in bed in the flat they'd shared, and an accident of biology or a moment of carelessness or a deliberate decision on her part had decreed that what was happening tonight would happen.

Inexorably, between then and now, time had been moving towards this moment, and I'd had no idea.

It's so unfair! my mind screamed. But there was no point in thinking that way.

'Liv, I... I'm going to be a father, one way or another.' He lifted his shoulders then let them drop back down, squaring them as if he was bracing himself for something. 'I can be a shit, deadbeat one who sends money here and there, or I can do my best to be a good one. There's nothing between me and Rachel any more, but I want to be part of my son's life.'

'I understand.' I felt a rush of admiration for him – already, he'd made the decision. He'd chosen to do the right thing and not the easy one. He knew what it was like to grow up without a father and he didn't want that for his own child.

'Liv, I don't want this to change anything between you and me.' He was speaking in a rush now, as if he was desperate to convince not only me, but himself. 'I'll have to get a job. A proper one – either for a construction company or... something else. I can't make art pay, anyway. I might have to find somewhere else to live – somewhere closer to Rachel and the baby. But I still want to be with you.'

But it won't be the same. The knowledge lay heavily on my heart.

I heard Luke take a breath, and as he released it, he said, 'I love you.'

I reached for him and held him close, able at last to offer the comfort I'd wanted to give him back at the party.

My voice muffled by his shoulder, I said, 'I love you too.'

But already I was wondering how many more times I would get to say it before we weren't able to love each other any more.

FORTY-THREE

30 OCTOBER 2005

Since I told Livvie, I've been thinking about my daughter – about Aisling – all the time. If Livvie knew this, I expect she would think it peculiar that I didn't think about Aisling all the time anyway, but the truth is I didn't – not any more than I think about my arms or my toes or my spleen.

They are all just part of me; I take them for granted. And I've come to take her absence – the absence of that being that grew inside me and was part of me for nine long months – for granted too.

I've been remembering those months, too, which I've never properly done before. All those conversations with my grandmother, going round and round in circles.

Can I not keep the baby?

That would be impossible, Orla.

Can I not go to England and... you know?

That would be illegal, Orla.

Isn't there someone – a midwife or someone – who could help me here?

That would be wicked, Orla.

So she took over and arranged everything.

It will be for the best, Orla.

I believed her; I trusted her. There was no one else I had to trust. And it did seem like it was for the best, right up until that moment when I lay alone in my bed in the maternity hospital, my body opened and stitched together again, my breasts swollen, surrounded by women nursing their babies, their proud husbands visiting them, their relatives bringing flowers and teddies.

In the weeks that followed, I thought something would happen, somehow, to change it. Declan would come and find me and say he knew why I had dropped out of college. He'd say he had never loved his wife but did love me, and wanted to be with me and our baby. The nuns would say that the couple who wanted her had changed their minds and were giving her back to me. My grandmother would say she'd had a change of heart and realised that she wanted to raise her great-granddaughter as her own, and we could all be a family together.

But none of those things happened, and I did nothing to make them happen. I stayed at my grandmother's house in Clonmara for six weeks, until I knew that the adoption was final, until my body had healed. Then I left for England and I never went back. I ran away.

Now, I have the chance to run away again. It happened yesterday, when I was returning from the supermarket laden with vegetables, tins of food for Maud and a pack of chicken breasts for Beatrice.

Approaching the house, I saw a young man putting a leaflet through the letterbox, and I knew straight away who he was and what he was doing there. All the places I've lived in the world, I've noticed that estate agents all look the same, with their cheap suits and their sharp haircuts, and I recognised him as one of that tribe.

When he saw me climb the stairs, he launched without hesitation into his sales pitch. This was a fine home. He could see that I was renovating it – had I considered having it valued? The area was becoming highly desirable and original Georgian properties were like unicorns. With skilful marketing, the house could be worth a great deal of money. If I were ever to consider... etc.

And I am considering. The temptation is so great – I can sell this house, move away and stay away. I've done it before. If I do it again, she will never find me.

But there is another option. I could, finally, apply to have my name on the Adoption Contact Register.

I can face my past, or I can leave it behind forever.

FORTY-FOUR

It was late on Saturday night when Beatrice and Neil arrived back in London. They'd spent Friday afternoon sightseeing, but Beatrice hadn't been able to focus on the statue of Oscar Wilde, St Patrick's Cathedral or the Guinness Storehouse. She'd tried to be enthusiastic because Neil was – she sensed because he was trying to take her mind off what they had discovered – but in her mind all she could see was those lines of bland, official typescript laying out her history.

All she could think was, *Is she my mother? How will I feel if she is?*

Ever since the idea of tracing her birth mother had occurred to her, she'd imagined what their reunion would be like. She'd dreamed of her pulling her into her arms, embracing her with tears of joy, saying that this was the happiest moment of her life. Or, at other times, she'd imagined her coldly rejecting Beatrice, saying that she'd never wanted a child and that hadn't changed.

Now, she tried to picture Orla in those scenarios. But she couldn't do it. Partly, she told herself, it was because of the shadowy presence of that possible sister – the out-of-favour one, the disgraced one. That prospect gave rise to other imaginings –

which one would she want as a mother: cool, rational Orla or the hot-headed, rebellious other one?

She didn't know. She couldn't decide and it was all fantasy, anyway, until she did what she probably should have done months ago, back when Neil's grandfather had confirmed that number five Damask Square had been the Doyles' property, and simply come out and asked Orla.

Back then, she had been stopped by the fear that if Orla simply denied all knowledge of Beatrice, there would have been nothing she could do about it. Now, there was still that uncertainty but she had more information, more ammunition. She knew that the Doyle family had owned the house on Damask Square. She knew it had never changed hands until it passed from Orla's grandmother to Orla. She knew that an unmarried woman named Doyle had given birth to a baby with Beatrice's birth name on her birthday.

It was enough. It had to be enough.

So she had explored Dublin with Neil, eaten dinner and drunk a couple of pints with him, and gone to bed in her single room with only one thought on her mind: *Tomorrow. Tomorrow I'll talk to her.*

But their flight home had been delayed by bad weather so by the time Beatrice reached the house it was after midnight and the place was in darkness. Despite her impatience, she knew that bursting into Orla's bedroom and demanding answers while her landlady lay in bed would not lead to any desirable outcome, and besides, she was exhausted.

Not bothering to unpack her bag, she fell into bed and slept for twelve hours.

When she woke up, she had a text message from Neil.

Everything ok? Call me if you need me. x

He'd added a kiss, which made Beatrice smile.

She got up, showered and sorted out her things. She put her dirty clothes in a bag to take to the launderette and made toast. She monosyllabically answered Livvie's questions about how her trip had been, noticing with only mild interest that Livvie seemed somewhat monosyllabic herself.

Orla was out somewhere and so was Luke. Beatrice waited in an agony of impatience for the opportunity to catch her alone, but it was mid-afternoon before it came. From her bedroom window, she saw Orla in the garden below, alone. Luke and Livvie were nowhere to be seen and even the cat would be unlikely to brave the outdoors on this raw, overcast day with the promise of rain in the lowering clouds.

Orla was kneeling on what looked like a folded newspaper, digging in the earth with a trowel. From her high vantage point, Beatrice could see the thin curve of her spine under her waxed jacket, the strands of grey in her short hair catching the dying afternoon light.

Abruptly, she pushed herself away from the windowsill she'd been leaning on and hurried downstairs, bursting out through the kitchen and into the garden.

'Beatrice.' Orla greeted her with her usual friendly but guarded smile.

'Hi. You look busy.'

'I'm planting tulip bulbs. This looks like it's the last chance before it gets too frosty.'

'May I speak with you?'

Orla smiled again, but there was a flash of something like alarm in her eyes.

'Of course.' She gestured with her trowel, but there was nowhere for Beatrice to sit and she didn't fancy joining Orla on her knees on the newspaper, so she remained standing.

'There's something I wanted to ask you.' Now that the moment was upon her, all the opening lines Beatrice had researched seemed to have deserted her. 'Are you – have you ever been married?'

Orla looked surprised. 'Yes. A long time ago, when I was living in South Africa. His name was Adrian. It didn't last very long but I kept his surname. I don't really know why.'

Beatrice nodded. 'And, Orla – do you have a sister?'

Orla's look of surprise turned to one of suspicion. 'No. I'm an only child. My parents' marriage didn't last long either; I suppose it must run in the family. Why do you ask, Beatrice?'

Beatrice didn't answer her question. Instead she asked another of her own.

'You had a baby, didn't you? At St Gerard Majella hospital in Dublin in February 1983.'

Orla turned her whole body towards her now, swivelling her knees around on the newspaper. Her face was as bleak as the bare branches of the chestnut tree, disappearing now against the clouds in the dying daylight.

'That's right,' she said weakly. 'A daughter.'

'And you gave her up for adoption, didn't you?'

'Yes, I did.'

Orla's face was still; Beatrice had no way of reading her thoughts. Her own were in turmoil: torn between fevered anticipation of a conclusion she'd longed to reach, longing for recognition and – overwhelmingly – fear of the response she might be about to receive.

'And you never tried to make contact with her. Not even when the contact register thing opened this year.'

'Beatrice.' Orla extended a hand. There was earth on her fingers; beneath it, they were bone-white with cold. 'Are you telling me you are Aisling?'

Beatrice nodded. All the scenarios she'd imagined seemed to have vanished in the wind; there were only Orla's eyes, confused and impossibly sad. Beatrice shivered, wishing she hadn't done this – not now, not alone.

Orla stood up, slowly, as if her knees hurt from kneeling on the cold, hard ground for so long – but Beatrice couldn't bring herself to reach out her hand and assist her.

'After all these years,' she said slowly, 'I never imagined this would happen.'

'Because you never wanted it to happen?' Beatrice demanded.

'Because it was impossible. There was no question of me ever seeing my daughter – seeing you. That was how it was then. How it's been all along, until very recently. Everything was a secret, and you get used to keeping secrets if you do it for long enough. I'm sorry. Sorry you've waited so long. Sorry it happened in the first place. Sorry for it all.'

She took a step towards Beatrice, her arms lifting.

Now, Beatrice thought. *This is the moment – the embrace.*

But Orla didn't touch her. Helplessly, she spread her hands up to the sky.

'Sorry I was born?' Beatrice asked, her voice tight and angry.

Orla's hands dropped to her sides. 'Of course not.'

Beatrice didn't believe her. 'Why did you do it? Why did you give me away?'

'I had no choice. It's hard to understand now, I know. But for women who – women like me – there was so much disgrace, so much shame. All we were left with was the possibility of pretending it had never happened. And the only way to do that was to give the – to give my baby away.'

'But you wanted to. You must have wanted to.'

Orla tucked her hands under her arms, hunched against the cold. 'I wanted you to have a good life. Better than you could have had with me. That seemed like the only good choice there was – the best thing for my baby.'

'But I didn't get to decide what the best thing was for me!' Even as she said the words, Beatrice realised how irrational they were.

'Well, no. You didn't.'

'What about my father?' Beatrice demanded. 'Couldn't you have married him? Isn't that what people did then? Or didn't he want you, same as you didn't want me?'

'He never knew. But even if he had, he wouldn't have married me.'

'Why not?'

'Beatrice.' Orla sighed. 'It's cold. Why don't we go inside and have a cup of tea, and try to talk about this more calmly?'

Beatrice looked at her, blazing with hurt and anger. 'I don't want a cup of tea. I don't want to talk to you. I'm going out.'

She turned and ran into the house, through the kitchen and the hallway and out of the front door, slamming it behind her. She ran – but not fast enough to miss hearing the first sob break out of Orla's throat. With every step, she felt her anger abating, shame and regret replacing it.

So now she knows, she thought. *Now she knows what it's like to have me as a daughter.*

FORTY-FIVE
31 OCTOBER 2005

Beatrice. Aisling. Beatrice. Aisling.

The names have been spinning through my mind all night, robbing me of sleep, and so now, still awake, I find myself writing them down. But however often I do so, I can't reconcile myself to them being the same person. My fingers are so numb I can barely hold my pen, my mind so blasted by shock I can barely think coherently.

Beatrice. The girl who came into my house with an agenda – How? How did she even begin to find out, to guess? – violated my privacy, shut my cat in the cellar. The girl I tried to like but barely tolerated.

Beatrice. The vulnerable young woman I knew must be inside there somewhere – a woman only just finding her way in the world, deeply conflicted, uncertain of who she was and doing her best to find out.

Beatrice. My baby, who I have thought of all these years with pain and longing and worry, whose face I have tried to capture on paper year after year. Aisling – my child.

I tried so often to imagine how she would turn out – what kind of woman she would have become. But how could I? I never knew her. I never even saw her. And now I know. Now things make sense: Beatrice's prying through the house. Beatrice's antipathy towards me. Beatrice's paintings, so similar to my own work in so many ways.

How she must hate me. Down in the garden, yesterday afternoon, when she confronted me, when she confronted me, she was so filled with rage. I understand her anger. Ever since she found out she was an adopted child, however carefully those parents of hers couched it, she must have carried that with her.

But I am angry too and I have also been angry for a long time – furious at the injustice of a system that forced women like me to abandon babies in their thousands and put secrecy above all else. Anger at my grandmother for colluding with it, refusing to countenance any other possibility. Anger at Declan and all the other men who carried on with their lives untouched by the devastation they had caused.

Yes, anger at Aisling – at Beatrice – too. Indignation that she could be there in my body in the first place, unasked for and unwelcome, sharing my blood, making me sick, having to be cut out of me when she was good and ready.

We aren't supposed to feel anger towards our babies, we women. I wonder if I am the only one? I think I am not.

And what did Beatrice want, anyway, when she came to me in the garden? Some moving, emotional reunion – an instant recognition, an embrace, tears of joy? Oh, Beatrice. So did I. But life is not like that, not a fairy tale where we go off together into a happy-ever-after future.

I know that I am the adult in this situation – I am the mother. I am the one who is supposed to make it all okay, dry her tears and heal her wounds in the way I never could when she was a little girl. But what about my wounds?

And what will I do now?

I feel I must get rid of this house. Beatrice and I surely

cannot live under the same roof as things are now, and I cannot possibly ask her to leave. A second rejection would be too much, too cruel. I must tell her that finances dictate it will have to be sold. I must call the young estate agent in the cheap suit.

I must move out and move on.

Only then, perhaps, Beatrice and I will be able to heal, to have some sort of relationship.

I know I am not the mother she wanted to find. I am only her mother in the most basic, biological sense. But perhaps I can change that. Perhaps now that she has found me, I can find the part of myself that has been lost, but was always there. Perhaps I can learn, at last, how to be a mother.

FORTY-SIX

Beatrice might have burst out of the house on Damask Square, but she didn't go far. Her keys were in her pocket but she didn't have her phone, bag or a coat, so she let herself into the garden square, sat down on a bench and cried.

All this – all her work, her research, travelling halfway around the world – and it had come to this. Orla hated her. She didn't blame Orla for hating her. She'd behaved terribly, alienating the one person in the world she most wanted to have close to her.

But she hated Orla, too. She hated her for reacting the way she had – for trying to explain and justify what she had done. She hated her for all the months she had spent preferring Livvie to Beatrice. Most of all, of course, she hated her for that first, irrevocable abandonment twenty-two years ago.

It was over. She would have to leave Damask Square and move into the spare room in Frances and Peter's apartment, if they'd still have her there. She'd have to explain to her parents what had happened – or alternatively lie to them and say that she hadn't been able to trace her birth mother and had decided to give up trying.

There was nothing here for her any more. Nothing left.

Half an hour later, she was still sitting there. She'd stopped crying and was beginning to shiver with the cold, but she barely noticed that, like she barely noticed the fox that drifted past, its rough coat amber in the light that fell from the windows of the flats opposite. She didn't respond when a group of young men called out, 'All right, darling?' to her. A light came on in the upstairs room of one of the neighbouring houses but she didn't look up to see who was there. The sky lanterns hovering in the darkness from a Diwali display somewhere might as well not have been there.

It was only when a man sat down next to her that she jerked back to consciousness, the awareness of potential danger tensing every muscle in her body.

'Beatrice? I thought it was you. Are you okay?'

'Neil.' He was like an apparition from another world – a world before she had confronted Orla in the garden. A world where there had been hope instead of only despair. 'What are you doing here?'

'Been visiting Gramps. Mum made chicken soup and I took him a load for the freezer. I thought I'd come by and see if you were okay, because you didn't answer my text.'

His text – the one with the kiss at the end.

'My phone's indoors,' she said.

'You must be freezing.'

Beatrice realised she was shivering. 'I guess so.'

'You look like you could do with some chicken soup yourself. Has something happened? Did you speak to Orla?'

Beatrice nodded.

'Here. Take my gloves.' Neil slipped them off and handed them to her. The warmth from his hands enveloped hers as she fumbled her stiff fingers into the rough wool. 'Do you want to get a cup of tea somewhere? Or a drink?'

Beatrice shook her head. The thought of being somewhere with bright lights, other people, the world carrying on as if nothing had changed, was overwhelming.

'I told her. Well – I asked her, first, whether she'd been married and whether she had a sister. She never had a sister, and she married some guy called Clifford years ago and kept his last name when they split up.'

'And so is she...?'

'She gave birth to me.' Beatrice found she couldn't use the word 'mother'.

'How does that make you feel?' Neil asked gently.

Guess he's had some therapy in his time, Beatrice thought.

'Honestly? Messed up. Not anything like I thought I'd feel.'

'Go on.' His steady gaze remained on her face.

'I thought... All my life, when I imagined I might meet her one day, I thought there'd be this instant connection. You know, you read stories and it's all fairy tale and heartwarming. Like recognising yourself. But I've lived with her for months and there's been nothing.'

'You've lived a whole life apart from her,' Neil said. 'And fairy tales aren't real. Relationships take time.'

'That's with other people, though. People you date, friends, colleagues. Not your own fucking—'

She stopped, holding back the wave of rage that threatened to overwhelm her. She hadn't wanted it to be like this – she still didn't want it to be. She wanted the moment she'd imagined so many times, looking up into a pair of eyes as familiar as her own, saying the words she'd dreamed of saying, feeling warm arms enclose her as if they'd never, ever let her go.

She remembered the two women she'd seen in the Dublin hotel all those months ago – *Haven't I waited twenty years to buy my daughter tea and scones at Bewley's?* Orla had offered tea and she'd rejected her.

That was what she'd yearned for, that touching reunion, that promise of future closeness. But it was too late. Orla already knew her. She knew the sides of Beatrice that Beatrice hadn't wanted her to see – her anger, her insecurities, her deceptiveness. Orla hadn't recognised her when she'd met her, hadn't loved her at first sight – so how could Beatrice expect her to love her now?

'It's not the same, I know,' Neil said. 'But my sister's baby – Aaron, my nephew – he was the most wanted kid ever. Claudia and her other half tried to get pregnant for ages, but it didn't happen. They had IVF and all sorts. It took years. When Claudia finally got pregnant, she couldn't believe it. She was so happy, but super worried, too. She obsessed about eating all the right food, doing exercises, all that stuff, so that the baby would be okay. Jon basically wouldn't let her wash a plate the whole nine months.'

Beatrice listened impatiently. Neil must have been telling her the story for a reason, but she couldn't see what relevance it had to her. But listening was easier than talking.

'Aaron was born just over a year ago,' he went on. 'My first nephew. My mom and dad's first grandchild; Gramps's first great-grandchild. The whole family was doolally over him.'

'That's nice,' Beatrice said.

'I'm sorry.' In the half-light from the windows of the flats, Beatrice could see that Neil was blushing. 'You don't want to hear all about my family.'

'It's okay.' Beatrice felt a stab of guilt. She hadn't meant to sound contemptuous, but she had. Neil was being kind to her, trying to help, and she'd made him feel bad. Him, on top of everyone else.

That was the kind of person she was – someone who took

advantage of others' kindness, threw it back in their face. Her mother and father had loved her unconditionally for twenty-two years, but that hadn't been enough for her. Orla had treated her with nothing but generosity and respect, giving her a place to live, cooking meat for her in her vegetarian kitchen, and how had she thanked her?

But her guilt was short-lived. Nothing Orla had done for her over the past months could ever outweigh the first thing she had ever done to Beatrice: rejecting her, abandoning her.

Giving her up.

'I was just going to say,' Neil was ploughing on, knowing his story wasn't landing well but not knowing what else to do, 'Claudia told me, just a couple of months ago, how hard she found it with Aaron at first. She didn't bond with him right away. It took months and months. That was my point – you have to give it time.'

'I've waited twenty-two years,' Beatrice said furiously. 'How much time does she need? She could've tried to track me down, and she didn't. She could've applied to be on that register thing and she never did. I've been living in the same fucking house as her for months and she hasn't even recognised me.'

'I get it,' Neil said. 'I understand how much it must hurt. It's hard. But she didn't know who you were. How could she have known?'

Beatrice didn't want to hear that, even though she knew it was true.

'She should have known. She should have asked. She never asked me anything about myself. She was never interested in me.'

'Now that she knows, she'll be interested,' Neil said. 'Of course she will. She'll want to hear all about your life. I bet she's been wondering, all these years, what happened to you. Now she'll be able to find out. She'll be massively relieved. It must have been...'

'It must have been what?'

'It must have been hard for her, too,' Neil muttered.

Part of Beatrice – the rational part, the part who'd been through years of therapy – understood that. But there was no way she was ready to hear it, especially not from Neil.

'What do you mean, hard?' she demanded. 'Hard would have been keeping her baby, bringing me up like I was – you know – her literal daughter. Having the courage to do that. But she didn't. She was just like, "Take my baby away and I'll get on with my life." She's lived all over the world, for God's sake. She's had all these experiences she wouldn't have been able to have if she'd actually had the balls to stick around and be a mother.'

'I'm sure it wasn't as easy as that,' Neil said. 'If it had been, I'm sure she would've done it. I don't know what it was like, in Ireland back then, but it was very religious, very Catholic, wasn't it? I'm sure she never wanted to give up her baby. I'm sure if she could have, she would've—'

'Why are you defending her?' Beatrice exploded. 'Whose side are you on? You asked me if I was okay and I'm not. I'm telling you I'm not. I never asked you to come and sit here – you chose to. And now you're lecturing me about the Catholic church and telling me all about your sister's baby.'

He looked mortified. 'I didn't mean to—'

'I don't care what you meant.' Beatrice stood up. Her legs were so numb with cold that she almost fell over, but she regained her balance and turned away from him. 'I'm going home.'

Then she realised where home was. Home was the house on Damask Square – the house her great-grandparents had bought, the house that had led to the death of her great-grandfather. Home was where Orla was.

She couldn't face being under the same roof as Orla. Or worse, watching Livvie with her – seeing the easy affection between them, the natural understanding she'd never managed to achieve. The kind of relationship that should have been her birthright but somehow wasn't there at all. Every shared smile between them felt like another door closing in her face.

Orla loved Livvie. If she could have chosen, she would have wanted Livvie to be her daughter, not Beatrice.

FORTY-SEVEN

The flat in Shepherd's Bush where Emily lived was buzzing with the early stages of her birthday party. I'd been looking forward to this – in the two weeks since Halloween, I'd been greeting each day with trepidation, and trying to hide it from Luke. It would do me some good to spend this evening outside of the house, outside of my world at Damask Square. When one of Emily's housemates let me in, I added the gift I'd brought to a growing pile on the coffee table. 'I Bet You Look Good on the Dancefloor' was blaring from the stereo and a group of her friends were chattering over the music. In the kitchen, Emily was stirring a vat of mulled wine on the hob, wearing a sparkly top, skinny jeans and heels.

'You came!' She hugged me, smelling of red wine and cloves.

'As if I'd miss my best mate's party,' I joked, hugging her.

'There's some fizz open,' she said. 'This will be ready in a few minutes, but don't wait. I've been on the booze since four. Would you mind cooking those cocktail sausages? There's a pan in the drawer there.'

I found it, poured myself a drink and stationed myself at the cooker next to her. It felt blissfully normal to be here, surrounded by music and friends. I realised how quiet the house on Damask Square always was, how empty – even more so now that the first floor was finished and the ground floor almost done, too.

It felt almost as if I'd emerged from some kind of time warp where I'd spent months in the past, and now I was back, blinking and startled, in the twenty-first century.

'No Luke tonight?'

'No Luke.' I sighed. 'Rachel's due date is in a couple of weeks but he's convinced she could go into labour at any moment. He's been twitchy as hell – he doesn't want to miss it.'

'He's not going to be there when she gives birth, is he?' Emily grimaced.

'God, no. Her mother's going to be with her for that bit. But he wants to be there when the baby's born and see it – see him – as soon as he can. He wouldn't believe me or even Orla when we told him these things take ages and he could basically go to Scotland if he wanted to and still make it back in time.'

'He's taking it all very seriously, isn't he?' She stirred the mulled wine, tasted it and added more brandy.

'He even went to an antenatal class with Rachel. He said it was awkward as fuck explaining where he fitted in and why he hadn't been before, but how else was he going to learn to change a nappy?'

'Riiight,' Emily said slowly. 'But things with you are still all good?'

I added the sausages to the hot pan and let them sizzle for a minute before giving it a shake.

'Honest, Em? When it's just him and me, they're great. But it's not like before. There's always this – thing – hovering over us. I feel bad because I know he wants to do the right thing – he is doing the right thing. But still.'

'So what's actually the plan? Once the baby's here? He can't bring it to live in that house every other weekend, can he?'

I felt the beginnings of tears prickling my eyes and poked the sausages forcefully.

'He's not going to be living there any more,' I told her. 'Not all the time, anyway. He's got a job. He starts in January, as a junior graphic designer. He's been rushing like crazy to get the house finished because he feels bad about leaving Orla in the lurch.'

'So where is he going to live?'

'The plan is, he's going to rent a room from Rachel's mum. She lives really close to Rachel's flat, so he'll be able to see lots of the baby. And then when he's not seeing it – him – he'll come and spend nights with me at Damask Square.'

'Well, that all sounds like it's going to work out splendidly,' Emily said sarcastically.

'I know, right?'

'And what about you in all this? Here, have a taste of this.' She passed me a spoon and I dipped it into the mulled wine and slurped.

'I guess I'll just carry on as normal. Living with Orla, working, seeing Luke when he's free.'

Fitting in around Luke and Rachel's plans. I didn't say this to Emily – I could barely say it to myself, and I hadn't to Luke, either – but that was how it felt. Like I'd become of secondary importance – not so much to Rachel herself, but to the child she and Luke were going to have and do their best to raise together.

And how could I admit that I felt sidelined by a baby? That would make me the most selfish and pathetic person in the world.

'You're allowed to have a voice in this too, you know.' Emily turned the gas flame down and started rummaging in a cupboard for glasses. 'You matter just as much as some random sprog.'

I laughed. 'Luke says that too. He says he loves me and he wants things to work out. He doesn't call it a random sprog though.'

'Course he doesn't, what with being father of the year and everything. But seriously, Liv. Have you thought about how this is going to work? Like, not in the first few months while they're figuring everything out, but longer term?'

I started lifting sausages out on to a plate. The truth was, I had and I hadn't. I'd imagined that, somehow, Luke and I would figure it out. That because we loved each other, we'd find a way. I hadn't allowed myself to look much further than our love for each other and the respect I undeniably felt for him wanting to step up and be a good dad to his son.

'You're twenty-two, Liv,' Emily went on. 'Do you really want to be a stepmother? Seriously?'

'Of course not. But I wouldn't be. I won't have to have anything to do with Luke's son unless I want to.'

'Right. So what happens when you and Luke get married, say? Or even just live together? When it's his turn to have his kid to stay with him? You fuck off to Butlin's for the weekend?'

'That won't be for a while,' I said defensively. 'Not until it's weaned, apparently. Rachel wants to breastfeed, so he won't be able to leave her for ages.'

'Sounds like Rachel's got it all figured out,' Emily said. 'Hey, listen. I care about you, Liv. I just don't want you to get sidelined in all this.'

Then she put down her soup ladle, stuck her head round the door and yelled that sausages and mulled wine were up, and moments later the kitchen filled up with laughing, half-drunk people.

I helped myself to another drink and a handful of cheese footballs and tried to enjoy the party. But I found I couldn't. I knew that what Emily had said was true – that if things worked out between Luke and me, my life would look a whole lot different from Emily's and her friends'.

If Luke and I ever had our own home, it would never be just ours – there'd have to be a bedroom for Luke and Rachel's son where he'd spend half his time. No matter what Luke promised now, I'd become involved – maybe just helping out at first, but ultimately sharing responsibility for a child who wasn't mine.

And if things really worked out between Luke and me and we eventually got married and had children of our own, those children wouldn't be Luke's only ones – not his first.

Much later, as I was leaving, Emily hugged me again, tipsily this time.

'I'm sorry if I came across like a bitch,' she said. 'I just think you need to talk to him.'

'I know. I know you're right.'

Outside, the cold air shocked my lungs. Behind me, the warmth and noise of Emily's party faded with each step. Ahead lay Damask Square – and the careful fiction of my life with Luke that was already unravelling. I walked faster, as if I could outrun what I knew had to happen next.

FORTY-EIGHT

'Ready for the bucking bronco, Slate?' Beatrice asked. 'Hold on tight.'

On all fours on the floor, she hunched her back, raised her hands, hunched again, hopped into a half-handstand, then repeated the process – only faster. She twirled around and went again.

Slate clung on, his knees digging into her ribs, his hands twisted into the shoulders of her sweater, shrieking with laughter.

Now, more than ever, Beatrice was taking comfort from every moment she spent with the children. After her argument with Neil – although she had to admit to herself that it hadn't been so much an argument as a rant on her side – she'd returned reluctantly to the house on Damask Square, purely because she had nowhere else to go. All her things were there. The Dublin trip had used up the last of her wages so she had no money for a hotel. And part of her – a wilful, stubborn part – felt the need to cling to the house as persistently as the ivy that blanketed its back wall, threatening to bring damp back into the upstairs rooms despite Luke's best efforts to eradicate it.

To cling – despite everything – to Orla and her distant dreams of how things might have been between them.

She'd texted Neil and apologised and he'd graciously accepted, saying that it was completely understandable that she felt as she did. When she'd taken the children to the library earlier that day, he had been as friendly to them as ever, but Beatrice had noticed a stiffness and formality in his manner towards her that hadn't been there before.

Orla, in contrast, had been as gentle with Beatrice as if she was a child recovering from an illness. She'd cooked her favourite meal on Monday evening, and the next morning when Beatrice was leaving for work she'd brushed Beatrice's hand and said, 'Please let me know when you're ready to talk.'

Beatrice hadn't been ready to talk, and more than two weeks later, she still wasn't. She didn't know whether she would ever be. She kept meaning to ask Frances about the possibility of her moving in with them, but she hadn't been able to bring herself to do that, either. The possibility of escape from Damask Square and all it represented felt alluring, but it also felt final – as if she would finally be turning her back on everything she had hoped to find there.

'Come on, Bibi,' Slate urged, his heels drumming against her ribs.

Beatrice snorted theatrically, produced a semblance of a neigh, reared and bucked again. Her laughter was rapidly turning to panting – the kid was heavy. But he wasn't letting go.

'You've won!' she gasped at last. 'Cowboy Slate is king of the rodeo!'

'My turn!' Parker squealed. 'Me now, Bibi, me!'

'No, me again!' protested Slate. 'Be the big, wild black horse.'

'Just a second.' Beatrice collapsed on to the floor on her front, laughing helplessly. 'The horse needs a rest.'

Then she heard Parker's voice say, 'Mommy!' and Slate released his grip on her shoulders.

She rolled over. Frances was standing over her, looking down, an expression on her face that Beatrice was completely unable to read.

'Oh, hi, Frances.' She struggled to her feet. 'You're back early. We were playing cowboys. It's too wet out there for the park so I thought they'd better let off some steam before they have their dinner.'

'So I see.' There was a hit of acid in her employer's tone that Beatrice couldn't remember hearing before. She squatted down and pulled both her children to her in a brief embrace, then got up again and headed for her bedroom. 'I'll let you get on with it, then.'

Beatrice was puzzled. In the past, on the rare occasions when Frances had returned early from work, she'd taken over the kids' bedtime routine, allowing Beatrice to have the rest of the evening off. Clearly that wasn't going to be the case today. And there'd been a hint of – what? Resentment? Disapproval?

Surely Frances couldn't object to a bit of rough-and-tumble play? It wasn't like Slate could have been hurt – earlier, when he'd fallen off Beatrice's back on to the thick shagpile rug, he'd jumped up right away and demanded to go again.

Oh, well – doubtless if Frances was going to chew her out over something, she'd do so once the children were asleep.

'Come on then, you two,' she said. 'Chicken stir-fry for dinner.'

'But you said we could have burgers and chips,' Slate objected. 'You said that's what cowboys eat.'

'Burgers and chips!' his sister echoed, her lower lip sticking out ominously.

Damn it. Her attempt to sub out the original menu with something more likely to win Frances's approval had been foiled. She hesitated. What was worse – being caught out giving the kids junk food or Parker throwing an epic tantrum on her watch and both of them most likely refusing to eat anything at all? Besides, she'd made a promise and she didn't want to break it.

'I forgot. Burgers and chips it is. But you'll have shredded lettuce on them.'

She fed the children, tidied away their toys while they ate, ran their bath and stacked the dishwasher, then went to sit with them while they splashed happily in the water. Through the closed door of the master bedroom, she could hear Frances on the phone, long snatches of her talking interspersed with longer pauses. But over the kids' laughter and chatter, she couldn't make out any of the words.

While Slate put on his pyjamas, she wrapped Parker in a towel and recited 'This Little Piggy', relishing the drowsy warmth of the little girl's body and the pink perfection of her toes. She ushered them both to bed and read *Llama Llama Red Pajama* until Parker fell asleep, then read *Funnybones* to Slate, who'd been obsessed with it since Halloween.

'Bibi?' he asked sleepily, once she'd closed the book. 'Can I be a cowboy when I grow up?'

'Maybe you can.' *Are cowboys still a thing?* Beatrice wasn't sure. 'If you work hard at school, you can be whatever you want.'

'I want to ride wild horses.'

'Maybe you should start off on tame ones. Even those are much bigger than pretend horses.'

'Will you take me to ride a horse?'

Beatrice didn't know if there were horses in London. But she could find out – she'd google it, or ask Neil. Neil would know. An idea struck her – she could find a place with ponies and take the kids as a special treat, maybe just before Christmas. She'd have to clear it with Frances first, but she saw no reason why she would object.

Excitement filled her – the thrill of being able to make a small boy's dream come true, even just for a day, with a bit of simple organisation.

'Maybe,' she said. 'We'll see. Now it's time for you to go to sleep.'

'Night night, Bibi.' Slate snuggled down into the pillow.

Beatrice pulled the duvet up under his chin and kissed his cheek, noticing how it was losing its pre-schooler plumpness. He was transforming right before her eyes – he was already halfway to his fifth birthday and then he'd be starting school.

'Sleep tight, Slatey.'

Turning away to dim the light, she saw Frances standing in the doorway. She had no idea how long she'd been there.

'That looks like a wrap,' Frances said. 'Would you like to join me for a glass of wine?'

'I... Yes, thank you. That would be lovely.'

Frances led the way into the living area, quiet without the children and tidy as Beatrice had left it. She took a bottle of Sancerre from the fridge and poured two glasses, then gestured towards the stools at the kitchen island before perching on one, her long legs in their opaque black tights elegantly crossed.

Beatrice joined her, feeling scruffy and homely by comparison, conscious of how much she'd sweated playing horses in the warm apartment.

'Cheers.' Frances raised her glass and clinked it against Beatrice's.

'Cheers.'

Frances cleared her throat. 'I guess I should say thank you. You've done a great job with the kids.'

'It's my pleasure.' Beatrice was taken aback, but also relieved. This didn't feel like it was going to be a telling-off. 'And my job, obviously. But they're amazing kids. I... I've become really fond of them.'

'Yes, well.' Frances sighed. 'I'm afraid I have some news for you, Beatrice.'

Normally, even once the children were in bed, Frances called her Bibi.

She took a gulp of wine. 'What's that?'

'Peter had a call today from his CEO in New York. There's been a restructure in the senior leadership team. Someone's had to be let go, and they need Peter back at HQ as soon as possible.'

At first, Beatrice didn't understand what she was saying. 'Peter's moving back to New York?'

'We all are,' Frances explained slowly, patiently, as if Beatrice was a child. 'There'll be a handover period with his cover here, but he'll be starting full time back at the Wall Street office in January.'

'January?' Beatrice echoed.

'Yes. But there's no point me and the kids shuttling back and forth, or staying here while he's in the transition period. I gave notice at work today, and I've got holiday saved up, so I can wrap things up in a few days.'

'You mean...?' Beatrice's whole body felt numb and floaty, as if she'd necked the whole bottle of wine instead of just taking a couple of sips.

'We'll be home by Thanksgiving. The kids' grandparents haven't seen them since we moved here – they're delighted.'

'So are you saying I...?'

'Sadly, of course, we won't be needing you any more. Juanita, who was our nanny in New York, was temping while we've been away and she's free to start back with us. But we'll pay you two months' wages, as per our contract, and we'll be sure to give you a glowing reference. We've been very happy, all things considered, with how you've grown into the job and especially how you've bonded with the kids. We can't thank you enough for all that you've...'

Frances carried on, heaping fulsome praise on Beatrice. But Beatrice barely heard a word.

She waited until Frances finished speaking, slowly draining her wine. Then she returned her employer's thanks, said goodnight and put on her coat, all on autopilot. She didn't see the elevator door sliding open or the lights glinting on the river when she emerged at street level.

All she could see was the children's faces and how they might look when she said goodbye to them for the final time. That, and Orla's face.

I never understood, she thought, almost in wonderment. *I never had any idea what it must have been like for her. But now, even though it's only a fraction of what she must have felt, I know.*

I understand now.

FORTY-NINE

For quite a long time, I was unaware of what was going on between Beatrice and Orla. Their relationship had been tense for so long that the new, additional tension passed me by unnoticed. Besides, Rachel's revelation and the shockwaves it had sent through my relationship with Luke took up almost all my attention. With the end of the year approaching, work was busy and I was getting back to the house later than usual in the evenings, and Orla herself was absent more often.

That is, until one Friday night. I'd managed to leave the office on time – the first time in a while – and returned home just before seven. Orla had mentioned that she had been persuaded to go to the pub with the committee of the historic buildings Preservation Trust, which had roped her in as a member. Beatrice, I presumed, was still at work, and as for Luke – I didn't particularly want to speculate about where he might be.

So, unusually, I had the house to myself. With winter drawing in, it was cold – the sort of cold that seeps into your bones and can only be banished by getting into bed or having a hot bath. I opted for the bath.

For once not having to worry about hogging the bathroom, I filled the tub with hot, scented water, watching in satisfaction as steam rose up to the high ceiling, fogging up the mirror and probably adding to the damp problem. I lowered myself in and wallowed, in between shaving my legs and putting a treatment on my hair, for almost an hour until I'd exhausted the boiler's supply and my fingers and toes were shrivelled like prunes.

Finally warm, I got out, wrapped myself in my dressing gown and hurried along the chilly landing to the relative warmth of my bedroom.

Beatrice was there. She was sitting on my bed, still in the jeans and red wool jumper she must have worn to work. Her feet were tucked under my duvet and she was crying.

'Hey.' I paused in the doorway, dismayed. 'Are you okay?'

She shook her head mutely.

'Can I get you anything?'

Again, the head shake.

'Do you want to talk?'

I made the offer somewhat reluctantly. Any hopes I might have had of Beatrice and me becoming friends had come to nothing, and her behaviour over the past weeks had made my wariness of her sour into something more akin to dislike. But I couldn't ignore someone so clearly distressed – especially since she was on my bed.

Beatrice nodded, and I stepped over and sat down on the end of the bed by her feet.

'Did something happen at work?' I asked.

'No.' She took a tissue from the box on the floor and blew her nose. 'Well, yes, actually. I've been let go. Peter and Frances are leaving London.'

'Oh, no. I'm so sorry. That's awful. What are you going to do?'

'Probably go back to the States and move back in with my parents.'

'You'll miss the kids, I guess,' I hazarded.

That seemed to hit a nerve. Beatrice put her hands up to her face and started to cry again. I reached out and patted her knee in what I hoped was a reassuring way.

'What about them missing me?' she said, taking a couple of goes to get the words out between sobs. 'They'll think I didn't want to be their nanny any more. They won't understand.'

'Oh, Beatrice. Of course they'll miss you and they'll be sad. You've been an amazing nanny.' I had no idea if that was true, but I said it anyway. 'But their mum and dad will explain why you couldn't carry on working with them, right? They'll understand. Maybe you can even visit them.'

'That's not how it works.' She looked at me, her tear-stained face furious. 'You can't explain that shit to kids.'

Taken aback by her vehemence, I said lamely, 'Well, they'll try, I'm sure.'

'Like my parents tried to explain to me.'

I had no idea what she meant, but I could tell that there was deeper hurt at play here. 'Explain what? I'm sorry, Beatrice. I don't understand.'

'I'm adopted.' She almost spat out the word. 'I was the most wanted baby in the world ever, my mom and dad always said. But that wasn't true, because before I was wanted, I wasn't. And that never goes away.'

Her revelation blindsided me. Everything she had told me about her family – which admittedly hadn't been a great deal – had suggested a life of adored privilege as the only child of doting, if overprotective, parents. But it made sense – of course it did.

Only child of doting parents and an adoptee – both things could be true at once.

'I didn't realise,' I said gently. 'I totally get why that would make leaving Slate and' – I couldn't remember the other child's name – 'leaving the kids harder. You poor thing.'

But it seemed like Beatrice wasn't thinking about them any more – or not only about them. She lifted her face and looked not at me but past me at the wall, and carried on as if she was talking to herself.

'My father worked in Ireland for two years, before I was born. He and Mom had been trying for a baby for ages but it wasn't happening. There weren't that many newborns you could adopt in the States by then – women were already keeping their babies if they could, or having abortions if they couldn't. But in Ireland it was different. So Daddy found a baby in Ireland, through some nuns or something, and when they went back home they took me with them.'

'Wow. You must have made them so happy.'

She grimaced. 'When I started talking about wanting to track down my birth mother, not so much. But they kind of went along with it. I guess they thought I'd never manage it.'

Did you find her? Have you found her?

But before I could ask the question, I realised I already knew the answer: it had been there all along, right in front of my eyes. The only reason I couldn't have realised was that, until now, I simply hadn't been aware that Beatrice was an adopted child.

Still, wanting to give her space to tell her story in her own way, I kept my question vague.

'Does Orla know?' I asked.

'I wanted it to be her, but also not. I imagined she might have had a sister – someone else, anyone but her.'

In spite of Beatrice's distress, I felt a stab of jealousy. It took me a moment to work out why. If I could have exchanged my own mother for Orla, I would have done in a heartbeat. The squalor of the house where I grew up, my mother's obsession with the piles of meaningless stuff that surrounded her which took precedence even over her own daughter, the way she passively let everything sink into chaos and decay – compared to Orla's serene resilience, compared to this house emerging into its rightful beauty, compared to the certainty that, here, I was someone who mattered.

Then I tried to see things from Beatrice's point of view, and it was with a guilty, sinking heart that I realised how it must look.

Still, I asked, 'Why do you think that was?'

'Because Orla doesn't like me,' Beatrice said in a small voice. 'I made her not like me – it was my fault. It could have been different. I'd thought that when I told her, she'd change her mind about me.'

'You knew, Beatrice,' I said, 'but she didn't. It would have been a total shock for her. She'd have needed time to process it all.'

Beatrice shook her head, tears starting again in her eyes. 'I've fucked it up. It was what I always wanted and now...'

'Hey, don't be mad. It's not too late. You just need to give it time, let her get used to the idea. It's hard for her, too.'

Beatrice looked at me and I saw a glimmer of her usual confidence.

'You might not look that similar to her,' I went on, 'not on the surface, anyway. But there are things about you that are just the same. When I hear you walk across the landing, it often takes me a few seconds to realise it's not her. Your singing voice is the same, even though you can hold a tune and she can't. Your hands are the same. She's your mother. You'll get there.'

A smile appeared on Beatrice's face, sudden and shining, the way Orla smiled.

'You need to give each other a chance,' I urged.

'I was so angry,' Beatrice whispered. 'About her having given me away. I was horrible to her. And I was mean as hell to Neil, too.'

Neil? She'd mentioned going to Dublin with someone called Neil – presumably her boyfriend.

'If he knows what you've been going through, he'll understand,' I said. 'And if he doesn't, then he's not worth having, right? Talk to him. Say you're sorry. It'll all work out. I promise.'

'Really?' She looked up at me, hopeful as a child. Then her face fell again. 'But – Slate and Parker. Nothing can make that work out.'

'Beatrice.' I tried to keep my voice gentle, to scrape together reserves of kindness and wisdom I didn't know I had. 'Sometimes things change. Sometimes you lose people not because you've done anything wrong but just because stuff happens. Life happens. And then you just have to make the best of it.'

Abruptly, she pulled her feet out from under my duvet and stood up, leaving the wad of damp tissues on my bed.

'Thanks, Livvie. Thanks for listening.'

'That's okay.'

'I should let you go to bed.'

'It's fine. Honestly, you can talk to me any time you want.'

'Thanks,' she said again. 'I'm glad I came. I'm sorry I haven't been a better friend.'

She hasn't really been a friend at all, I thought. But that hadn't only been down to her.

'Me too,' I said.

She reached down and gave me an awkward half-hug, her long hair brushing against my lips.

She doesn't much like touching people, I thought. *Same as Orla.*

'Goodnight, Livvie.'

She left. I heard her bedroom door open and close, and I was alone. I'd planned to make myself something to eat, but I didn't feel hungry now. I turned out the light and lay on the bed in the warm place Beatrice had left, staring up at the ceiling in the dark.

I couldn't heal the wounds that had been left on Beatrice's and Orla's hearts. But I felt the beginning of a realisation that hurt so badly I almost started crying myself: if they were to reconcile, salvage any kind of relationship as birth mother and daughter, the relationship I'd come to cherish between Orla and me would be a barrier between them.

My own words, uttered on the spur of the moment like an agony aunt on a deadline, came back to me: *Sometimes you lose people not because you've done anything wrong but just because stuff happens.*

Things change, I'd said. Things were going to change for me – it was inevitable. For me and for Luke and for Orla as well as for Beatrice. They'd have to change.

I would have to leave Damask Square.

FIFTY

Beatrice looked around the apartment, her hands on her hips. The pictures had been removed from their hooks on the wall, swaddled in bubble wrap and stacked in a corner. The children's clothes had been laundered, neatly folded and placed in their suitcases; their cabin bags were equally carefully packed with drinks, snacks, crayons and paper, their favourite teddies perched on top ready to accompany them on the journey. What remained was only what belonged to the landlord, not the family – larger items of furniture; crockery and glassware – and Peter's clothes and enough towels and bedlinen for him to use during his handover period.

There was nothing more for her to do here. Well – one thing. The most important thing.

She heard the swish of the elevator doors and Frances came in with Slate and Parker, raindrops sparkling on their hair.

'I went down the big slide, Bibi,' Slate told her proudly.

'You did?' Beatrice squatted down in front of him. 'That was brave. Were you scared?'

'A bit. But Mommy was waiting for me at the bottom and it was my last chance.'

Parker thumped down on the floor, her thumb in her mouth. She'd been tetchy all day; Beatrice hoped she wasn't coming down with something, but suspected it was just the knowledge of impending change.

'Library,' she said, her voice muffled.

Beatrice stroked her hair. She'd put it up with a new hair tie that morning, brushing it carefully, conscious that it was the last time she would do it.

'There's no time to go to the library,' she said gently. 'Your daddy's going to be home soon and then you're going to go to the airport and get on an airplane and fly back to America.'

'The place looks great, Bibi,' Frances said. 'I'm so grateful for all your hard work.'

'You're welcome,' Beatrice replied automatically, scrambling to her feet. 'I think I'm all done here. The courier isn't due until the morning but I'll leave my key with the concierge – he knows to expect them.'

'That's right – there's no need for you to hang around,' Frances said, and Beatrice filled in the rest of the sentence in her mind: *It'll only upset the kids.*

'Right,' she said. 'Come on, Parker and Slate, give me a cuddle.'

She pulled the children towards her, pressing their small bodies against hers, breathing in the smell of them for the last time. She'd never see Slate ride a pony, never read Parker another bedtime story. Within a few weeks, they'd probably have forgotten all about her.

The pain was intense – almost physical. But she couldn't let the children see it; she had to stay strong and calm for them. She held on to them for as long as she dared, then quickly kissed each of their heads in turn and stood up.

'This is for you.' Smiling, Frances handed her a small bag, duck-egg blue, printed with the Tiffany logo. 'It's just a trinket, to say thank you from all of us.'

'Thank you.' Beatrice leaned in for a kiss, breathing in Frances's Shalimar scent, feeling the sharpness of her jaw against her cheek. 'I'll treasure it. I've... It's been wonderful, getting to know Slate and Parker. And you, of course. So thank you for that, too.'

Frances looked at her, her gaze astute. *She knows*, Beatrice realised. *She knows exactly how I feel, but neither of us can acknowledge it.*

'I'd best be off, then,' Beatrice said.

'You take care, honey.'

Beatrice nodded miserably and Frances leaned in, patted her cheek and whispered to her, 'Don't be too sad.'

Almost blinded by tears, Beatrice turned away and pressed the button to open the elevator. There was no looking back now – no going back. Even a final glance at the children, a final hug, would only postpone the inevitable parting by a few seconds. There was no point. She stepped in, keeping her back to the elevator doors, hearing the swish and soft thunk as they closed.

Down at street level, she said her goodbyes to the concierge, leaving him with the neatly printed list of instructions and contact numbers she'd prepared as well as her key to the apartment. Then she walked slowly out into the rain.

It was only four o'clock, but already dark. She had nothing to do and nowhere to go. She felt bereft, alone with her sadness. She let her legs carry her automatically towards the bus stop, barely noticing the brightly lit windows of the library as she passed it.

Then its door swung open and, glancing reflexively over, she saw Neil emerging, his leather satchel slung over his shoulder, a knitted beanie pulled down over his shaven head. He recognised Beatrice too and waved, jogging over to catch her up.

'Hey, Beatrice. Long time no see. How're you doing?' he asked.

Beatrice told him, just managing to keep her tears at bay.

'Ah, that sucks.' Neil's voice was sympathetic, his eyes kind. 'Those cute kids. You must be gutted.'

Beatrice nodded. 'It's just – I'm so worried they'll miss me. Slate worries about monsters under his bed at night – what if the nanny in New York forgets to check for them? And Parker will only eat her toast if you put the butter on when it's hot but then wait for it to get cold. But she's too little to explain that – I only found out by trial and error.'

'Hey.' Gently, Neil punched her bicep. 'Parker's not going to starve and Slate's not going to get eaten by monsters. You know that.'

Beatrice sniffed. 'I know.'

'Still sucks though,' he said.

Beatrice nodded, then she said, 'Neil? Remember you asked a while back – you said maybe we should go for a drink sometime, and we did, but I said I didn't want it to be a proper date?'

Neil laughed. 'That feels like quite a long time ago. I mean, we've basically been on holiday together since then.'

'I know. But that was just as friends, right? I'd like... I'd like to see if we could be a bit more than friends. If you would. I know I've been shitty to you and I'm sorry, and I'll understand if you say no.'

His face lit up in a grin, and Beatrice had her answer.

Half an hour later, she arrived back at the house on Damask Square. The comfort of Neil's company gone, sadness had settled over her again like a damp, heavy blanket. She knew she'd get over it; she knew the kids would be all right, loved and cared for by their parents and Juanita, who'd known them long before Beatrice had. But the sense of loss was still raw, as painful as anything she'd ever known.

She slipped her key into the lock and pushed open the door, hoping she could steal unnoticed up to her room and cry, alone, until the worst of her sorrow had passed. But as soon as she stepped into the hallway, she stopped.

The house smelled different. It was as if she'd been transported somewhere else – back to her childhood home. She could almost feel the rug beneath her feet, although she knew it was bare floorboards. The music she could hear coming from the kitchen was Radio One on Orla's boombox, but at the same time it was her mom playing Mozart on the piano in the living room.

It was the smell that was confusing her. A smell of childhood, rich and warm and comforting, sweet and savoury and spicy. As eagerly as she had when she was a little girl, Beatrice followed it through the house.

Orla was in the kitchen, cocooned by warmth and light and that familiar childhood aroma.

She smiled when she saw Beatrice, though uncertainty flickered in her eyes.

'Hello,' she said. 'You're home early.'

Beatrice felt the scent surrounding her, almost as if she could reach out a finger and touch it. Cinnamon, nutmeg, butter and brown sugar – the exact smell that had filled her mom's kitchen every autumn. She felt saliva fill her mouth at the same time as tears sprang to her eyes, and stood frozen in the doorway. All her emotions – sorrow at the loss of the children, regret at how she'd treated Neil, anger at Orla – swept over her in a wave. But as quickly as it hit her, the anger vanished.

Orla had never been her mother: never had the chance to buy her presents or dry her tears or bake her favourite things. But she was doing so now.

'I made a pumpkin pie,' Orla said, then added hesitantly, 'I thought you might be homesick, as it's Thanksgiving tomorrow.'

Beatrice dropped her bag and crossed the kitchen in three quick steps, throwing herself into Orla's arms.

FIFTY-ONE

I was in my bedroom, folding the washing I'd taken to the launderette earlier and putting it away in my drawers, when I heard Luke come home. I recognised the sound the door made when he closed it – not a gentle click like Orla's nor a vigorous slam like Beatrice made, except when she made no sound at all – and the tread of his boots on the wooden floor. Over the months, I'd become attuned to the noises of him in the house, and each one brought me joy.

Now, though, I heard him speaking to Orla: the note of excitement, almost wonderment, in his voice and her soft responses, congratulating, questioning, comforting.

I knew what had happened and I knew what I was going to do.

I scooped up the last of my underwear and threw it into the drawer, followed by my unpaired socks, sat down on the bed and waited. A few minutes later I heard Luke's feet on the stairs and a tap on my door. He didn't wait for me to answer but opened it instantly, bursting into the room, his face alight with happiness in spite of the dark shadows beneath his eyes.

'Rachel had the baby,' he told me. 'A boy, obviously, like we knew it was going to be. She's called him Charlie, after her grandpa.'

'Congratulations.' I got up off the bed and hugged him, feeling the strength of his arms around me. 'Is she okay? Is the baby okay?'

'Mother and baby doing well, like they say in those swanky birth announcements in *The Times*. Me, not so much. I'm knackered and starving. I've ordered a pizza – you want some?'

'I'm all good. Was it... Did it take a long time?'

'Thirteen hours from when she went into hospital.' He sat down on my bed abruptly, as if imagining what Rachel had gone through had sucked the last of the energy from his body. 'Apparently that's about average for a first baby. Her mum was with her the whole time and I waited at the hospital, but I got to give him a cuddle afterwards. I've got some photos on my camera but I left it at Rachel's mum's place. He weighs seven pounds four ounces and he's eating like a champion. Takes after his dad.'

Tiredness and pride shone out of him. I ached with love for him and sadness at what I was about to do.

'Is she still there, in the hospital?' I asked.

He nodded. 'They still need to do some checks, but they should be okay to go home tomorrow. Rachel's mum wanted her to go back to hers for a couple of days but she wants to go back to her flat because all the baby stuff's there. I said I'd go there in the morning and help. Apparently I need to figure out how the car seat works – my first dad job.'

'Beats changing nappies,' I said.

'Oh, I've already done that.' He grinned.

'Wow. Hands on, or what?'

'I know, right? God, he's adorable though, Liv. His little hands. And he's got a good pair of lungs on him. I can't believe someone so small can make that much noise.'

I listened to him, the pleasure and enthusiasm in his voice

just the same as when he talked about some breakthrough he'd made on the house, or a painting he'd finished. But those were achievements I'd been able to share with him, triumphs I'd experienced at first hand. This was different. What had happened in that hospital had created a distance between us that hadn't been there before; the arrival of this new life marked the end of our old one.

No matter how much Luke intended that not to be the case, it was – and there was nothing either of us could do to change it.

'Maybe in a few days you can meet him,' he said tentatively. 'I said, when Rachel feels ready, I'd like to take him out for a walk in his buggy, show him the world, while she gets some rest. If she's okay with it, you could come.'

'Luke,' I said, as gently as I could, forcing the words past the lump in my throat. 'I don't think I'm going to do that.'

'Why? I mean – okay, I guess it might be a bit weird. But later on, when you're ready. Only they change so much, so quickly, Rachel's mum says. Literally from one day to the next.'

Like everything else, I thought.

I said, 'Luke, there's something I need to tell you.'

He literally winced, then looked horrified, and I realised how badly I'd messed up.

I couldn't help laughing. 'It's not that. Don't panic. One baby is great, but another would be a bit much, right? I'm not pregnant.'

'Thank God.' He laughed as well, a bit shakily. 'I know you didn't mean to but you had me there for a second. What is it? Is everything okay?'

'I'm okay,' I reassured him. 'But us – I'm so sorry, but I don't think this is going to work.'

'What? Liv, what are you saying? I know I haven't been focused enough on you. I'm sorry. But I love you. The way I love Charlie – it's completely different. It doesn't mean anything in terms of us.'

'It does, though.' I reached out and took his hands. 'I can tell how much being a dad means to you. And you're right – it should. But I can't be part of it. I'm not ready. I don't want to be.'

'Then don't.' His hands in mine had gone still – he didn't pull away, but I could tell he wanted to. 'It's fine. You don't have to meet him, ever, if you don't want to. It doesn't have to change things between us.'

'It would, though. It already has. You're a father now, Luke. That's a massive change – it hasn't just changed your life; it's changed you. And it should. I admire what you're doing – I really do.'

'You just don't want to be with me while I'm doing it.' Now he did pull his hands away.

With a lump in my throat, I said, 'That's right. I don't. I think you need to focus on Charlie, and I know if you did that, I'd end up resenting you for it. And that's not fair – it's not right. I'd end up hating you and you'd end up hating me.'

'I could never hate you.'

I wouldn't bet on it. Already, I could see anger in his face, alongside hurt. I had wanted to keep my own expression calm but I could feel my lips twisting into the grimace of a sad clown as I fought back my tears.

'It's just not going to work,' I said again.

'Liv, this is bullshit. I thought we had something special together.'

I felt my hands reach out for his as if he was the only thing saving me from drowning, but I forced myself to pull them back.

'Me too,' I said. 'But I don't want to be a stepmother. Not now and probably not ever.'

'So you're saying you don't want me to be part of Charlie's life? You're asking me to choose between you and a one-day-old baby?'

'I'm not saying that. There's no choice for you to make – he's here, he's your son. It's a done deal. I just can't be part of it.'

'I can't deal with this right now.' He put his head in his hands.

I longed to hug him, tell him I'd made a mistake, that everything would be all right and somehow we'd find a way through it – a way to make everyone happy, him and me and Rachel and Charlie.

But I knew there wasn't a way.

I heard a knock on the door downstairs and Orla's footsteps as she hurried to answer it.

'I think your pizza's here,' I said.

Luke looked up, tiredness and hunger overcoming emotion for the time being.

'I'll eat downstairs,' he said stiffly. 'We'll talk in the morning.'

'Okay.'

He got up and left, not dramatically, not slamming the door or swearing at me or anything. I'd been holding off crying, but now I found I didn't want to cry any more. I felt numb and empty, like all my feelings of love and loss and sadness had passed through the door along with Luke. I ached for him. I hoped that Orla would be able to offer him the comfort I could not. I hoped when morning came he would see things the way I saw them.

Because I knew there was no other way it could be, even though my heart was breaking.

FIFTY-TWO

As had become her weekly habit, Beatrice was perched on the stairs with her laptop on her knees. The balustrade had been stripped and varnished all the way up now; under her hands she could feel the smoothness of the freshly sanded stair she sat on. She and Orla had been looking at carpets earlier – Beatrice wanted blue but Orla had said grey would be more versatile and Beatrice suspected she was right.

Beatrice sensed that Orla was approaching their relationship in the same way she was – tentatively, yet with a growing sense of trust. She'd told Orla details of her childhood, yet Orla had so far declined to be introduced to Beatrice's mom and dad over Skype, saying it was too soon for her and probably also for them. Orla had unearthed a box of old photographs in the cellar and shown Beatrice pictures of her own parents and her grandmother. Sometimes Beatrice stood and looked over Orla's shoulder while she painted, admiring her skill but reluctant to interrupt her work by speaking.

Before she went upstairs to bed, Orla would say goodnight to Beatrice and, just a few days ago, she'd leaned over to drop a kiss on Beatrice's cheek. The imprint of it seemed to linger there, so precious that Beatrice had been reluctant to wash off her make-up.

The stairwell was as warm now as it had been back in summer – although now it was thanks to the new boiler and radiators that had been installed all through the house. The repair of the roof was complete and the attic rooms above her were dry and empty, waiting to be converted into bedrooms and a proper studio for Orla. A new bathroom was being installed there too – Luke's final job before he moved out.

Livvie, too, had given Orla notice and was leaving before Christmas. After that, it would be only her and Orla living here.

Beatrice heard the familiar acoustic modem handshake as Skype on her computer reached out to Skype on her parents', and seconds later their faces appeared on the screen. They were downstairs in the living room today, not in her dad's office, and Beatrice could see the Christmas tree behind them, laden with glass baubles in shades of red and gold and sparkling with white lights.

'There you are, honey.' Her dad beamed. 'You're looking well.'

'I hope you're getting plenty of rest now you've got some time to yourself,' her mom said.

'We just wish you were going to come home for Christmas,' said her dad.

'I know.' Beatrice smiled. 'I'm going to miss you both, and Sligo. I sent gifts for you all. But I wanted to spend a bit more time getting to know Orla. And – well, there's this boy I've kind of been seeing. Neil. I'd like to get to know him better, too.'

'Oh, sweetie.' Her mom's face fell. 'You know we were worried you'd fall in love with someone out there.'

Beatrice laughed. 'Take it easy, Mom. I'm not in love with him. You don't need to start thinking about grandchildren just yet.'

'And what about your – what about Orla?' her dad asked.

'Like I said, it was awkward at first,' she said. 'But we're getting to know each other now, and we've got lots in common. She keeps a journal – she calls it Morning Pages – and every time she needs a new notebook she spends ages choosing a special one, just like I would. She's a really gifted artist. She's been doing some sketches of me and they're beautiful – she's asked me to sit for a proper portrait and I think I will.'

Her mom sighed. 'So it sounds as if it'll be a while before we see you again.'

'I think so.' Beatrice knew so, but she'd been planning to break it gently to them. 'I could get another job as a nanny easily, but I think I'd like to study, or do some work experience in early years education. Maybe even a course in counselling or a master's in social work. I could – I thought, I'd love to work with children who've been adopted, like me.'

'I understand.' Beatrice's dad reached over and took his wife's hand. 'I guess we'd better start planning a trip out to London then, hadn't we, Ruth?'

'That would be so cool! You can meet Orla and Neil, and see the house.'

'Did you say Orla went to art college in Dublin?' her father asked. 'Was it the IADT?'

'No, I don't think so. She hasn't been back to Ireland since – you know. She doesn't talk about that time much.'

Beatrice felt her mind turning over the conversations she'd had with Orla, all the details she'd gleaned about her past. She'd spoken at length about her childhood – the huge grey house where she'd spent holidays with her grandmother, surrounded by fields where horses grazed; the terms at boarding school, where teenage Orla had rebelled and been expelled; the turbulent relationship between her glamorous mother and hard-drinking, feckless father.

But Orla was vague about the time surrounding Beatrice's conception and birth. It was understandable, she thought –

eventually, Orla would open up more about what must have been a deeply traumatic period in her life.

'And you told us she never got to see you after you were born,' her mom was saying. 'Poor woman.'

'It was a Caesarean section,' Beatrice said. 'And they took me away from her right after. It sounds brutal. But then I got to go home with you, didn't I?'

'You sure did.' Beatrice's dad smiled.

'Well, mind you come home again,' her mom said. 'I feel for Orla, losing you. Really, I do. But that doesn't mean we want to lose you too.'

'You won't,' Beatrice reassured her. 'I'm only a flight away and there's plenty of me to go around. More than enough for you and Orla.'

And Neil, she thought.

Then the internet connection began to drop as it often did and Beatrice said goodbye, promising to Skype again on Christmas Day, after her parents had got back from church.

'Love you, Mom. Love you, Dad. Tell Sligo I love him too.'

Her parents' answer broke up into crackling and the screen went blank. But that was okay – Beatrice knew what they'd been saying.

She put her computer back in her room and went downstairs.

Orla was in the kitchen, sitting at the table with the cat on her lap. She was writing in a notebook – not one of the special ones she used for her Morning Pages but an ordinary spiral-bound one from the newsagent. Beatrice could smell soup – carrot and coriander, maybe. She didn't mind eating Orla's vegetarian food so much now – she no longer felt she had any point to prove.

'Hello.' Orla smiled. 'Everything all right with your parents?'

One day, Beatrice thought, *maybe one day she'll say, Hello, darling. Just not yet.*

'All good.' She sat down across from Orla. 'They're not thrilled about me staying here over the holidays, but they understand.'

'They've had you all your life, and now it's my turn?' Orla smiled.

'Something like that.'

They both laughed, even though neither had said anything particularly funny. Beatrice relished the moment of connection – one of many moments there had been over the past couple of weeks as they'd grown to understand each other – tentative at first, but growing more confident with familiarity.

Then Orla said, 'Beatrice. There's something I want to speak to you about.'

Beatrice felt her stomach turn over anxiously. Had she done something wrong? Had something happened to disturb the fragile accord she was building with Orla?

'It's nothing bad. It could end up being a good thing.'

But the churning didn't subside. 'Go on.'

'It's about this house,' Orla said, looking down at her notebook. Beatrice could see columns of figures on its lined pages – that and a doodle of a robin on a sprig of holly. Orla always drew when she was thinking, Beatrice had learned.

'What about it?'

'Yesterday I had an estate agent come round and value it. The renovation's almost done, you know, apart from extending out down here and putting in a proper kitchen to replace this mess. And I can't afford to do that now, because all the money from that grant's been spent.'

'It doesn't matter,' Beatrice said. 'I like this kitchen.'

'So do I.' Orla smiled. 'But the rest of it – it's too big for just the two of us, you know. And now the heating's in it's going to cost a fortune to keep warm. The estate agent said – well, he said lots of things, they always do. But he said it'll be worth a lot of money.'

'You're thinking of selling this house?' Beatrice couldn't keep the shock from showing in her face.

'Just *thinking*,' Orla said hastily. 'I haven't made a decision yet. But I wanted to talk to you about it because – well, it'll be yours one day. The house or the money I sell it for.'

'I don't want money. I don't want to even think about – you know. That.'

'I'm not going to drop dead any time soon.' Orla looked up from her notepad and her steady hazel eyes met Beatrice's. 'Please don't think that. But although you're welcome to live here for as long as you want, it won't be forever. You might want a place of your own. You might want to go back to America. And I can't be rattling around here on my own.'

'You could get more lodgers,' Beatrice said. 'Like me and Luke and Livvie.'

'Believe me, I've thought about that. But much as I've loved the past few months, I'm not sure I can face doing it again.'

Once again, there was that moment of connection, and they both laughed.

'I get that,' Beatrice said. 'But I'm still here. I'm not going anywhere.'

'Not yet. I hope not for a long time. But you will.'

Beatrice looked around the cosy, shabby kitchen – the only thing left of the dilapidated wreck Orla had inherited. She knew, now, what it had cost to bring it all back to life – not just in terms of money, but in terms of Luke's labour, Orla's anguish and Livvie's heartbreak. And as for her – only now did she realise how precious number five Damask Square had become to her. It was here that she'd confronted truths about herself, come face to face with the mother she had lost and left behind the child she had been.

'Don't,' she said. 'Please don't sell it, Orla.'

'I won't right away. I promise. It – and I – will be here for as long as you need. But eventually, it's something I'll have to consider.'

'There's a way.' The idea came to Beatrice all at once, fully formed. 'My dad – he teaches history of art at a private university. His students are all from wealthy families, and every summer they come out to Europe on their grand tours. They come to London first and visit the National Gallery and Tate Modern and everything, and then they go off to Paris and Florence and Vienna and whatever.'

'Go on,' Orla said, her face intent.

'Well, when they're in London, they'd need somewhere to stay,' Beatrice went on. 'Somewhere comfortable, with someone who can help them plan their travel itinerary and introduce them to London. Someone who knows art.'

'Someone like me,' Orla said.

'Exactly! They'd pay a fortune – much more than we've been paying. And they wouldn't stay long so they wouldn't have a chance to – you know.'

'Become annoying?'

They laughed for longer this time, in shared silliness and relief.

'It's a good idea,' Orla said. 'It really is. We'll talk about it some more in the new year.'

Next year, Beatrice thought. *Next year, I'll still be here.*

'Shall I get a couple of bowls for our soup?' she asked.

FIFTY-THREE
10 DECEMBER 2005

I can hear the shower running and Beatrice singing. Don't Cry for Me Argentina – she has sung it while she gets ready almost every morning since she moved in. I wonder what it is about that particular song that appeals to her? Is it a favourite of her mom's – that musical woman who has a baby grand piano in her front room and sings in the church choir?

Perhaps someday I will ask her. If I did, she would probably look at me in surprise, unaware of this habit she has.

Then she might become self-conscious and stop doing it. And I don't want her to stop – I don't want to make her feel anything other than at home in this house. Having lost her for so long, I don't want to do anything that might frighten her off.

Even my portrait of her I am working on in snatches – a few brush strokes here, the adjustment of a line there – because I do not want to ask her to sit still for too long lest she becomes restless and makes a run for it.

It reminds me of those early days when Maud turned up at the house and I tempted her with tasty food and warm places to sleep, but always left a window open for her so she could come and go as she pleased.

But even when I work on the portrait alone, my charcoal and my brushes seem to capture her as if she were there in front of me: the smooth curve of her cheeks, the gleaming curtain of her hair, her delicate hands. How beautiful she is. Any mother would swell with pride at having produced such a girl, with all her flaws and complexities. A young woman who, despite her privilege, has been dealt a difficult hand and is playing it as best she can. I find myself admiring her – her energy, her spirit, her courage in coming here to seek the truth about who she is.

I am full of wonder now that I know she is my daughter. I have never felt the connection I felt with Livvie – that meeting of minds, like falling in love. But I cherish her – I want to protect her, to be here for her, to keep her safe from harm.

Perhaps, then, this is what mothers feel, and what I felt for Livvie was something quite different.

I don't know. I have never been a mother before. I am working it out as I go along.

I wonder how different she would have been if she had grown up with me, in the house in Clonmara, learning to ride a pony and running wild in the fields before being ordered inside to wash and change for tea and hold her knife and fork like a lady.

I wonder what would have happened if I had told Declan about her. Sometimes I used to imagine that he would leave his wife and be with me. God, how stupid I was! As if he would have done that. Declan was no fool – I was the fool and I know in hindsight that I was not the first of his students with whom he'd had such a dalliance.

He would never have left her – that pretty woman in the photograph on his desk, taken on their wedding day, her dark hair crowned with flowers. All that would have happened is I would have been kicked out of college in disgrace instead of choosing to leave with my head held more or less high.

Is it all worth it? The pain, the shame, the years of hiding and running away?

To hear my daughter singing in the mornings like a lark – yes. To know that even if I couldn't hear her, even if I had never met her, she would be alive and singing?

Yes, it is.

FIFTY-FOUR

I descended the stairs slowly, my bag over my shoulder. It was eight in the morning – a cold December day. The high-ceilinged, airy rooms on the ground floor of the house were almost as bright as outdoors, their huge windows reflected in bright rectangles on the glossy polished floors.

I glanced through to the kitchen, where I'd spent so many evenings at the rickety pine table, chatting to Orla. Soon it would be gone – the shabby 1960s units stripped out, the chipped freestanding cooker consigned to a skip, replaced with fresh new cupboards and counters where Orla and Beatrice would sit.

Outside, the trees in the square were bare, the black metal railings rimed with frost. In a couple of months, snowdrops would appear in the grass, followed by crocuses and, later, daffodils would herald the proper start of spring. I knew that when I saw them it would be with a start of surprise, rather than the gradual, almost imperceptible transition I'd observed from summer to autumn and autumn to winter.

I paused and looked back at the house – the tall, elegant facade that had welcomed me so many times, the high-up window that had been mine now in darkness. I felt the need to find some way of saying goodbye to it, fixing it in my memory forever, only I couldn't think what that might be.

The sound of footsteps and voices disturbed me and I looked around. Three people were approaching the house: a young man carrying a briefcase and a couple a few years older than me, who were holding hands. She was wearing a long red coat that flew out behind her in the sharp morning breeze; he had blond hair that shone almost golden as they passed beneath a lamp post.

Then I recognised the man with the briefcase. He was the estate agent who'd come to the door in summer, interrupting me and Luke in the garden, insistent on seeing Orla. Surely he wasn't coming to her house now, not coming to show this couple round and persuade Orla to sell it to them?

But it was the house three doors away that they were approaching: number eight.

'Now I'll be straight with you,' the estate agent said. 'It's not pretty in there. It's an ambitious project.'

'We're ambitious people,' the blond man said.

'Speak for yourself,' the woman teased. 'I just want a place to live.'

'Then let's take a look.'

I watched as the estate agent fumbled a key into the lock, turned it and opened the door, but I couldn't see what lay inside. It didn't really matter, because whatever it was would soon change. That young couple would move in and set to work as Luke had done, ripping out plasterboard, sanding floors, evicting spiders. Before long the rooms would fill with the clink of their wine glasses at dinner, the voices of their friends, the laughter of their children.

I took a last look at the closed door of number five, but I didn't feel the need for a farewell any more.

I felt as if I had been released from a spell.

Slowly, I began my usual walk to the bus stop, my shoulders hunched beneath my coat and my eyes watering from the cold.

With the same inexorable progress as the changing seasons, my life would move on – I knew that. Emily had talked about a girls' holiday to Ibiza in the summer. I'd been awarded a Christmas bonus that I planned to spend on some new clothes, the knowledge and skills I'd gleaned from Orla allowing me to pick out pieces that suited me and adjust them so they fitted perfectly.

I wondered if I'd ever thread a needle or pin a dart without thinking of her, remembering the quizzical tilt of her head as she assessed the drape of a fabric, the scent of her skin as she leaned in towards me to pull up a zip, the touch of her cool fingers on my skin.

At first, I thought the hand I felt on my shoulder was my imagination, my mind playing tricks on me as I thought of Orla.

But then I heard a voice say my name.

'Livvie? I thought it was you. You were miles away.'

It was Samantha, my old housemate. She, too, was bundled up in a winter coat, a bright red scarf with reindeer faces knitted into its pattern wound tightly round her neck. A strand of hair clung to her lipgloss.

I anticipated the sinking feeling of anxiety I'd felt when I'd seen her in the past, but there was nothing.

'Hi,' I said, smiling as naturally as I would on seeing any other old acquaintance.

'On your way to work, then?' she asked. 'Daily grind, nine to five?'

'That's right. You too?'

'As per. I started a new job in October. Me and Mands are living in a flat just over there.' She gestured. 'I'm surprised I haven't bumped into you before. Do you still go to the Crooked Billet on a Friday?'

'Not really,' I said.

'Listen.' She fell into step next to me. 'About that night – that time you were there with your friends.'

It felt like a long time ago – but Samantha was capable of nursing a grudge for far more than a few months, I knew. If she'd held Beatrice's actions that night against me, no doubt I was going to hear all about it.

'Go on,' I said.

'Remember – your mate snogged Gary on the dance floor?' To my surprise, she laughed, as if it was some hilarious memory we shared and dug out every now and again to giggle over together.

'Yeah, I remember that.'

'I broke up with him that night. I should have done it sooner – he was always a cheater. I don't know why I couldn't see it before. He treated me like shit, always trying to make me feel bad about myself, about other girls.'

'Sounds like you're well rid of him.'

'Too right I am. What an arsehole! And you know what, I've got your friend to thank for making me realise it. That night – it was like the straw that broke the donkey's back, you know.'

Camel, I thought. 'It must have been hard at the time.'

She laughed. 'He cried and everything. Loser. I chucked him out into the street and threw his stuff out the window. It was great.'

I couldn't help smiling, imagining Samantha's rage directed in the right direction for once.

Encouraged, she went on, 'But anyway, Livvie. That whole thing made me realise how badly I'd behaved towards you. I was a right bitch. It was my own insecurities, the way he kept going on about you. Amanda tried to tell me but I wasn't having any of it.'

'Sometimes it's hard to see these things when you're in the middle of them.'

'Yeah. You always were a wise owl, weren't you? Anyway, I guess I owe you an apology. So, I'm, like, sorry. And everything.'

'You don't have to apologise.' It was true, but I was touched all the same. I reached out and gave her a clumsy half-hug.

'I've moved on,' she said proudly. 'I'm seeing such a nice guy now; he's a branch manager at Tesco. Are you dating anyone?'

'Not right now. I was, but not any more. We broke up.'

'Dean's got loads of single friends. We should have drinks down the Crooked Billet one evening – I'll introduce you.'

'That would be great,' I said, knowing it would never happen.

'And listen – I don't suppose you're looking for a place to stay? Only Mands and me have got a spare room in our flat. The girl who was living with us is moving in with her bloke. It's lush – there's an en-suite and everything, so you wouldn't have to fish my hair out of the plughole.'

I laughed. 'Sounds like an offer I couldn't refuse. But I'm all sorted – I'm actually moving to West London, to live with my friend Emily.'

'Ooooh, West London? Fancy.'

'It's only Shepherd's Bush.'

'Nice. Anyway, I just thought I'd ask. Drop us a text if you change your mind.'

'I will.'

We'd reached my bus stop by now so I stopped walking, hoping in spite of myself that Samantha wouldn't be getting the same bus.

But she said, 'Is this you? Going into town as usual? I'd best be on my way too or I'll get a bollocking from my manager. Let me know about that drink, all right?'

'Of course,' I said. 'And merry Christmas.'

'Merry Christmas.'

We leaned in and hugged each other briefly, then she waved

a mittened hand and turned away, walking as quickly as she could in her high heels on the frosty pavement.

I remembered how much power she'd had over me – how I'd almost feared her. All that was gone now – she was just another young woman, making her way in the world as best she could. Ultimately, I supposed I had Beatrice to thank for that.

I wondered if Beatrice even remembered that night, kissing a random man to prove a point. I wondered if I'd ever tell her about seeing Samantha that morning, and the epiphany she'd unwittingly caused.

But I doubted I ever would.

FIFTY-FIVE

Beatrice stood in the front room of the house on Damask Square, looking out at the street. Someone had wound fairy lights around the iron railings, and they twinkled merrily in the gloom of the winter morning. Between the bare branches of the trees, she could see one of the tower blocks on the estate, most of its windows lit up and – she counted – Christmas trees glittering in twelve of them. Behind her, she could hear the gentle crackle of a log fire; Orla had hired a chimney sweep and, after years of rubble and abandoned sparrows' nests had been removed, the house was cosier than she had ever known it.

She turned around, feeling her long skirt swish against her tights. The skirt was wool, finely woven and beautifully tailored; it had belonged to Orla's grandmother in the 1950s, Orla had told her, and now that the seams had been let out it fitted her perfectly. From the kitchen, she could hear the clatter of pans and smell the mouth-watering savouriness of roasting turkey. Orla had insisted on buying a turkey crown for Beatrice, and Beatrice in turn had consulted Delia Smith online and found a recipe for a nut roast with cranberries and made it for Orla.

The room was still only part-furnished: apart from a worn brocade chaise-longue Orla had bought in the market and a teak coffee table Beatrice had found on eBay, it would have been empty but for the huge Christmas tree that stood in the corner. It was a Norwegian spruce, almost seven feet tall, and they'd had to pay extra to have it delivered to the house. On its branches hung an assortment of cheap baubles Beatrice had picked up in Woolworths, alongside delicate blown-glass spheres that were family heirlooms of Orla's. Maud had already smashed one of them, but Orla had only laughed, carefully sweeping up the fragments lest they hurt the cat's paws.

On the mantelpiece stood a meagre selection of cards: one from Imran at the newsagent's, one from the historic buildings Preservation Trust, one for Beatrice from her mom and dad, one from Luke and one from Livvie. They flanked the largest one, at the centre of the display, which had been sent from America. In it was a note from Frances wishing Beatrice well and saying they all missed her, along with Peter's scrawled signature and notes from the children. Slate had written 'Merry Christmas Bibi' in wobbly crayon and Parker had drawn a wonky, bright red heart, her colouring-in scribbling beyond its outlines.

She and Orla had exchanged gifts that morning. Beatrice had bought Orla a cashmere jumper from Selfridges, which had cost a good chunk of the cheque her parents had enclosed with their Christmas card and was the same tawny gold as Orla's eyes.

Orla's gift to her had cost nothing but been worth far more. Beatrice had cried when she'd opened it, looking down at the paint-stained ellipse of birch wood in her hands and knowing straight away what it was.

'My palette from when I was at art school,' Orla had explained. 'In case you want to try your hand at oils sometime.'

Beatrice heard the crash of the door knocker and hurried out of the room. She'd never answered the door here before, she realised – she'd always left it for someone else to do, assuming whoever it was was nothing to do with her.

But today was different.

She pulled open the door. Neil stood on the threshold, smiling, a bunch of red roses and a bottle of champagne in his hands.

'Hello,' Beatrice said. 'Merry Christmas. Come in before you freeze.'

'Merry Christmas.' He followed her along the hallway, glancing in at the Christmas tree as he passed. 'That's how it's done! Impressive.'

'Let's go and find Orla.' She led the way through to the kitchen, feeling suddenly shy. She'd never introduced Neil to anyone before, nor introduced Orla as her birth mother to anyone.

But Neil seemed entirely comfortable with the situation. He handed over the bottle and the flowers, returned the kisses Orla planted on his cheeks and wished her merry Christmas, saying how excited he was to meet her.

'We're so pleased you could come,' Orla said. 'I've heard a lot about you from Beatrice. I'm glad your family could spare you for the day.'

'We were lucky with the dates.' Neil smiled. 'Hanukkah starts tomorrow and then I'll be knee-deep in family – that, and ninety per cent potato latkes before New Year.'

'You're our first official guest,' Beatrice said. 'We thought we'd be spending the day just the two of us, then Orla said I should invite you.'

Because she was eager to meet my kind-of boyfriend? Or because she didn't want to spend the day alone with me? But Orla's face when she'd made the suggestion had given nothing away.

Not that Beatrice cared. She was here, spending Christmas

with her real mother, as she had dreamed of doing ever since she'd been old enough for the concept of having a different, separate mother from the one she'd always known to be a thing. She was in the house she'd come to love, with a man she suspected would fall in love with her in due course. Contentment swelled inside her as satisfyingly as if she'd already devoured a whole Christmas dinner.

Which, after a couple of hours, they had. Orla opened Neil's champagne and then a bottle of red wine. Neil carved the turkey, saying that as the oldest son, it had always been his job at home and he was an expert at it, with Maud twining round his legs mewing for scraps. Beatrice over-boiled the brussels sprouts, but the others said it didn't matter. Everyone found an abundance of silver five-pence pieces in their Christmas pudding.

When everything was cleared away, Beatrice said, 'Should we go for a walk? Isn't that what you do on Christmas Day in England?'

Orla laughed. 'It's certainly what we used to do in Ireland. Rain or shine – and it was usually rain – my grandmother would insist on it. She said it was good for digestion. But it's raining now, so...'

'My digestion could use all the help it can get,' Neil said. 'But what I'd really like – if you wouldn't mind, Beatrice – is to see some of your paintings. May I?'

'I... All right. Of course. I'll just finish off here and then I'll get my portfolio from upstairs.'

She dried the last of the plates efficiently, stacking them away in the cupboard. Then she hurried up to her bedroom, retrieving the plastic folder from its shelf. She glanced through the pages inside, suddenly filled with doubt.

Neil would be uncritically enthusiastic about her work, she was sure. But Orla – the only work of hers Orla had seen was the roses Beatrice had painted for her by way of an apology.

She'd praised that – but what would she think of these? Beatrice found herself craving Orla's approval.

She carried the folder downstairs and joined the others in the living room, where they were sitting on the chaise-longue finishing the red wine. Beatrice folded herself down on to the floor, feeling the fire warming her back.

'These aren't very good,' she apologised. 'I've got a lot to learn.'

'Never apologise for your work,' Orla reprimanded her, smiling.

'I'm sure they're brilliant,' Neil said.

'Okay, so...' Beatrice extracted a page from the folder and handed it to Neil. Orla leaned in close so she could see too. 'These are some of the paintings I brought with me when I came out here, to remind me of home. This is the view from my bedroom – that's a maple tree.'

'Gorgeous colours,' Neil said.

'There's beautiful brushwork on the leaves,' Orla observed. 'Real delicacy.'

'And this is Sligo, our dog.'

'He's adorable.'

'You've captured his face perfectly. The playfulness and the eagerness to please.'

'And this...' Beatrice looked at the painting. It was the best thing she had ever done, painted shortly before she'd left for Europe, full of apprehension about what she might discover and sorrow for what she was leaving behind.

'Go on, show us,' Neil urged.

'This is my mom and dad – my adoptive parents. Ruth and Declan.'

Shyly, she handed it over. Neil studied it with all the seriousness of someone seeing potential in-laws for the first time. But Orla's face had gone as still as marble.

I shouldn't have shown her, Beatrice thought. *She can see how much I love them and I've hurt her feelings.*

'Are you all right?' she asked.

'Of course.' Orla's smile had returned as if it had never not been there. 'That's a wonderful portrait. You should be proud of it. Perhaps you could have it framed and hang it on the wall in your bedroom?'

She doesn't mind, Beatrice thought with relief. *Or if she does, she'll mind less and less when she understands she isn't going to lose me again.*

'The rain has stopped,' she said. 'Maybe we could go for that walk after all?'

Outside, the wind whipped Beatrice's full skirt around her legs, hobbling her steps. But she barely noticed. Her eyes were fixed on the twinkling lights in the windows above; Neil's hand clasped hers and kept it warm and on her other side, Orla's shoulder pressed strongly and steadily against her own as they linked arms.

I will paint a portrait of Orla too, she decided. *I can frame that as well and hang it next to the one of Mom and Dad, and every morning I'll be able to wake up and see them there.*

My family.

FIFTY-SIX

'Liv?' Emily called across the landing, her voice reaching me over the opening chords of 'You're Beautiful' blaring out of the speakers downstairs. 'Can I borrow your Russian Red lippie?'

'Only if you zip up my dress.'

'Deal.'

Her heels clattered over the floor and she burst into my room in a cloud of L'Eau d'Issey and hairspray. 'Love the dress. Foxy. Is it new?'

'Mango sale,' I confirmed. 'But the zip's fiddly as fuck. Here.'

I turned my back to her and felt her cool fingers on the skin of my back as she fumbled with the zip pull. For a moment, I was transported back to the basement at Damask Square.

But I wasn't at Damask Square any more, although the Schiaparelli dress was. I'd left it, shrouded in a polythene bag from a specialist dry cleaner, hanging over the door of what had been my bedroom, pinning a note to the front.

I can't take this with me – it's too special. Thank you for letting me wear it, and for everything else. All my love, Livvie.

That had been two weeks ago. Since then, I'd moved into the free room in Emily's house share, spent a dutiful Christmas with my parents in Nottingham, and returned with relief to London in time for the New Year's Eve party Emily and her other housemates, Vanessa and Josh, were throwing.

Only two weeks, but already Damask Square seemed distant, almost like all the months I'd spent there had been a dream. Already, I'd grown used to being woken by the roar of the Westway in the mornings, rather than the song of blackbirds in the square. I'd become accustomed to the smell of Josh's shower gel in the mornings, not Luke's. I barely noticed that when I walked into the kitchen, it was Vanessa I saw chopping vegetables for a stir-fry, not Orla preparing dinner for the four of us.

If I came into my bedroom to find someone sitting on my bed wanting a chat, it was Emily and not Beatrice.

This all felt normal – it felt like real life. I'd return to work in a couple of days, face a new year filled with what my manager was fond of calling Challenges and Opportunities. I'd travel east on my journey to work instead of west. Emily had suggested I go along to the pub quiz on Tuesday nights with some of her other friends, promising that my knowledge of English literature, added to theirs of politics, sport and popular culture, would make us unbeatable.

In my heart, there was still an ache where my feelings for Luke had been, a space as empty as the side of my bed where I'd grown used to him sleeping.

'Friends?' he'd said the last time we saw each other, drawing me into his familiar embrace.

'Friends,' I'd agreed, knowing that meant only the liminal space between 'enemies' and 'lovers', and not the true friendship I had with Emily.

I'd probably never see him again, and I was okay with that – there was really no alternative.

Saying goodbye to Orla had been harder. When I'd gone into the kitchen for the last time, she'd been there as I'd expected, temporarily distracted from the pile of bills she was sitting over, chequebook by her side, by Maud settling down, purring, on top of her paperwork.

But Beatrice had been there too, pouring water from the kettle into the teapot.

'You heading off, Liv?' she'd asked, the morning sun from the window falling on her face as she'd smiled at me. 'Take care. We'll miss you.'

'I'll see you out.' Orla had stood up and walked with me to the front door. She'd opened it, a blast of cold air enveloping me before she pulled me close into her warm arms, whispering, 'You could stay, you know.'

'I couldn't,' I'd said into her shoulder. 'I have to go. But I'll stay in touch.'

'I hope so.' There had been a sadness in her voice. We both knew I would, but that it would be faithfully at first, then intermittently, then probably not at all.

The relationship I had with her – not like a mother and daughter and not like friends, but something else, something special and unique – would never be replaced in my life. But in Orla's, it had to. By something not like a mother and daughter and not like friends, but something special and unique. Only with Beatrice, not with me.

As for Beatrice herself, when I'd told her I was moving out she had nodded calmly, like I was confirming something she already knew.

'I'm sorry,' she'd said. 'I wish you could stay.'

'I know.' It would have been more honest if I had said, *I know you don't.*

'You must visit. Come and see the house when it's finished, ready for the students to come and stay.'

I imagined the upstairs rooms that had been silent and

empty filling with laughter, trainers clomping on the stairs, voices in the kitchen enthusing over Pre-Raphaelite art. I imagined walking in and faces turning to look at me – *Who's she?* – and not knowing. And Beatrice, the daughter of the house, central to it all.

'Maybe it would be better if we met for a drink somewhere else,' I'd said.

'Maybe it would,' Beatrice had admitted, smiling her smile that was like Orla's, yet not Orla's.

'You're all good,' Emily said now. 'Come on, hand over that lippie. Not that it'll last, the amount I plan on drinking tonight.'

'It's New Year's Eve.' I watched as she carefully coloured in her full lips. 'If you can't get shitfaced tonight, when can you?'

'Exactly. Vanessa's promised a fry-up and Bloody Marys in the morning, so let's do it.'

'Let's do it.'

With a final swish of our hair, we headed downstairs. Guests had already begun to arrive, spilling from the kitchen into the front room, plastic glasses of cava in their hands, chatting and laughing and slotting CDs into the stereo. I fetched myself a drink and poured a packet of crisps into a salad bowl, handing them round as an excuse to introduce myself to people.

By midnight, the flat was heaving. I'd danced with Vanessa's brother and had an incoherent conversation about politics with a group of Josh's friends. I'd jokingly reprised my long-running argument with Emily about whether pineapple on pizza was sacrilege or the food of the gods. I'd kicked off my shoes to join the pile of other discarded heels people kept tripping over on their way to the toilet. I'd laughed until my face hurt.

Now, I found myself face to face with a man I'd never met before. He was blond and stocky, taller than me but not as tall as Luke, his hair standing up at random angles as if it had been carefully combed into place earlier in the evening but disarranged by his fingers running through it. His eyes were green and smiling.

'Who are you?' he asked. 'And where have you been all night?'

'I've been here,' I said. 'I live here.'

'That would explain it.' His voice was soft, his accent noticeably posh. 'Since I've only just arrived. I'm Tom. I work with Emily.'

'I'm Livvie,' I echoed. 'I share the house with Emily.'

'Then we've got something in common already. And soon we'll have something else.'

'What's that?' I couldn't help returning his smile – his confidence was infectious.

'We'll have seen the New Year in together. Hello 2006, adieu 2005. A turning point in our lives.'

'Which way are you thinking your life's going to turn?' I asked.

'Oh, upwards. Always upwards. And onwards, obviously.'

'Okay,' I said slowly. 'That sounds good to me, Tom.'

He leaned in towards me to say something else and I caught the scent of his cologne, smooth and expensive like his leather jacket. But whatever he was about to say was drowned out by the voices around us beginning the countdown and the chimes of Big Ben coming from the television.

Around us, voices erupted into shouts of, 'Happy New Year!' and several champagne corks exploded at once.

Tom smiled at me and I smiled back. The rims of our plastic glasses touched each other and then, with what didn't feel like any conscious decision on either of our parts, our lips met too in a kiss that was something less than passionate but definitely more than friendly.

'Happy New Year, Livvie.' He laughed down at me once the kiss had ended.

'Happy New Year, Tom.'
And in that moment, I truly believed it would be.

FIFTY-SEVEN
1 JANUARY 2006

It is after midnight and therefore a new day, but more importantly a new year. It is also the first time I am picking up my pen to write these pages since Christmas morning, and it is only the knowledge that if I did not, I might never begin again that has impelled me to do so. In all these years – not when I left Adrian, not when I learned of my grandmother's death, not when Beatrice revealed that she was my daughter – have I not written my Morning Pages.

But Beatrice's inadvertent revelation on Christmas Day left me reeling with shock to the extent that I have been unable to find words to write until now. At first, when I saw his face in her painting, I thought I might be sick or faint, but I didn't. The fresh air helped. I managed to get through that walk – barely feeling the ground beneath my feet or the cold air on my face – and then I said I had a headache and came up to bed, leaving Beatrice and her Neil downstairs alone.

Was it some trick – some kind of cruel joke Beatrice was playing on me? It was the kind of thing she might have done months ago, when she first came to Damask Square, but not now. Surely not now. And there was nothing in her face to suggest that – she was full of diffident pride at the beautiful portrait she was showing us.

The portrait of her parents. Ruth and Declan.

It was unmistakably him. Beatrice's style is immature but her talent is unquestionable and she has captured his likeness perfectly – the strong arc of his jaw, the lines around his eyes, the dimple in his chin all there, reproduced on paper with familiarity and love.

But how? How can it have been allowed to happen? In fact, having thought of little else this past week, I can see exactly how. Declan never knew I was having a baby. I could never have told him; no one knew but me. When my grandmother went to register the birth, in the space where her father's name would have been, there would only have been a dash – a strikethrough.

I remember Declan saying to me, that first time, after he had removed his jacket and hung it over the back of the chair, tenderly taking my face in his hands before kissing me: *I won't tell if you don't.*

I never told. Not anyone. The conspiracy of secrecy, silence and shame we were all part of did its work.

And so he adopted her, not knowing. He has raised her, not knowing. She does not know; her mom does not know.

I myself did not know. Even when letters came to the house addressed to Beatrice Walsh-Seymour, I thought nothing of it. Walsh is as common a name as Murphy, Kelly or Smith, and the addition of what must be Ruth's maiden name made it spark only the barest glimmer of memory in me the first time I saw it.

Now, though, I do know. I cannot unknow. So what will I do?

Declan has loved her all these years. It would bring him joy, I am sure, to learn that she is his daughter in every sense. But does he deserve that, after what he did to me, to Ruth?

Ruth – that shadowy woman. The bride with flowers in her

hair, the wife unable to have a baby of her own, the mother who lavished love on the daughter she was able to bring home at last. It would surely devastate her to find out the truth.

As for Beatrice – I do not know. Would she be horrified by what the man she knows as Dad did all those years ago, who he was? It could destroy her relationship with the father she loves. Would she be disgusted at me? When she asked about her father, I told her he was a man I met at a party, a fellow student called Andrew, whose last name I never knew. Perhaps she is already disgusted by that.

Perhaps not. Perhaps she would be delighted – her history complete at last, the final piece of the puzzle in place.

Only I hold the answer, the truth. And I do not know what I will do with it.

There is only one thing I know for sure.

Once again, this house here on Damask Square is hiding a secret.

I can hear Beatrice opening the door downstairs, Neil thanking her for the evening and saying goodnight and happy New Year, her laughter mingling with his. She is happy. My daughter is happy. Her happiness is something I hold in my hands like a baby bird – at once fragile enough to destroy and too precious to release.

Perhaps one day I will be able to tell her. But not now.

Not now.

A LETTER FROM THE AUTHOR

Huge thanks for reading *All Our Missing Pieces*. If you'd like to be kept up to date on my future releases, please take a moment to sign up to my author newsletter.

www.stormpublishing.co/sophie-ranald

Readers who are familiar with my previous novels – all sixteen of them; it quite honestly boggles my mind to think of it! – may feel that *All Our Missing Pieces* is something of a departure from what I have written before.

And you'd be right – but also slightly wrong. In fiction writing, more and more, genre is becoming paramount. The way our books are packaged, marketed and categorised is becoming increasingly rigid as the size of the market burgeons and publishers endeavour to make it as easy as possible for you – our readers and customers – to identify books you'll love.

So when I came up with the idea for *All Our Missing Pieces*, with its serious and sometimes heartbreaking themes, it was clear that representing the book as a romance or a comedy would be misleading to my readers and lead to disappointment and confusion. There are – I hope at least – elements of humour in this novel and there is certainly romance, but above all it is a story of women's choices: the decisions we make; the context of society, of family and of home within which we make them; and the impact our choices have on our lives and those of others.

All that said, I do hope you have enjoyed reading *All Our*

Missing Pieces. Writing it has been an arduous and exhilarating journey that has included brain-frying hours at my keyboard, a lightning trip to beautiful Dublin, and way too many 5 a.m. starts. If you enjoy novels of the fluffier kind, I invite you to dive into my sixteen romantic comedies – while they also include some serious themes, they're lighter and perhaps easier reads. If you've loved this book, please look out for my next Damask Square-set novel, out in September 2025.

As always, please take a moment to leave a review on Amazon and connect with me on social media – I'd love to hear from you. And, as always, thank you from the bottom of my heart for giving your time to read this novel.

Much love,
Sophie

www.sophieranald.com

facebook.com/SophieRanald
instagram.com/sophieranald

ACKNOWLEDGEMENTS

Often, authors come up with ideas that seem like strokes of genius but end up being rods for their own back. That's how it is for me, at least – and that's how it was when I made the entirely impulsive decision to place adoption at the heart of a novel that was originally intended to be just the story of some people living in a house.

I quickly realised that in order for the chronology to work, the adoption would have to have taken place in Ireland. There, the law around adoption has evolved significantly since 1953, when the 1952 Adoption Act was enacted. My research led me down multiple rabbit holes and my brain was soon filled with dates and details of various consultations and statutes as well as heartbreaking and heartwarming stories.

In an attempt to get my head around it all, I reached out to the children's charity Barnado's. Very shortly after sending my email, my phone rang with a Dublin number and I spent a hugely informative half hour picking the brains of Andrew Walker, who provided context, anecdotes, recommendations for further reading and an insight into the boundless compassion of the people who work in this field. Thank you, Andrew.

Subsequently, though, I realised that in order to achieve a degree of authenticity in the storyline, a trip to Dublin would be necessary. Until 2020, when Covid intervened and changed this practice as it has changed so many others, adoptees looking to trace their birth parents often had to visit the Research Room at Dublin's General Register Office and comb through birth records, as I describe in the novel. When I visited, I met the wonderful Liam Harris, whose huge generosity with his time and experience helped me enormously. Thank you to Liam and his colleagues Noelle and Grainne, who helped me plan my trip to coincide with the reopening of the Research Room following refurbishment work.

In 2005, when Beatrice and Neil travel to Dublin, the Research Room would have been located at its former site on Lombard Street; I have taken a creative liberty and described the current premises on Werburgh Street. This and any other errors are entirely my own.

Back in London, my research took me to Dennis Severs' House in Spitalfields, a kind of architectural amber within which centuries of historical artefacts are preserved, giving a glimpse into the lives of Huguenot silk-weavers in a Georgian home. Damask Square, however, is fictional and any inaccuracies are again my own.

Addressing any other errors and inaccuracies in this novel was the task of copy editor and proofreader dream team DeAndra Lupu and Becca Allen – thank you both. Audio narrator Lucy Paterson has brought the story to life for listeners, and Rose Cooper is responsible for the beautiful cover.

I am incredibly privileged to be published by Storm, where my wonderful editor Claire Bord has worked tirelessly to improve every aspect of this novel, with the support of a brilliant team: Founder Oliver Rhodes, Editorial Operations Director Alexandra Begley, Publicity Manager Anna McKerrow, Head of Digital Marketing Elke Desanghere, Digital Operations Director Chris Lucraft and Editorial Assistant Naomi Knox.

Thanks as always go to the amazing Alice Saunders and her colleagues at The Soho Agency and to my beloved crew at home – my partner, Hopi, and cats, Purrs and Hither.